AWAKE, MY HEART

What happens when a young man and a young woman, each bitterly distrustful of the opposite sex, not only meet but find themselves sharing the same country house? At first Luisa, returning home from abroad, finds herself hating Martyn Saunders, a young vet injured in the war. Martyn becomes engaged to Luisa's best friend, and too late he and Luisa discover their love for one another. First loyalty, then an accident, contrive to keep them apart, and when reconciliation seems likely, another woman from Martyn's past interferes, until love at last finds a solution to all their problems.

Awake, My Heart

by

Patricia Robins

Magna Large Print Books
Long Preston, North Yorkshire,
BD23 4ND, England.

British Library Cataloguing in Publication Data.

Robins, Patricia
    Awake, my heart.

    A catalogue record of this book is
    available from the British Library

    ISBN   0-7505-2436-7

First published in Great Britain

Cover illustration © Len Thurston by arrangement with
P.W.A. International Ltd.

The moral right of the author has been asserted

Published in Large Print 2005 by arrangement with
Claire Lorrimer

Magna Large Print is an imprint of Library Magna Books Ltd.

Printed and bound in Great Britain by
T.J. (International) Ltd., Cornwall, PL28 8RW

FOR MY SISTERS,

EVE AND ANNE,

WITH LOVE

CHAPTER I

1950

To Luisa, who had been away from England since the end of the war, Cavin Woods, as they were on this gentle, early Spring morning, seemed breath-takingly lovely. The soft, spongy moss was still damp with yesterday's April shower, and the beech leaves, just unfurling, were yellow-green like unripened lemons. Underfoot the twigs and bracken of last year crackled and snapped beneath her light tread, and the shafts of sunlight filtering through the branches overhead, touched her face and hands with warm fingers.

"It's beautiful!" she thought, inhaling the rich odour of damp leaves and earth. "I've longed for this and now I'm here, here for as long as I choose. And it's mine – all mine."

She felt strangely happy, content, at peace. Strange, because for the last three years she knew she had been numbed of all feeling. Purposefully, she had deadened them and allowed herself only those thoughts and actions and responses that were necessary for existence.

'Boot!' she called, and the black Labrador

7

came bounding through the undergrowth, his tail swinging furiously to and fro, his eyes gazing at her adoringly.

Luisa smiled at the dog and stooped to pat him.

'You haven't forgotten me, have you, old fellow!' she whispered. 'Faithful old boy!'

Luisa walked on, the dog now following quietly at her heels as if aware of her mood of thoughtfulness, of retrospection.

"My life!" thought the girl. "What have I done with it since the war ended? Nothing – nothing – nothing! I've wasted three years; it's taken me that amount of time to escape. And now I'm free."

She forced herself to think of those years. Her parents having died suddenly just before the war ended, she had returned from her life as a V.A.D. to live with her aunt – her rich relative who offered her a home and security.

'I want a companion, Luisa,' she had said in her patronizing tone which she always used to 'inferiors'. 'In return, I'll give you two pounds a week pocket-money and a luxurious life such as you've never dreamed about. A chance to meet some eligible young men with money, too. Now come, child, don't hesitate. This is a chance in a lifetime for you. There isn't a girl alive who wouldn't jump at it.'

And yet Luisa hadn't 'jumped at the

chance'. Perhaps some premonition had prompted her hesitation. Perhaps it was just a natural longing to stay on in the old vicarage where she had known such happy childhood days – stay among the comforting possessions that were part of her home.

'May I think about it, Aunt Ellen?'

'But my dear girl, what is there to think about? You haven't a penny in the world – nothing but the old Vicarage and that bouncing great dog of yours. What will you do? How will you support yourself?'

'I could get a job,' Luisa had answered. 'I'm a trained V.A.D., and the country needs nurses.'

'A life of drudgery, my dear,' her aunt had dismissed this idea with a wave of her lavender-gloved hand. 'Besides, there's the house itself. It's in ruins. It needs repairs. You haven't any money.'

'I've my gratuities, Aunt,' said Luisa, thinking, 'You could easily afford to do up the house for me, with your thousands. But you wouldn't do that. You never helped Mother and Father since Mother married "beneath her" as you called it. Just because you married into a title and money, you thought that could make Mother happy, too. But you were wrong. She was happy with Father. She loved him. They...' she cut short her bitterness, remembering that in her own way, her Aunt was trying to help her now.

'Much better sell the place and be rid of it. You'll marry soon and then you won't want it. At least you've got looks, child, even if you haven't a penny. Not that you make the best of yourself. But we'll soon see to that. I shall be spending the winter in Monte Carlo. We'll get all your clothes there. At least we don't have to be bothered with coupons...'

"But I don't want to leave home!" Luisa had cried silently. 'I don't want to go.' And yet even while her heart spoke the truth to her and her Aunt chattered on about clothes and hotels and the Casino, Luisa knew that she would have to go. Nursing wasn't a paying career. She wouldn't have enough to keep the Vicarage going. Besides, if she lived in a hospital, she couldn't live here.

That was what she really wanted. To live here as she had done before the war – quietly with Mother and Father and Boot, looking after the garden and the orchard and the house. That, alas, was impossible. Money – or lack of it – made it impossible. But she wouldn't sell the house. She'd let it – on a short lease – say three years with an option each way. That would mean a small income. And if she saved the salary her aunt was offering her, she might after three years be able to afford the repairs and find some local job in the village that would support her.

Finally, this had been arranged. The house

had been let after she left England, to a young ex-Serviceman who was starting up a veterinary surgery. The idea pleased her, the Vicarage as a place for making dogs well again. She had wondered idly what the tenant was like. She had had one letter from him – curt but a kind letter which had brought her great happiness. It so happened that old Mrs Jennings who had done the weekly washing for the Vicarage, had agreed to look after Boot for her. But Boot had had other ideas, and every day, as soon as he was let out, he had returned to the Vicarage and lain there in his usual position just outside the front door, if it was fine, or just inside the hall if it was wet, until Mrs Jennings had come up to collect him. Only by chaining him up could Mrs Jennings keep him with her, and she didn't like to do this. Two weeks after the new tenant had moved in, he had written saying:

Your dog haunts the house and it's somewhat annoying to have Mrs Jennings constantly on my doorstep asking if I've seen him when I'm busy. Unless you have any objections, I suggest you let him live here as he seems to wish to do so.

The kitchen drain-pipe was leaking so I have had it repaired and will deduct the amount from the next quarter's rent.

Yours truly,
Martyn Saunders.

The letter had both pleased and annoyed her. How dared he start repairing the house at her expense without asking her first. Then she had forgotten the drain-pipe in her pleasure at knowing Boot to be back where he wanted. Leaving the dog had been like leaving part of herself behind, and the thought that he was haunting the Vicarage had caused her several sleepless nights.

She had replied immediately saying that she would be most grateful if he would care for Boot for her, and that he could deduct ten shillings a week for Boot's keep as this was what she had allowed Mrs Jennings. Perhaps from time to time he would be good enough to keep her informed of Boot's health. She had not mentioned the drain-pipe. But he hadn't written again until the last month before his three years' lease came up for consideration.

By this time, Luisa knew that she could not bear another year like the preceding three. It was not that her aunt had been unkind or inconsiderate. Her demands on Luisa as a companion were relatively few. But it was the life she could not tolerate. The dreadful artificiality of this existence led by the rich in such places as Monte Carlo. The futile frittering away of time at endless cocktail parties, evenings in the Casino, small talk and flattery that meant nothing underneath. At first she had only naturally been thrilled by the novelty of everything. Her exotic rooms at the hotels they went to (Aunt Ellen never stayed in one place for more than a few months); the beautiful clothes which seemed to her, brought up as she was to simple living in comparative poverty, an unnecessary extravagance, were to her aunt part of her job.

'My dear child, I'm not going around in the company of a badly dressed poor relation,' she said. 'What would everybody say?'

This expression, Luisa had soon discovered, was the key to Aunt Ellen's existence. All that mattered to her was what other people would say, especially if they were titled, or very rich.

At first, she had almost enjoyed her life. Aunt Ellen, too, had been seemingly content with Luisa. There had been several invitations from rich young men who would not otherwise have been bothered with Aunt Ellen, but who wanted to get in with her for Luisa's sake. She had, not unnaturally, been flattered at first by their attentions. It was a novelty to her to discover that she was considered beautiful by men, and that they were attracted to her. Then, when she came to know them better, she knew that their attentions were a poor compliment because they were, on the whole, so shallow and characterless, that their admiration could mean no more to her than the praise of an illiterate for a great writers' works. By that she meant that none of them had any worthwhile values and were for the most part as useless to the world as her aunt.

But Luisa's beauty was such that even while she took little pains to conceal her contempt for them, men still pursued her tirelessly. She had the kind of loveliness which they did not often find among their own set – a fresh passionate youthfulness and clear honest eyes that were nearly violet in their intense blueness. Her hair was naturally wavy, red-gold that did not come from clever dyes. Her skin was almost white and inclined to freckle in the sun, which added to her charm, for it made her look younger even than her twenty-four years. Her figure, too, was straight and slight and almost boyish with a tantalizing suspicion of awakening femininity about it.

Apart from her physical assets, Luisa also possessed for these rich, bored young men, another novelty – her unspoilt manner and complete lack of artificiality and sophistication. She could be young without being awkward; she could be poised and assured without being pretentious. She had, moreover, that air of promise which is seen in girls who have never been in love and are yet aware that it is there, in the future, waiting for them, and of their awaiting the right man to find the key to their hearts.

And so they pursued her, flattered her, proposed to her, and filled her life with meaningless empty offers of their undying devotion and admiration and love. Scornfully she turned them away, knowing only by her instinct that they knew nothing of the meaning of love as she would one day find it.

Aunt Ellen had at first applauded her on her skilful coquetry. She had refused to believe that Luisa was doing her utmost to put these men as far as possible out of her life. When, as Aunt Ellen put it, Luisa had turned down finally 'three very good matches' her aunt began to get annoyed.

'What do you think I've brought you here for, Luisa? Just to have a good time? I've introduced you to hundreds of eligible young men and you just turn up your nose at them. Well, you can't afford to, my girl. You're penniless. The sooner you marry, and marry well, the better. I shan't keep you for ever, you know.'

Luisa had turned from her in disgust seeing, for the first time, how thoroughly unpleasant her aunt was, wondering again and again how this could possibly be her mother's own sister. Whatever the reason, she knew she could not go on as her aunt's companion. Anything would be better than this.

And so her thoughts had turned to home,

and she started counting the days until the lease was up and she might return to the Vicarage. Daily her need grew more great. She felt that only England and the fresh countryside could wash away the stains that all this had left on her; cleanse the bitterness and disgust of life and these people. She had now nearly five hundred pounds in the bank. The Vicarage had been let at three pounds a week and she had saved a pound a week since she had started out with her aunt. With that she could repair the house and live for a little while until she could find a job.

And so it was by numbing herself to all feeling that Luisa had survived the last few months. Then she had written to her tenant to tell him she intended to return.

She had not been prepared for the shock of the letter she received in reply – not from the man, Martyn Saunders, but from his solicitor, saying:

You are no doubt unaware of the regulations concerning unfurnished tenancies now in force in this country. As my client has leased the house at the unfurnished pre-war rental, he comes under the protection of the Rents Restrictions Act and cannot be turned out...

In an agony of disappointment, Luisa had rushed to an English solicitor who had explained that the facts in the letter were, in part, true, but that she could, if she required the house for her own use, get the present tenant out if he were offered alternative accommodation.

'But there is nowhere else in the village,' Luisa had cried. 'Mrs Jennings wrote telling me that every nook and cranny was full. Oh, what am I going to do? This is awful, awful!'

'Perhaps, if I may make a suggestion?' asked the solicitor, affected by the girl's obvious distress.

Luisa nodded her head.

'If this house – it's a Vicarage, isn't it? – is fairly large, could you not have it made into two flats? You could then each have your own half.'

At first Luisa had rejected the idea. It was her home – hers, and she didn't want a stranger living there. And then reason had come to the fore. If she continued to rent half the house, it would be an enormous help financially. Besides which the Vicarage was far too big for herself alone. She would have had to close a number of the rooms anyway. She could afford the alterations and it would pay her in the end.

'This tenant, is he the sort of person who will agree to such a suggestion?'

Luisa came back to the present. She shook her head.

'I don't know. I don't know anything

about him, except that he's an ex-Service-man, and a vet. He uses the house as his surgery. I'll write.'

She had written, explaining at length how the house would divide. There were two bathrooms – a big scullery which would make a second kitchen. Each of them could have four rooms, two up and two down. They need not even use the same staircase. The Vicarage was old and rambling and would convert easily into two separate parts…

The answer had come a week later. Martyn Saunders had agreed to the arrangement. They would discuss further details on her return home.

And so she had left her aunt, trying as best she could to thank her for the three years of luxury living among the rich and élite, three years which she hated, and this morning she had arrived home. Mrs Jennings had been there to greet her; had explained that Mr Saunders was out on his rounds but that her luggage which had arrived last night was up in her rooms and all unpacked.

'That was sweet of you, Mrs Jennings,' Luisa said. 'Then I think I'll have a bath and change and go for a walk with Boot.'

'Have this cup of coffee first,' said Mrs Jennings, and patting Luisa's arm, she added: 'It's Mr Saunders' coffee and milk. I took the liberty. Still, I don't s'pose he'd mind. Easy going, he is, s'long as you leave him alone. Odd young gentleman. I expect it's all them years in a prison camp – and his hand.'

'Was he a P.O.W.?' Luisa asked, as she sipped the coffee gratefully.

'Four years, I believe. Never talks about it though. Still, my sister's boy was a prisoner of war, too, and he don't talk about it neither. He it was what told us Mr Saunders was in the same camp as hisself. Tortured, Jim says he was, too. But never told nothing. I dare say that accounts for him,' finished Mrs Jennings.

Not very enlightened as to her tenant, but not really wishing to be, Luisa had gone upstairs to have her bath, Boot following faithfully in her footsteps. She was tired of men and their attentions. She didn't want anything to do with them and if this Mr Saunders started following her around she'd – she'd get him out of this house somehow or other. All she wanted now was peace and quiet – time to readjust herself, to become herself again. And then, later, she would find a job. She put Martyn Saunders out of her mind, and with a little cry of delight, opened the door of the Vicarage and started off for the woods.

Martyn Saunders drove carefully along the lane that led to the road, his last call finished, for which he was thankful. It was nearly lunch time and Mrs Jennings' lunches were too good to be missed. A bit of luck finding her, he thought.

His mind swung away to the Alsatian he'd just been treating for hysteria fits. Nasty, but he'll pull through with care. Tricky animals to rear, he thought. Funny how people always imagine they are ferocious. No dog is really, if he's treated right. Any dog will be if he's treated wrong. Not that I've ever been particularly fond of Alsatians.

They reminded him of German patrol dogs ... his mind swerved quickly away from those memories. No, give me Labrador, he thought. Like old Boot there. Faithful old hound. He still won't accept me as his master. Still hankering after that girl, I suppose. Heartless little brute gadding off to Monte Carlo and leaving him behind with the char. Still, they're all the same. The more money they have, the less heart. Take Betty...

His mind turned again. He didn't want to think about Betty now. He'd almost succeeded in forgetting her. There was something about this village – a certain sort of peace one could find here. It was like living in a tiny world inside a world. One could escape down here. He didn't stop to ask himself from what he wanted to escape. The war, Betty, the post-war world – they were things he refused to allow himself to remember. But it wasn't so easy to forget. There was his arm to start with. It took time to get accustomed to having only one hand. Dreadful handicap to his work. But then he'd managed. He'd defied the lot of them. He'd proved it could be done.

A fierce pride of exultation surged through him, and he gave a short, happy laugh.

"I can drive, too," he thought. "I can do most things now."

He looked at his arm; at the sleeve of his coat where it was tucked into his pocket.

"I couldn't have looked there this time last year," he thought. "I'm improving. And nobody notices it much now. Everyone in the village is so used to it. Only a stranger would stare – like Betty when she looked and looked and turned her head away. Damn her! Damn her for her beastly pity and her silly squeamish..."

He caught himself up, aware that his one hand was trembling on the wheel.

"I don't mind about Betty," he told himself quietly. "I'm glad we broke our engagement – that she broke it..." he corrected himself with a bitter quirk to his lips. "She'd never have made a vet's wife with her horror of blood and deformity and anything unpleasant. Funny she never told me before. She knew I meant to become a vet. Well, I hope she's happy with that silly film crowd she works with. No doubt she'll make a great film star. She's beautiful enough, God knows..."

He bit his lip, angry that for once he could not put Betty from his mind so easily. His anger turned to the girl who was supposed to be arriving to-day.

"It's a confounded nuisance," he thought. "What on earth does she want here, anyway, with all that money? Why couldn't she stay at Monte Carlo or wherever she was? Currency restrictions, I suppose. Well, I've no doubt she won't stay here long. Too dull. Nothing to do. No parties. No drink. No young men – except one deformed veterinary surgeon. Perhaps she's hoping to amuse herself with me. What was it Betty had once said? 'Oh, but Martyn, I have been faithful to you – in every way. It's just that, well, you can't expect a girl like me never even to go out with a man, can you? I mean, you can't be jealous of just a few friends and an odd kiss good night. It didn't mean anything.' No, not to Betty perhaps, but it meant something to him who had thought of little else for four long, bitter, torturing years. It had all been for Betty. He had only lived through it because one day, one day he would be back with her. Because he had faith in her and thought her worth everything...

That had been the worst of all – the discovery that she was not worth it. That had seemed to him the cruellest part – the bitter knowledge that he had been suffering

22

for and worshipping a shallow, silly pretty young girl who had, yes, enjoyed the war. 'Really, Martyn, it was quite fun with all those American boys – except that I missed you, of course, darling. Positively heaps of drink and cigarettes – hand me one, darling … oh, I forgot. Never mind, I'll light yours for you.' And she had taken the packet of cigarettes from him as if he were unable to light one himself, or for her. He could have forgiven that, but not the way she thought about his hand – the other hand – the one that they had pulled slowly away from his wrist, finger by finger, joint by joint...

And this woman who was invading his home, Martyn thought. What would she say, if she got the chance to say anything, for he intended to keep well out of her way. 'Oh, I didn't know … I'm so sorry.' Or, 'If there's anything I can do to help, I mean…' Innuendoes – always. They never said it outright. They never said, like sensible Mrs Jennings: 'Oh, lawks, you'll have a job to manage without one hand. Do you miss it much, Mr Saunders, sir?' To which one could reply without hurt, 'A bit. But I'm getting used to it now.'

Martyn turned the car into the Vicarage drive and the expression on his face softened a little.

"You take things too seriously, Martyn, my boy," he told himself. "You think too much. Don't think. Except about lunch. I hope it's shepherd's pie..."

His arm swerved suddenly on the wheel as a black streak shot across the drive nearly under his car. He swore softly, and then recognized Boot as the car came to a standstill, one wheel on the turf bordering the drive. His fright had shaken him and for one moment he thought he had hit that black shadow.

'You silly fool, Boot!' he said roughly, opening the car door and stooping to pat the dog on the head. 'It's not like you to rush madly about like that, I...'

'I'm afraid it's my fault. I raced him home and he got rather excited. He's all right, isn't he? He's not hurt?'

Luisa, who had seen the near accident, had come running up the drive and was standing now by the car, her cheeks flushed, her hair blowing in disarray over her shoulders. She was wearing an old tweed skirt and loose sweater which she had had when she was eighteen, and she looked now very little older. Martyn stared at her, her beauty knocking away from him the angry words that had risen to his lips. He could only stare, wondering stupidly who she was. He'd never seen her in the village before.

Luisa, disconcerted by his penetrating glance, felt that she must say something. She supposed this was her tenant – this dark, glowering young man behind the wheel. Nobody else in the village had a car.

'I – you are Mr Saunders?' she asked, after a painful silence.

He nodded, dragging his gaze away from her and reaching into the pocket of his tweed jacket for a packet of cigarettes. He shook one into his mouth, put the packet down and felt again for his lighter. As he did so, he became aware again of the girl and knew she was staring at him.

Quite suddenly, anger caught hold of him. He didn't stop to analyse the reason except to know it had something to do with this girl's beauty. It reminded him of Betty. No one since he had known and loved Betty had had the power to touch him – the loveliness to twist his heart-strings into a painful knot of remembrance.

His face was distorted and his voice harsh as he said:

'Well, don't stand there staring, girl. I've only got one hand. Is there anything so unusual in that?'

The colour rushed into Luisa's face at his tone. Then receded, leaving her pale and quiet.

'Nothing at all unusual,' she said on a deep breath. 'But there is about your manners. You have no right and no cause to be so rude.'

And she turned away and ran, Boot following at her heels, back into the woods.

CHAPTER II

Martyn drove the car back the short distance to the house and went slowly in to lunch.

"What in heaven's name possessed me to behave like that?" he thought, feeling that he had made an unutterable fool of himself. "I suppose it was just – shock, or something. Why didn't somebody warn me she was like that? I didn't expect ... oh, confound everything! Why couldn't she be just plain and ordinary and comfortable?"

For Martyn knew that he could never be at ease with a girl like Luisa. She brought back the past far too vividly. She was an echo of Betty – of all the pain he had suffered loving and hating her.

Mrs Jennings came in with his lunch and a smile softened Martyn's face, making him suddenly young and attractive. His face, in repose, was strikingly handsome. It was only when the hard lines gathered about his mouth and face, his lips twisted, his eyes darkening from deep brown to near black, that he changed to something else. As Luisa had unthinkingly described him, he 'glowered' and looked both hard and cruel. And

27

yet cruelty was far from Martyn's nature. It hurt him almost physically to have to see an animal suffering in treatment. It was only himself he flayed, and others who encroached on the sealed bitterness of his heart.

But now he smiled, for Mrs Jennings was a kind, motherly soul who never bothered him. Moreover, she now carried in his favourite dish – shepherd's pie.

'Smells good!' he said, as she put the dish before him.

'Should be, too,' she agreed. 'There were three calls for you, Mr Saunders, sir, while you was out. One from the farm about their cow. Farmer thinks she'll have difficulty calving and he expects it to-night and says would you go along, sir, to see what you think. Other call was from White House. The Cairn's ill again. And Miss Mott about her cat.'

'Thank you, Mrs Jennings,' said Martyn. 'I'll see to it after lunch. You know, I really begin to think I'll have to get an assistant or a secretary or something. I've far more work on my hands than I can cope with, and when you've left after lunch, there's nobody to answer the telephone in emergencies.'

'You could do with help,' agreed Mrs Jennings. 'The practice is growing. Never thought it would, you know. People in these parts always treated their own animals. It's a feather in your cap, sir, if I may say so. Particularly that there Farmer Mills. Never thought to hear him ask for help, I didn't.'

'It's not been easy,' said Martyn reflectively; 'but I've enjoyed the struggle. Something to make me work and stop me thinking too much about myself.'

Mrs Jennings turned to go but remembered another message.

'Miss Luisa asked me to tell you she wanted to see you when you'd finished lunch, sir. About the house. She'll be in the back parlour.'

"Oh blast!" thought Martyn, as he started his meal. "Now I suppose she'll demand an apology or something. And why must she bother me about the house? That's her job. Doesn't she realize I'm busy? Well, I shan't go."

But he knew he must, and his meal over, he lit a pipe and still feeling resentful at being summoned like a naughty schoolboy to apologize to a parent, he went along to the parlour and knocked on the door.

Luisa, who had been thinking a great deal about this very odd young man and her encounter with him by the car, had decided that this first meeting was best ignored. Mrs Jennings had warned her he was 'touchy'. She recalled, too, that he was 'easy going' so long as you left him alone. Very well, she thought. That suits me too. I don't want him

29

bothering me any more than he wants me interfering. But I must see him about the house and make the necessary arrangements. I'll get that over and then we really needn't see each other except to say good morning if we pass in the doorway or something.

She was making a little list of the things she must discuss with him when he came in. She did not get up from her chair but turned to face him, her eyes avoiding his.

'I'm sorry to bother you,' she began awkwardly, 'but I'm afraid there are one or two things we must settle. Mrs Jennings' wages, for instance. I understand you employ her to clean and cook for you. I intend to do my own cleaning but Mrs Jennings has agreed to cook for me, too. She seems to think it would be easier if we pooled rations. We'd eat separately, of course. Would you have any objection to this plan?'

Martyn stared at her, shaken out of his resentment when he realized that she did not after all mean him to apologize. He stood awkwardly looking down at her, feeling that in some way she had had the better of him so far.

'No, I don't mind,' he said. 'I presume it will only be a temporary measure?'

She looked up at him then, not understanding his question.

'I mean, you ... will you be staying here

long?' Martyn asked.

'Always!' Luisa said firmly and definitely. 'This is my home. Why should you suppose I wish to leave it?'

A smile that was almost scornful flickered across Martyn's face.

'Won't you find it "frightfully dull" after Monte Carlo?'

The tone of his voice – the clever mimicry of the boredom about those words 'frightfully dull' that could only refer to the set she had been mixing with – Aunt Ellen's 'rich and élite' – came like a sudden insult. So he thought she was one of that crowd. Luisa's lips tightened and her face flushed with anger.

'I see no need to discuss my personal affairs,' she said pointedly. 'But since you have mentioned it, I have been in Monte Carlo because my financial state forced me to take a job with my aunt as her companion. I hated it. I'll never go back. Thanks to the rent you've been paying, I have enough money to see to the house and then I shall get a job.'

'What sort of job?'

"Now why did I ask her that?" thought Martyn. "To provoke her? I'm not really interested. Still, I've boobed, obviously. She's not an ex-débutante after all."

'I really don't know,' Luisa answered coldly. 'The only job I can do is nursing, but

I don't wish to leave my home to live in a hospital. I shall find some local work. I might even go on the land.'

'With those hands?' Martyn queried, before he could stop himself.

Luisa clenched the small white hands with their carefully manicured fingertips and the Irish temper she had inherited from her father's side rose inside her.

'Since I have arrived home, I have had the pleasure of talking to you exactly twice so far,' she said in an icy tone. 'In that short space of time, you have been exceedingly rude and insulting three times. Quite a record. But although it may amuse you, it doesn't amuse me. Now shall we get down to business and then we needn't bore each other with our company any longer.'

"She's right," thought Martyn. "I've been behaving disgracefully. She's got a temper though – and she can control it." Reluctantly he allowed himself to feel a twinge of admiration.

'I'm sorry,' he said briefly and with difficulty.

He sounded so unexpectedly like a small repentant boy, that Louisa's anger left her as abruptly as it had come. "I must remember," she told herself, "that my arrival home is a nuisance to him. It's really only by his good will that I'm here at all. And his money," she thought, recalling the weekly rent that had been paid into her bank.

'About the house,' she said. 'I intend to get the conversion started right away…'

'Do you think you'll get a licence so easily?' Martyn broke in.

'Why not?' Luisa asked in surprise.

'Well, I gather these things take time. There's a lot of form filling and it goes through about fifty government departments and even if they do agree to it, you'll have to wait for materials and so on.'

'I see,' said Luisa. She hadn't known about such things. She'd been away from England too long. 'Well, I suppose it can wait.'

'And in the meantime?' Martyn asked.

'We must just manage as best we can,' said Luisa quietly. 'I assure you I shan't encroach on you.'

'That's not the point. What are the village going to say?'

Luisa frowned.

'The village? I don't understand.'

'A young unmarried girl alone in the vicarage with a young unmarried man…'

'That's nonsense,' Luisa broke in, her cheeks flushing as the implication of his remarks reached her. 'Why, who would… I mean, they couldn't possibly think … well, even if they did, it's just ridiculous.'

'Maybe your reputation isn't important to you. Mine is. I work in this village and my livelihood depends on it. You know what village people are like.'

His words were provoking enough to rouse even a less spirited person than Luisa. A swift retort rose to her lips but she forced herself to ignore it. She did not intend to defend herself against such a person. He was best ignored. But her heart cried out against such injustice. He had no reason, could have no reason to treat her in this way. What had she done? Or perhaps it had nothing to do with her. Perhaps he was quite simply a misogynist. Without thinking, she said impulsively:

'Why do you hate women so much, Mr Saunders?'

She knew immediately that she had touched him on the raw, and momentarily was glad. Then, seeing the expression of his eyes, an expression of bitter pain and humiliation, she realized that unwillingly she had touched a wound still raw in him. Some girl, she thought intuitively. He's been hurt. That explains everything. Perhaps she left him because of his hand. How he must hate her. How he must hate any woman now.

He had not spoken and a painful silence had fallen between them. Luisa sought desperately for words to break it.

'I – I'm afraid I'm interfering in your personal affairs now. I'm sorry. But you … look, let's get back to this business of the house and... I'll ask Mrs Jennings if she could come and live here. With her as a "chaperone" no one could gossip.'

Martyn's voice was quiet and his face softened by her words. She had known she had hurt him – even if he'd deserved it – and she was sorry. He's been churlish and insulting and, really, it was quite unwarranted. With a great effort, he held out his hand, saying:

'I'm afraid we've started off on the wrong foot. It was my fault. I'm sorry. Let's start all over again.'

Luisa responded immediately, and her hand was clasped in his for a brief instant. During that time, she thought, "we could be friends, once we learnt to understand each other. I might even be able to help him somehow. He's not bad underneath. He's even quite attractive when he smiles."

But her feeling was impersonal ... sexless. She had had far too much to do with attractive young men showering attentions on her, trying to hold her hand, to kiss her, to make love to her – men she despised, whose attentions she despised so that now she had come to hate all thought of physical contact with a man. And because of this, her idea of love was always of a spiritual and mental emotion. When she fell in love, it would be as far removed from the physical plane as the sun from the earth. So thought Luisa who hadn't yet learned that her nature was such that one day she would love as passionately as any woman; that for her love would be the perfect combination of spiritual understanding and passionate adoration. Hers was the nature that could only love deeply, fully, with every fibre of her being.

'About Mrs Jennings,' Martyn was saying. 'I'm afraid we won't be able to have her. I asked her some time ago if she could come here as a housekeeper, but she has an aged invalid mother at home, apparently. Do you know anyone else in the village who might come?'

'I don't think I do,' Luisa said, after some thought.

'Then have you a friend, or cousin or relative who would come?'

'I have no relations,' Luisa said, and with a sudden laugh, 'except my Aunt Ellen, and I wouldn't have her if every village in England were gossiping about us. But wait a moment – I've a friend in London. She wrote to me a few weeks ago saying she had just finished her training and was going to have a long holiday before finding a job. She might come here temporarily. She's a secretary, or will be. She's young, though, only twenty-five. Would she be considered a chaperone?'

'I don't see why not,' Martyn agreed, and then an idea suddenly striking him, he said: 'You know, I've got to get an assistant some time soon. I've far more work on my hands than I can manage. But, meantime, until I do find someone suitable, perhaps this friend of yours would act as secretary for me – answer 'phone calls and keep accounts and so on. I could pay her – not much, but a little, and it would be training for her, too.'

Luisa's eyes shone.

'I'm sure she'd love that. She's crazy about animals. She wanted to be a vet, too, but the war came at the wrong time for her, and because she'd started training before the war as a secretary, she couldn't get a government grant for anything else, and she couldn't afford it herself. She'd be an enormous help, I'm sure.'

'Well, if you'd write or telephone, or something,' Martyn said vaguely. 'Then we'll know where we are. Meantime, perhaps Mrs Jennings could stay a night or two and find someone to look after her mother.'

They discussed further details of these arrangements, accounts, repairs and furniture, and with Martyn promising to see the necessary people about the conversion of the house, they parted company, Luisa to go to the 'phone to get hold of Bridget Castle. To her delight, Bridget jumped at the chance of a temporary job which would be a holiday as well, if she could spend her free time with Luisa, and said she would come down on a later train. There was no need, therefore, for Mrs Jennings to come since Bridget would be arriving to-night.

Martyn heard this news with a mixture of relief and perplexity. The chaperone was settled, and his assistant, but how had he possibly encouraged a situation where he now had two women in the house?

"I'm slipping," he thought with a grin of self-amazement. Then putting everything but work out of his mind, he set off for the farm.

A week later, Martyn knew that in some way his life had improved. It wasn't just that he had ceased to be bothered by Mrs Jennings about things like the laundry, or that there were new curtains in the kitchen, or flowers on his tables; but his work had been made a great deal easier by Bridget. She was enthusiastic and never too tired to work overtime, in spite of the fact that the salary he paid her was relatively infinitesimal. She was good with animals and equally good with book-keeping and his papers. He began to wonder how he could ever have managed without her help.

Apart from these qualities, he liked the girl herself. She was, to put her in a nutshell, a typical English girl. Not beautiful – for her hair was light-brown and only just missed being 'mousy' – her eyes hazel, and her eyelashes short and curly. She had a fresh complexion and an easy natural way of treating people. There was, in fact, nothing about her make-up that could cause Martyn to be affected by her in any way. She was a comfortable companion – and he found he could treat her as he treated another man.

Of Luisa, he had seen very little, only occasional glimpses of her setting off for a walk with Boot, or dusting round the house or working in the garden. She kept her distance and he was content that this should be so. Not that he disliked her, but in some odd way their natures clashed. They could never be long in each other's company without provoking each other's temper. And her beauty disturbed Martyn in a way he did not fully understand. He put it down to Betty, but did not stop to analyse it further.

Bridget, too, was settling down happily to her work. She and Luisa had been school friends and the complete oppositeness of their characters gave them a firm base for companionship. Bridget was without complexes or moods or violent emotions. Luisa, as a child, had been prey to all these. But she was controlled now in a way that puzzled her friend.

'Didn't you enjoy Monte Carlo, Luisa?' she had asked.

Luisa had shaken her head.

'No! Don't let's talk about it, Bridget. I want to forget it. I'm so happy to be home.

It's wonderful to have you here, too. I've almost forgotten what it's like to have a real friend around the place. I should have been lonely here, I think, on my own.'

'What, with Martyn around!'

'Martyn!' Luisa echoed. 'You don't surely find that boorish young man a companion, do you, Bridget?'

'I think he's extremely nice,' Bridget said. 'And most attractive. I can't see why *you* don't see it, Luisa. You're not blind, and to my way of thinking, he's God's gift to women. I envy you, Luisa. If I had your looks, I'd set my cap at our Mr Saunders.'

Luisa laughed outright, and then said seriously:

'Do you honestly find him attractive, Bridget? After all, you see more of him than I do. I suppose you ought to know. Personally, I think he's difficult and at times extremely rude and the very last thing I should have called him was a good companion.'

'But you don't know him, Luisa,' Bridget cried. 'Of course I've only known him a week, but you should see him with animals. You couldn't possibly dislike him if you had. He's so gentle and kind and...' she broke off, her face flushing a little at her own vehemence. It was unlike her to show so much emotion ... or to feel it. Could she be falling in love with Martyn Saunders?

Luisa spoke her thoughts.

'You wouldn't be falling for him, would you Bridget?' she asked. 'Because frankly I shouldn't, if I were you. He'd make an impossible husband, I'm quite sure. Besides, he's a woman-hater. I think there must have been some girl in his past or something. I accused him of being a misogynist the first day I was home. He didn't actually admit it but he didn't deny it.'

Bridget was silent and thoughtful and Luisa's face flashed with sudden understanding.

'Look, we won't talk about him, Bridget. I didn't really believe you were serious. I was just talking...'

'I'm not serious, Luisa, don't be so silly; why, I've hardly had two words with him except about work. It's just – well, don't you think he's rather like Bill?'

Luisa remembered for the first time Bridget's adored elder brother who had been killed in the war. Without doubt, Martyn did bear a marked resemblance to Bill. The same dark eyes and jet black hair. The same rather lean-drawn face. No wonder Bridget found so much in common with Martyn. It explained everything.

'It doesn't worry you, Bridget? Seeing someone so like Bill but who isn't him?'

'No!' said Bridget, a smile in her hazel eyes. 'They aren't really enough alike for that. But because he reminds me of Bill I could never dislike Martyn. I can't understand why you do.'

'I don't – really,' said Luisa. 'I'm just not interested. I suppose I'm not really interested in men at all.'

Bridget looked at Luisa in surprise.

'You've changed, Lis!' she said, using a pet name they had at school. 'I remember you telling me in full detail the wonderful husband and home and children you would one day have. You were longing, even at seventeen, to get married to some magical Prince who'd ride up on a white horse and claim you!'

They both laughed.

'I suppose I do want to get married one day. But – I don't know, Bridget. I suppose I must have changed. I want someone quiet and simple and good and kind.'

'Well, each to her own choice,' said Bridget, not understanding the reason for Luisa's changing. 'All the same I don't see how you can be with Martyn and not be affected by him. He's such a compelling person. He makes you feel things with a sort of desperateness and intensity. He...' she struggled for the right words ... 'he's so alive that he makes *you feel* more alive.'

'But that's just what I don't want to do,' said Luisa enigmatically. 'I want to be left in peace.'

Bridget shook her head and went off to

answer the telephone.

It was not, as she had expected, somebody wanting Martyn, but a personal call for herself from a Mrs Mathers.

'I'm an old school friend of your mother's,' the voice was saying. 'She has just written to tell me you are staying down here and I have a house about seven miles from your village.'

'Yes, of course,' said Bridget. 'I remember Mother mentioning your name.'

'I have my son coming down for the week-end and I thought perhaps you could come to tea on Saturday and meet us both. Could you do that?'

'I'd love to,' said Bridget. 'It's very kind of you to ask me. How do I get to you. Is there a 'bus?'

'Jim will come over in the car and fetch you,' said Mrs Mathers. 'I shall look forward to it.'

"That will be nice," thought Bridget. "I wonder what Jim is like. I believe Mother said he was a decent, well-mannered boy – a medical student, I think she said."

But her mind did not dwell long on Jim. It never could dwell on anything when Martyn was in the room. She had, she knew, misled Luisa. It wasn't Martyn's likeness to Bill, at least, not altogether, that had aroused her interest. But she hadn't wanted to admit even to herself, that she knew she was falling in love with Martyn. It wouldn't be any use and Martyn could never feel anything for her. Bridget knew only too well that she was no beauty. Beside Luisa she was positively plain, she thought grimly. I mustn't be so stupid.

But she knew when Martyn came into the room although she did not turn her head, and the colour rose to her cheeks at the sound of his voice.

'Well, Bridget, any calls?'

'Only one for me. Mother has some friends near here. I'm going over to tea Saturday, if that's all right.'

Martyn gave her a friendly smile.

'Of course,' he said. 'You've earned a rest. I've never known anyone work so hard for so little.'

'I like the work,' Bridget said simply, made happy by his praise.

'Could I drive you over there?' Martyn asked. 'There's no local 'bus, I'm afraid.'

'Her son is coming to fetch me, thank you,' said Bridget.

But when Jim Mathers arrived at the Vicarage, Bridget had gone out on an urgent call with Martyn, and it was Luisa who met him at the door.

CHAPTER III

Jim Mathers stood awkwardly on the doorstep of the Vicarage feeling rather annoyed that he must spend his weekend traipsing round the countryside in order to collect some girl or other for tea. He was a shy, reticent young man and intensely vague about everything except his work. He had a shock of untidy fair hair and very blue eyes, more often than not hidden behind a pair of spectacles, for he was short-sighted. Without these spectacles, Jim could be called attractive in a boyish way. He had a charming smile and a very clever and astute brain. His only other love beside his work was the country – for he was a nature lover in all senses of the word.

For this reason he was feeling peeved that his Saturday must be spoilt by idle chatter with some silly girl. Jim had little time for the female sex, unless they were ill or nurses. He had found little in common with the friends and sisters of his fellow-students and could not understand why they talked such a lot of rubbish about love. At twenty-two he was socially immature and mentally a good many years older than other young men of his own age. He was, in fact, a curious mixture of boy and man and one could not know Jim for long without one started musing about his future. That he would make a name for himself in the medical world was certain. But Jim, the shy, boyish good-looking young man – what would he develop into?

Viewing him from the hallway, Luisa could not have cared less. She, too, was feeling peeved with Bridget for not being on the spot to look after her own friends. That short note on the mantel-shelf– *'Have had to dash off to an urgent case with Martyn. Keep Jim Mathers entertained till I get back'* –had spoilt her plans for the afternoon.

'How do you do? I suppose you must be Jim Mathers,' she said with an effort at politeness.

Jim looked up at her with his usual short-sighted stare and became aware of a tall slim young girl in an open-necked sweater and tweed skirt. He wished he'd remembered to bring his spectacles. He really couldn't see properly without them.

'Yes. You must be Bridget. I've come to fetch you,' he said shyly.

'I'm afraid Bridget has had to go out with Mr Saunders on some important case,' Luisa said. 'I'm the friend she's staying with. Won't you come in?'

'Oh, I say, I didn't know there were two of you,' Jim said, stumbling over the top step into the hall.

A smile crossed Luisa's face at the dismayed tone of his voice. So young Jim Mathers had been sent against his will, by the sound of it. He looked very large and awkward standing in the hall with his hands in his pockets.

'Well, we weren't both coming to lunch,' she said. 'Only Bridget. Now it seems you'll have to stay and have lunch with me. Could you telephone your mother and explain?'

Jim looked rather like an animal that had been trapped. For the life of him he couldn't think of an excuse. It would obviously be stupid to suggest he went home for lunch and then drove back again to collect Bridget for tea.

'Yes, I suppose I could. What time will Bridget be back?'

'I'm afraid I don't know,' said Luisa, leading the way to her sitting-room. 'She just left this note. I expect one of the farm animals is calving or lambing or something. Mr Saunders is a vet, you know, and Bridget has been acting as his assistant. Will you have a drink? I think I can produce some sherry.'

Resigned, Jim sat down in a large armchair and accepted the sherry.

"I might as well give this Saturday up as a dead loss," he thought. "If only Mother wouldn't force me to meet all these girls. I suppose she thinks it's good for me, or

47

something. Oh well, lunch won't be long and I'm darned hungry!"

He nearly upset his glass of sherry by placing it on a book he hadn't seen. He apologized and explained that he was very short-sighted.

'Awful nuisance. Can't see a thing without my specs.'

Luisa smiled again. He really was incredibly young and clumsy. Rather like a big St Bernard puppy.

'I'm so sorry you've been put out like this,' she said. 'As a matter of fact, it is a bit inconvenient all round. I'd planned to go into the Market this afternoon and see if I could pick up a riding hack for some fabulously low sum...'

She broke off hurriedly, realizing that she was being more than rude suggesting that she didn't want him on her hands all afternoon as well as for lunch. But he did not seem to have noticed her *gaffe*.

'I say, are you fond of riding?' he asked, his face suddenly lighting up. 'I'm crazy about it and I've still got a very ancient old mare at home which I used to ride as a kid. She's really not fit for anything now except a quiet amble round the countryside. Do you hunt at all?'

'I've been abroad for two years,' Luisa explained, 'so there's not been much chance. But I'm afraid, now I am home, the old exchequer won't run to a hunter. I shall have to be content with a hack, if I can find one.'

'Well, please don't let me put you off your trip to the market,' Jim said. 'I can easily wait here on my own. Or... I say, perhaps I could run you in in the car? I'd love to have a look round. Father said he'd finance me a motor-bike next Christmas, but I really don't need it in town and down here I've got the Mater's car. I might buy a hack, too.'

Luisa smiled at his eagerness.

'Well, it's an idea,' she said. 'But suppose Bridget turns up in the meanwhile?'

Jim's face fell, and his expression was so ill-concealed that Luisa wanted to laugh outright.

'We *could* leave *her* a note,' she suggested, feeling suddenly rather young and naughty – as if the pair of them were planning something against the rules.

'I say, that's an idea,' said Jim, catching her mood. 'I'd better 'phone Mother and tell her not to expect us till tea-time. This is going to be rather fun after all.'

'Of course,' said Luisa, 'the others may be back before we're through lunch.'

'Well, couldn't we hurry it up?' Jim asked with a grin.

Fifteen minutes later, they had finished lunch, written a note for Bridget explaining their whereabouts, and were on the way to the market.

Bridget sat beside Martyn in the car wishing the drive home were not such a short one. When he was concentrating on his driving, he did not notice if she happened to be looking at him, and she could study his face to her heart's desire.

"Of course, I'm hopelessly in love for the first time in my life," she thought. "And I'm quite crazy because Martyn simply doesn't consider me in that light and never would. I'm more like a sister or a very good friend, judging by the way he treats me. Luisa's right. There must have been some girl in the past who handed him a raw deal. He doesn't like women as such, and even if he did, I wouldn't stand a chance. If I had any sense I'd get out before I fall so deep I shan't recover."

It wasn't only that she admired him as a person, she thought. It was something else which attracted her – his lean rugged face with those very brown eyes and dark hair; his essential masculinity. He had succeeded in awakening desires that she had not known existed. She had been kissed before, often enough by young men, and enjoyed the excitement. And there was Bob, of course, whom everyone expected her to marry one day. He was terribly in love with her and in a way she had been very fond of him until Martyn had come into her life. Now she knew she could never marry Bob ... that she had mistaken her fondness for him for something deeper. Martyn had quite inadvertently shown her that there was no breath-taking passion in the way she felt about dear old Bill. Her heart-beats never quickened when he turned his head and smiled at her, the way they did when Martyn gave her a friendly grin. There was no trembling when Bill's hand touched hers as Martyn's touch had the power to evoke. To be in Bill's arms was comforting and nice and agreeable in every way, but the very thought of Martyn's arms caused the colour to run into her cheeks. She adored him and tried to conceal it both from Martyn and Luisa. Luisa, she knew, did not like Martyn and would think her quite mad, or else silly. Of course, Luisa was the silly one really – not to see Martyn's immense attraction. How she could remain so impervious to him Bridget couldn't begin to understand.

'You're very thoughtful, Bridget,' Martyn said, casting a quick glance at her. 'Worried about the boy-friend? I'm sure you needn't. Luisa will have asked him to lunch and he'll be waiting to take you to tea. I'm terribly sorry I had to keep you so long.'

'You've no need to be sorry,' Bridget said. 'I love the work, Martyn. Besides, Jim Mathers isn't "the boy-friend", and I've never seen him before in my life and don't even want to go over to tea.'

His eyebrows raised at the vehemence of her tone.

'Why, what's the matter with the fellow?' he asked.

'Nothing, that I know of. It's just that – well, I'm not particularly interested in other young men.'

'Oh, so there's one in particular?' Martyn teased her.

A quick flush rose to Bridget's face. She turned her head quickly and looked out of the window so that he could not see her expression.

'In a way – yes!'

'Don't you know?' Martyn queried, his tone still friendly and teasing.

'I know that I'm in love – but he isn't in love with me,' Bridget replied.

'I say, I'm terribly sorry,' Martyn said quickly. 'I didn't mean to pry into your private affairs. I was just teasing you really. I'm so sorry – in every way.'

Bridget gathered herself together and was able to say easily:

'Oh, well, it's life, I suppose. Anyway, I'm not unhappy.'

'I'm glad,' Martyn said. 'You see, life treated me much the same way and I was unhappy and very bitter. It can hurt like hell. But in time you can get over anything, it seems. I don't care any more.'

'I – I thought perhaps something like that had happened, Martyn. You see, you're so obviously a misogynist.'

Martyn gave a quick laugh.

'Am I? I suppose I am – or was. But I must be softening or something, seeing that I've got two women around me most of the day – and that I don't mind it.'

It was Bridget's turn to laugh.

'You're hardly complimentary,' she said.

'As a matter of fact it was meant as a compliment,' Martyn said seriously. 'I was fed up to the teeth with the whole situation when I heard Luisa was coming home. I never realized then that she'd be responsible for introducing the most efficient secretary and assistant I could have hoped for – and a very good friend into the bargain.'

Bridget flushed again at the warm tone of his voice. Something in her prompted her to ask:

'You do like Luisa, don't you, Martyn?'

'Oh, she's all right, I suppose. I don't think she likes me very much though, judging by the way she avoids my company. But it suits me.'

'She's very beautiful,' Bridget said quietly.

'Is she? I suppose she is, if you're looking for beauty. I'm not. My work is all I care about. Besides, facial beauty isn't everything. It's what there is underneath that counts in the long run. I'd rather have someone like you, Bridget, who's thoroughly decent and honest underneath.'

'But Luisa's decent and honest, too, Martyn. I can't understand why you two don't hit it off.'

Martyn gave her a quick look.

'My dear young girl,' he said, 'I trust you're not trying a little match-making on me, are you? Because, if you are, I wouldn't marry Luisa if she was the last woman on earth.'

'Why?'

Martyn frowned, not understanding himself the vehemence with which he had spoken.

'I don't know. I – well, I really don't know!' he said awkwardly.

'Because she reminds you in some way of that other girl?'

Martyn remained silent, thinking to himself that Bridget had hit the nail on the head. She'd guessed at something he hadn't yet analysed himself. Luisa did remind him of Betty. Her beauty had the same breath-taking quality. And underneath, no doubt, she was just as hard, just as shallow.

'You're very discerning, Bridget,' he said, evading a direct answer. 'But, for heaven's sake, don't repeat what I've been saying. Not that you would, but Luisa and I have only just reached a footing where we can be polite to each other.'

'You're impossible, Martyn,' Bridget said.

'You just refuse to see Luisa as she really is.'

'There you go again, trying to get me to like her,' Martyn said laughing. 'I really believe you're just a match-making old hen at heart.'

'On the contrary,' said Bridget, forcing her tone to seem light and teasing, 'if you weren't such a hopelessly confirmed bachelor, I'd set my own cap at you – not Luisa's.'

Martyn laughed again, not taking her seriously.

'Thanks for the compliment. Still, I'd be a rotten bargain for a girl – bad-tempered and surly and moody and this – this damned handicap,' he added savagely, looking at his empty sleeve.

Bridget looked at him and said quietly:

'I can't see why you mind so much, Martyn, about your hand. You manage very well without it. I think you take it far too seriously. It isn't, after all, in the least disfiguring. And even if it were, girls don't mind that sort of thing when they are in love. Look at the women who married those R.A.F. boys whose faces were so badly burnt.'

'Pity!' Martyn said curtly.

'No, not pity – love,' said Bridget. 'You know, Martyn, a woman's love is so much more worthwhile than a man's. Beauty matters a lot to him, even while he loves. It doesn't to a woman.'

'You're very young and you talk a lot of

nonsense,' Martyn said brutally. 'Women do care, and they don't hesitate to show their revulsion at an ugly sight. Don't talk about things which you don't know about.'

'You're speaking of one incident, aren't you, Martyn? One woman. I think I do know what I'm talking about. If that woman behaved in such a way, she couldn't have loved you. I'm sorry if that hurts, but it must be true. You've been unfortunate.'

Listening to those words, Martyn's bitterness vanished. Perhaps Bridget was right. After all, no one else but Betty had ever shied from the sight of his missing hand. Bridget, for instance, never even noticed it. Nor had Luisa seemed in the least affected except at that first meeting when he had imagined she was staring at it. Maybe he had only imagined it. Maybe Betty's behaviour had given him a complex.

'You know, Bridget, you're a great girl!' Martin said. 'You're so wonderfully matter of fact about everything – and sensible. You do me a world of good. I think you're reforming me. It was a lucky day for me when Luisa invited you here in more ways than one.'

Bridget felt her heart thudding. Was there a deeper meaning in Martyn's words? Could he, after all, care for her a little? She wasn't really plain, except beside someone like Luisa. Bob thought her beautiful and loved her. Why not Martyn one day? And yet Martyn could have meant nothing more than he said – just a friendly remark, a show of gratitude for her companionship.

But because she wanted to, Bridget could not stop herself hoping, believing that Martyn was turning to her after all.

He was unaware of the emotions of the girl at his side. He had, in fact, meant nothing more than he had said. He liked Bridget, tremendously, and was grateful to her and enjoyed her company. He took her untiring efforts to work for him for granted, knowing she, too, loved the work. It never occurred to him that the girl might be falling in love with him. The thought had not entered his head. Nor did he think of the repercussions of such an event. If he had done so, he would realize that inevitably Bridget would go back to London, and would have been horrified at the thought. He depended on her, even in the short time she had been here, a great deal.

'Well, here we are. Let's hope Mrs Jennings has kept us some lunch. I'm starving,' he said cheerfully, and then: 'Wasn't your friend coming by car? I don't see it in the drive.'

'Perhaps he decided not to wait,' said Bridget.

Inside the house, she found Luisa's note, and showed it to Martyn, feeling relieved that Luisa had made it possible by taking Jim Mathers off for the afternoon, for her to have Martyn to herself. Every minute with him was precious now and she had been wishing all morning that she had not accepted Mrs Mathers' invitation to spend the day there.

She was quite unprepared for Martyn's sudden flare up.

'Of all the damned cheek,' he expostulated.

'Well, really Martyn, I don't see why,' Bridget said, amazed at his anger.

'Well, he's *your* boy-friend, isn't he? I suppose Luisa thinks she has a right to walk off with any man who finds her in the least bit attractive. And she calls herself your friend.'

'I think you're being ridiculous, Martyn,' Bridget said calmly. 'To start with, Jim Mathers isn't my boy-friend; and secondly, Luisa had to keep him entertained, anyway. I think it was very nice of her.'

'The trouble with you is, you're too damn nice yourself. You can never see the worst in other people,' said Martyn, feeling brotherly and protective for Bridget.

'The trouble with you, Martyn, is that you always see the worst in other people,' said Bridget.

Martyn laughed unexpectedly.

'Maybe! Anyway, at least I avoid unpleasant let-downs. Come on, let's have some lunch and forget about it.'

But inwardly he had no intention of forgetting about it. And later that afternoon, when a laughing Luisa returned with a glowing Jim Mathers, all his anger and resentment returned.

'May I introduce Jim – this is Martyn, and Bridget,' Luisa said. 'We've had a wonderful afternoon and I've gone quite mad and bought a hack. He's ninety at least, but Jim says he'll keep up with his old mare. It was enormous fun, Bridget. I do wish you'd been able to come with us.'

'It's a bit late, don't you think, to consider that. As a matter of fact, Bridget and I were back by two-thirty. Had you waited a little longer she could have gone, too.'

Luisa's face flushed angrily at the reproach in Martyn's voice. Jim was staring at him in surprise and she felt very embarrassed. An awkward silence fell as Luisa curbed her angry retort out of consideration for Jim.

Bridge spoke hurriedly:

'Really, Martyn, how stupid of you. As a matter of fact I've had a lot to do this afternoon and it's given me an opportunity to catch up on my work. Tell us more about the horse, Luisa. And I do want to apologize, Jim, for not being here. I hope Luisa made my explanations and excuses.'

'Of course I understood. I hope you'll come over to tea. I've asked Luisa and maybe you would come with us, Mr Saunders?'

Jim did not ask Martyn because he wanted

his company but felt that politeness demanded it. An odd sort of chap, he reflected. What on earth made him go off the deep end like that? Obviously he didn't care for Luisa. He must be mad. One afternoon had sufficed for Jim to realize that Luisa was the nicest girl he'd ever met, and the most fun. They had had a wonderful afternoon and behaved just like a couple of silly kids, eating ice cream from cones and wandering round the market.

'I'm afraid I have work to do,' Martyn said curtly. 'As a matter of fact, I was hoping Luisa would be here this afternoon so that we could go over some accounts; but, of course, if you've made other plans, Luisa...'

Luisa bit her lip angrily. Martyn, it appeared, was trying to prevent her going with Bridget and Jim. Perhaps he imagined she was trying to steal Bridget's boy-friend, or something. Well, she liked Jim Mathers, and if she wanted to go on seeing him she would. Besides, Martyn must be blind not to see that Bridget was in love with him (heaven alone knew why) and therefore not the slightest interested in young Jim. Well, he shouldn't have a chance to criticize her. Bridget could go to tea and wish all the time she were back at home with Martyn. She could blame him for that.

'Of course I'll stay and do the accounts,' she said. 'You'll excuse me, won't you, Jim?

But Martyn is so busy these days, I don't want to waste a few spare moments when he has them.'

Jim looked crestfallen but managed to say:

'That's all right. I quite understand. Well, shall we go, Bridget? Mother will be wondering what's happened to us.'

'I'll just fetch my coat,' said Bridget, knowing she had no alternative.

Once they had gone, Luisa turned on Martyn furiously.

'I think it would be a very good idea if in future you refrained from making such comments on my behaviour in front of strangers,' she said, her green eyes blazing with irritation.

'And I think it would be a good idea if you stopped trying to steal Bridget's friends. You think just because you're pretty you can walk off with any man, no matter who else you hurt by it. I thought you called yourself a friend of Bridget's.'

The angry retort died on Luisa's lips. And quite suddenly she laughed. Martyn must be quite mad. He was making a huge issue out of nothing. It was utterly ludicrous. Surely he saw how ridiculous he was being.

'I'm sorry. I fail to see the joke,' he said bitingly.

Luisa controlled herself, and her anger returned.

'I'm sorry, but I fail to see what business it

is of yours.'

'It's my business because I'm fond of Bridget, and she's too thoroughly decent to see you as you really are – another pretty little flirt.'

Luisa felt the last vestige of control leave her. This was really too much, and utterly unjustified. She took a step towards him and said furiously:

'You're rude and quite mad, Martyn Saunders. And blind into the bargain. And since you're so worried as to Bridget's feelings, I suggest you do something about it yourself instead of worrying about how I behave.'

'And what exactly do you mean by that?' asked Martyn, his temper rising to match hers.

'I suggest you stop dangling her on a string and tell her where she stands. Don't pretend you don't know she's in love with you,' she added, seeing the expression on his face. 'Anyone but a fool could see it...' she broke off, her anger suddenly deflating as she realized that she had behaved unforgivably to her friend, giving her away like that. Bridget had tried hard to conceal it from her as much as from Martyn.

'I'm sorry,' she said awkwardly. 'I – I didn't really mean that. You – you provoked me ... I didn't mean it...'

And covered in confusion, she turned and ran out of the room.

CHAPTER IV

Martyn did not try to follow Luisa, but sat quite still, her words echoing in the silence as he tried to sort their meaning.

At first he was sure Luisa was talking nonsense. It was absurd! Why, he had only known Bridget a few weeks and there had been no sign ... no indication ... or had there? he asked himself, doubts suddenly rising. The truth of the matter was, he had simply never given Bridget a thought in that light. She was to him just his assistant, a companion and a very good friend. But that didn't prove he meant the same to her. Bridget – in love with him! Of course it wasn't true! Why, she had only this afternoon told him she was in love with some fellow who didn't return her affections.

And remembering this, Martyn suddenly realized that Bridget could have been referring to him. He was profoundly embarrassed. After all, it was a very awkward position for him. He couldn't possibly continue on the same impersonal footing with her in the future. If it were true she loved him, it wouldn't be fair to her unless there were some chance that he might fall in love with her – and that was quite out of the question.

'I'm still in love with Betty,' he told himself bitterly. 'Although I despise and hate her, I still love her. I've nothing to offer a girl – even if I wanted marriage, and I don't.'

But his unspoken thoughts only led to further self-questioning. Ever since Betty had chucked him over he had shied away from probing his emotions. It hurt too much to do so. But now, suddenly, he knew that he couldn't avoid life, however much he may have tried to do so. First Luisa had broken into his house, and then Bridget ... now this. And yet, oddly enough, he had hardly noticed this invasion into his solitude except to realize that his life was considerably more comfortable. His meals were better cooked. His laundry was dealt with by someone who had had it mended and put back in his room where before he had to call Mrs Jennings' attention to the fact that he hadn't one pair of socks without a hole in them. And the other domestic worries – ration books, housekeeping – it had all been taken out of his hands. And then there was his work – Bridget had helped enormously and his practice had definitely grown. There had been no working until the early hours of the morning trying to sort out his papers and accounts. Bridget had had everything filed, sorted, and typed ready for him to sign in the morning before surgery.

"In fact," thought Martyn, "I've thoroughly overworked the girl and never thanked her for it. I've been devilishly selfish. She's been the one to work late at night to have everything ready for me. And now I've got to do something about it. The question is – what?"

That Bridget was only working on a temporary basis he knew very well, and yet since the day she had started work and he had begun to rely on her help, he had not considered her going. The thought appalled him. He hated changes and he would undoubtedly have to get some other girl. And however efficient, he was quite sure he would never like her as he liked Bridget.

Martyn swore softly to himself as he thought over the position. Everything pointed against Bridget leaving, and yet he couldn't do the one thing that would make the arrangement permanent – marry her. If only he loved her everything would have been so perfect – a home, a companion, an assistant, and a wife who loved and understood animals as he did and was equally interested in his work.

'Other men have married for less,' Martyn said quite suddenly. Then he rejected the idea. It simply wasn't fair to Bridget. After all, he was a hopeless bargain for any girl with his moods and that damnable handicap – let alone the fact that he couldn't offer them love as women wanted it. But Bridget's words that afternoon in the car came into his mind with great clarity. If a woman loved you, she had said, she wouldn't mind the absent arm. Pity didn't come into it. It was all a question of love.

Bridget had said Betty couldn't have loved him to let him down like that. Perhaps she was right. Perhaps it would turn out for the best. Betty would never have made him a good wife and with her shallow, pretty, affected ways, he would probably have ended up by hating her ... hating her as he hated Luisa who seemed to him to be just another Betty. It was no good pretending he liked her. Somehow he simply wasn't able to do so. Luisa inevitably rubbed him up the wrong way. They were always having rows or scenes about something. No doubt it was equally his fault, but the reason didn't really matter. The result was clear to them both. They just didn't make a team the way he and Bridget did.

'Am I trying to make myself fall in love with Bridget?' Martyn asked himself. 'If only I knew what to do. If only Luisa hadn't had to flare up like that and let the cat out of the bag!'

But he knew that was an escapist thought. Sooner or later he'd have found out for himself and then his position would have been the same. At least now he had time to think what to do. Bridget didn't know yet that he knew. He could carry on as usual until he'd made up his mind what was best for all of them – unless Luisa went and told her. But that was unlikely. It was hardly the sort of thing Luisa would care to confess to. He presumed women maintained some kind of honour between themselves and didn't go around betraying confidences. Or, if they did, like Luisa, they took care not to be found out responsible for it.

The telephone rang and, with some relief, Martyn answered it and was called out to a case. He shelved the question of Bridget and turned his mind to his work. There were no awkward problems about that, he thought thankfully. One had a job to do and one did it. If only life were as easy! He collected his instruments and hurried out to the car.

Luisa walked hurriedly through the woods, Boot bounding along beside her. She had no destination in mind and her pace was set entirely by the emotions that were troubling her.

"I hate Martyn Saunders," she thought furiously. "He's rude and interfering and irritable and warped. Just because some girl let him down he has no right to take it out on me. And it's his fault I've given Bridget away. She'll never forgive me. I only hope he doesn't take what I said seriously."

A little calmer after she had walked two or three miles, Luisa felt slightly reassured. Martyn knew she had lost her temper. No doubt he would attribute her remark entirely to feminine spitefulness or something of the sort. Her first inclination had been to tell Bridget of the whole scene, but now she felt that it might not, after all, be necessary, and might only cause Bridget a lot of embarrassment. In any case, she, Luisa, was only assuming Bridget's feeling. It might not be true at all, in which case, nothing mattered. But supposing her suspicions were right, as she was convinced deep down they were, then it would be far easier for Bridget to behave normally in front of Martyn as long as she supposed he had no idea how she felt.

Luisa threw a stick for Boot, who started tossing it about like a two-year-old. But she was not really watching him. She was considering her future. It was high time she got a job. Her resources were dwindling, and the builder's estimate for the job of converting the Vicarage, so far not yet started, had been higher than she anticipated.

For the first time since she had discussed the idea of converting her home, Luisa was not so sure that she wanted to go ahead with it. For one thing, she and Martyn Saunders were clearly not going to hit it off. For another, supposing Martyn did marry Bridget, they'd want a home of their own.

But immediately she knew that it was impossible for Martyn to make his home elsewhere unless another house became available in the locality. His work was here and he had, undoubtedly, built up a big practice for himself and was doing well.

Luisa sighed, the problems seeming to have no answer but that they continued as they were. What happened between Martyn and Bridget really didn't concern her and she would do far better to keep out of it. Indeed, she had never meant to come into it at all, only Martyn's interference had provoked her to it. He was, without doubt, the most difficult person to deal with. After all, what right had he to criticize her behaviour with Jim Mathers, which had been above reproach in any case? It was utterly ridiculous of him to imagine she was trying to 'steal' Bridget's boy-friend. To start with, Bridget had never met Jim before. To second it, Luisa had no intention of turning Jim Mathers into a 'boy-friend'. She had liked him as a person and after their afternoon together, had known they could be good friends. Why must people always bring an emotional side into the picture? Couldn't a girl be friendly with a man without people bringing in 'love' or sex?

But then, Martyn was undoubtedly warped in his outlook, Luisa decided. Nothing else could explain away his extraordinary behaviour. Bridget's life had nothing to do with him, unless he were himself in love with her, and had that been so, he would obviously have been glad if Luisa had removed a prospective rival instead of accusing her of 'stealing' Bridget's friends in her absence.

No, it did not make sense whichever way she looked at it. Only one thing was quite clear, and that was that Martyn didn't like her, and she certainly didn't like him. She had come home intending to be friendly and considerate and live her own life without bothering him, and this was the result. The fact that he took all she had done about the house quite for granted, didn't really matter. She hadn't taken the domestic worries off his shoulders in order to have him show a little gratitude. It merely seemed the obvious thing to do. Someone had to give Mrs Jennings orders and see that the house was kept clean and running well. At the same time, she had had sufficient time to see to Martyn's laundry and mending and so she had done it along with the rest of the household stuff. But now she wished violently that she hadn't bothered. Why put one's self out for a man who went out of his way to dislike you?

Luisa called Boot away from a rabbit hole and continued her meditations. The past didn't matter much. It was the future she bothered about. She must get a job of some sort. If only she had a few more horses and could open a riding school! What tremendous fun that would be. There was a boys' preparatory school only five miles away and she could get plenty of custom, she was sure. With a little more capital, she might have bought two more hacks and started in a small way. The Vicarage was an ideal starting ground. The old stables were untouched since the days of her grandfather when they had had no other means of transport. Only one had been converted into a garage, which Martyn used for his car. And there was plenty of grass, for the Vicarage boasted five acres of pasture which were let off to a neighbouring farmer for his cows.

Luisa's face lit up with growing enthusiasm. It would be a wonderful job. There was nothing she loved more than riding and caring for horses. Martyn would be conveniently on hand to see to the animals if they were sick or needed attention. If only she had a little capital – another horse or two.

Luisa halted in her tracks and sat down suddenly on a tree stump. Supposing she held up the conversion of the house and used the money to start? Martyn might object, of course, but as far as Luisa was now concerned, Martyn could put up with it. In a year or two, she might be able to make the capital back. Anything might happen before then and the conversion might not be necessary after all.

She tried to quell her excitement and think more practically. Could she get food for the horses? Were there restrictions on such things? Ought she to be doing something more worth while to benefit the country? Would it be a paying proposition or was she going to run herself into debt? There was so much to be considered. She could go along to the school and see the headmaster first – see if he could give her some idea of the number of children who might be taking riding as 'an extra'. She could start with fairly low prices seeing that the horses were old and slow. That was just as well for young children. Then she could keep them out at grass and avoid extra expense on food and so on. Saddles, bridles, stirrups – all those would have to be bought. And the horses.

"I'll ask Jim's advice," Luisa thought, jumping to her feet. "He's reasonably sensible and knows about costs of upkeep and so on. I'll ring him this evening when Bridget gets back, and see what he says."

Feeling in a very much happier frame of mind than when she had left home, Luisa returned to the vicarage, and being impulsive, decided not to wait for Bridget's return but to cycle over to Jim Mathers' house. She had, after all, been invited to tea, and Martyn had prevented her going from sheer stupidity. Well, she would have missed tea, but she would still go. Then she'd kill two birds with one stone – snub Martyn and see Jim about the new idea.

Half an hour later, she was being welcomed by a smiling Jim.

'I say, I'm terribly glad you could come,' he said. 'Mater was sorry you hadn't been able to make it. So was I. We were trying to persuade Bridget to stay to supper but she was saying she thought she ought to get back and give you a hand or something. Now you're here, you must both stay. Come and meet the Mater.'

Jim's mother was a charming grey-haired woman of fifty or so. She obviously adored her only son and ran her life entirely for him. Having been widowed nearly ten years ago, she had not married again, and her one reason for living was to see Jim established and happy. She worried about him a good deal and felt that he took life a little too seriously, and having decided that he didn't mix enough with young people – girls in particular, was trying hard to find him some friends.

As was inevitable, Jim never seemed to like the girls his mother had chosen for him and she had almost despaired of him marrying. Of course, he was very young yet to think of marriage but, being a sensible woman, Mrs Mathers felt that young men ought to meet and get to know about as many girls as possible so that when he did meet the 'right' girl, he would know her true value and make a sensible and happy marriage. She was utterly unlike the selfish mothers who try to prevent their sons marrying in order to keep them at home, although, living alone as she did, Jim meant everything to her. Unselfishly, she desired only his happiness.

Now, at last, Jim appeared to have met some girl and taken a most unusual fancy to her. All through tea, he had been plying Bridget with questions about 'Luisa' and her name had cropped up so consistently that Mrs Mathers' suspicions had been aroused. Bridget seemed to be a thoroughly nice girl and had only the nicest things to say about her friend 'Luisa'. Mrs Mathers felt a great desire to meet this girl – the first Jim had shown the slightest interest in – and when Luisa arrived, she was delighted.

Jim, it seemed, had certainly picked a very beautiful girl. Luisa was flushed and rosy from her cycle ride and her red-gold hair, wind-blown and curly, was only rivalled by the incredible beauty of her green eyes.

Mrs Mathers studied Luisa unobtrusively and saw that she had personality as well as looks – and instinctively, she liked her. Yet something warned her that this was not the right girl for Jim. She was too alive, too vital, too beautiful for her son. Jim was a shy, simple, studious person. One day he would be a great man in the medical world. But brain alone would never satisfy this glowing young woman. Bridget had given her age as twenty-six, only four years older than Jim, and yet the discrepancy seemed far greater. Luisa was a young woman. Jim still seemed a boy.

Luisa, however, was feeling very young and enthusiastic as she explained her scheme to Jim and Bridget.

'I'm sure it would work out,' she said. 'And I'd adore the job. Of course, I do feel I ought to be helping the nation in some way or another, but then if I run the riding school entirely for pupils of the preparatory school, it will be in a sense school work, won't it? And giving children healthy exercise is important.'

'I think it's a wonderful idea, Luisa,' Bridget was saying. 'I'll give you all the help I can with stable work and so on – that is, if I have any time to spare. Martyn keeps me pretty busy.'

'Of course it'll work, Luisa,' said Jim, pulling out a pencil and paper. 'We bought that hack to-day – I mean you did – for sixty pounds. I'd lend you the mare and you'd only need two more ponies to start. That's about a hundred and fifty pounds. Say another fifty for saddles and gear if we're lucky. Two hundred pounds. I'll come in fifty-fifty, Luisa, and take a half share of the profits. Of course, you'll have most of the work to do, stable work and so on, so we'd better make it a seventy-five, twenty-five financial basis. Then on Sundays we can use the horses for riding ourselves.'

'Oh, but I couldn't accept your help, Jim. I mean, I think it's a bit risky, really, and it doesn't matter losing your own money as much as it matters losing someone else's. It's very nice of you to offer but...'

'Luisa, don't be difficult,' Jim said, pleading with her. 'Do please let me help. I'd love to be in on it. Don't you think it's a good idea, Mater?'

Mrs Mathers smiled at her son. It was unusual for him to show so much enthusiasm and he seemed as excited about the idea as Luisa.

'It's up to you, Jim. You must decide for yourself. It's your money.'

'Then say yes, Luisa,' said Jim.

For a moment, Luisa considered it, and then something forced her to refuse. It wasn't that she was too proud to accept financial help – just that she didn't feel justified in taking it from Jim Mathers, who, after all, she had only met for the first time to-day.

'Really, Jim, I think I'd rather try to make out on my own. But I will accept the mare on a sort of share basis, and be most grateful for any advice and help.'

Jim looked pleased and Mrs Mathers felt a moment's admiration for Luisa. The girl had spirit and was independent. And she was quite right. It was far better not to bind oneself with financial ties which for all one knew might turn out to be difficult.

Bridget repeated her own offer to help as much as she could and then rose to her feet excusing herself.

'I really think I ought to go back,' she said, 'although it's most kind of you to invite me to stay to supper. But it's Mrs Jennings' afternoon off and someone ought to see to Martyn's supper.'

'I'll go, Bridget, if you like,' Luisa suggested.

'Look here, must either of you go?' Jim asked, hoping against hope that Luisa would stay.

'Luisa, you stay,' Bridget said. 'Martyn may have work for me anyway. You understand, don't you, Mrs Mathers? But Mr Saunders is so busy and I am his assistant, so I feel responsible, if you understand.'

It was quite clear to Luisa that Bridget, however much she liked the Mathers, was aching to get back to Martyn, so she did not offer again to go herself. It was finally decided that Bridget would go home on Luisa's bicycle and Jim would run Luisa back in the car after supper.

Bridget had just finished her own supper

when Martyn returned. She fetched his from the oven and sat talking to him while he ate it. They discussed the case he had been on and Martyn was relieved that everything seemed normal and Bridget her usual cheerful self. Perhaps after all Luisa had been wrong.

'Where is Luisa?' he asked.

'Discussing starting a riding stable with the Mathers,' Bridget told him.

'So she went after all,' Martyn said, feeling angry and irritable.

'Martyn, why ever not? I don't understand what you're fussing about. First when we came back at lunch time and now this. Why shouldn't Luisa go to the Mathers? She was invited, you know. Besides, it'll be company for her. She must lead a very lonely life here. We're working all day and she has no one to talk to except old Mrs Jennings.'

'Then she should get some work,' said Martyn. 'Do her good.'

Bridget sighed. It really did seem an impossible job getting Luisa and Martyn to like one another.

'That's just what she is going to do,' she told him. 'I think it's an excellent idea.' And she told him more about it.

'Oh, well, I suppose it might work out,' he said. 'As a matter of fact, this place lends itself very well to being a riding school. Who's financing it?'

'Luisa!' said Bridget.

'But I thought she was hard up?'

'She is. I think the idea is to hold up the conversion of the house for a while. She's going to talk it over with you. I hope you won't raise any difficulties, Martyn – about the house I mean. After all, it seems to work out all right as it is.'

Put in Bridget's calm, practical way, Martyn could see no objections. It was fortunate for Luisa that Bridget had, so to speak, cleared the obstacles before she herself spoke to Martyn. Undoubtedly had Luisa raised the subject, Martyn would have found something wrong with the idea.

'Yes, I suppose the conversion is really hardly necessary. It was only decided in the first place on moral grounds. Obviously Luisa and I couldn't share the house alone or we'd have had the whole village gossiping. But as long as you stay, there's no need to go ahead with it.'

'Yes!' was Bridget's only comment, thinking, "As long as I stay. But how long will I stay?"

Martyn was thinking along the same lines.

'As a matter of fact, I wanted to talk to you about that, Bridget. I mean, you came here temporarily with the idea of getting some other job in London, didn't you? Is there any chance you might leave me?'

Bridget poured out the coffee, feeling her

heart thudding painfully. If only she could tell him how she really felt – that if she had her way, she'd never leave him.

'No, I like my job here, Martyn. I'd like to stay on as long as it suits you. At least, that's the way I feel at the moment.'

'Well, if you get bored with it, just give me the word,' said Martyn. 'I suppose I could always get someone else, although I must say, I should hate the idea.'

'Yes – I – I shouldn't want to go,' Bridget said awkwardly, and then hurriedly collected the dishes and disappeared into the sanctuary of the kitchen.

It was those few words and her hurried retreat that made Martyn realize there was, after all, something in what Luisa had said. The question was, what did he intend to do about it.

CHAPTER V

Jim Mathers drove home, having deposited Luisa safely at the Vicarage, his mind in a whirl of excitement. To-morrow, Sunday, he was driving her up to the boys' preparatory school to see the headmaster about pupils for her riding school. That meant he would be able to spend the best part of the day with her before he had to return to London.

'I've fallen in love!' he told himself ecstatically. 'For years I haven't believed there was such a thing – not the way you read about it in books – the way the rest of the fellows talk about it. But it's true. Absolutely true. I'm just crazy about her.'

Thinking about Luisa and how beautiful she was and how wonderful a companion, Jim drove in a dream. He did not try to analyse his feelings. The thought of marriage simply had not crossed his mind. If it had, he would probably have turned a fiery red and told himself not to be so silly. Nobody as wonderful and marvellous as Luisa would ever think of marrying a chap like himself. No, Luisa was a person to be loved, admired, and respected. At a distance.

The fact that he had only known Luisa a

day flashed across his mind for a brief instant but settled comfortably into its niche. When you fell in love like this, it always happened suddenly, magically. One minute you were yourself. The next you were transported into the realms of fantasy. You could think of nothing but the girl you adored and the wonderful thought that you'd be seeing her again to-morrow.

He was glad that his mother had already gone to bed when he reached home and that he could go quietly to his room and lean out of his window until the early hours of the morning dreaming happily to himself and wondering if Luisa could by any miraculous chance be thinking of him.

Luisa, however, was not thinking of Jim Mathers. She was sitting on Bridget's bed having a feminine heart-to-heart talk with her friend. Jim couldn't have been further from her mind.

Bridget, unable to keep her feelings to herself a day longer, had confided in Luisa how she felt about Martyn. She had told her, too, for the first time about Bob, the young man in London who wanted her to marry him.

'Of course, it's utterly hopeless now,' she told Luisa. 'I had told Bill to give me a year to make up my mind. I suppose I always knew in the end I would meet someone like Martyn and then really fall in love. I shall have to write to Bill and tell him the truth. It's not fair to keep him hanging on a string now my mind is made up.'

Luisa frowned and looked more than a little disturbed.

'Do you think that's altogether wise, Bridget, my dear?' she asked gently. 'After all, you've admitted you don't think there is much chance of Martyn returning the compliment. Suppose there were no hope, then you may turn to Bill after all. He sounds so nice and comforting and reliable.'

'If Martyn never loves me, it wouldn't alter a thing,' Bridget said firmly. '*I* couldn't change. I could never love Bill properly now. It wouldn't be fair to him just to have him as second best, even if I wanted to – which I don't.'

'Perhaps Bill wouldn't mind,' Luisa suggested. 'He may trust to luck that you'd fall in love with him after marriage.'

'That's what he's always said,' Bridget admitted. 'But it's quite out of the question, Luisa. How can one love two people? And I shall love Martyn as long as I live.'

Luisa gave Bridget's hand a quick squeeze.

'Then I hope he'll soon feel the same way about you, Bridget.'

Bridget smiled wryly.

'So do I, Lis. But I can't say I feel any more convinced than you sound. He's much too good for me. I'm too ordinary for him.

He needs someone more exotic and exciting – like you, Luisa.'

'What unutterable rubbish,' Luisa said indignantly. 'Firstly, I'm neither exotic nor exciting. Secondly you know as well as I do that Martyn and I just don't hit it off. We're all right apart but whenever we're together we flare up and become rude and impossible. No, Bridget, you're just what Martyn needs – someone steady and reliable and kind. I think you'd make him a wonderful wife.'

Bridget sighed.

'I wish I felt it, Lis. But I don't. Deep down inside, I think I'll end up by boring Martyn. Maybe now, while he's still on the rebound from this girl, Betty, and still touchy about his arm and that sort of thing – I do suit him. But I'm sure Martyn when he's his real self is a different person – amusing, vital … oh, I don't know. I just feel I couldn't hold him.'

'You suffer from an absurd and quite unjustified inferiority complex, Bridget. Martyn would be darned lucky to get a wife like you. He doesn't deserve anyone half as nice. Personally I don't think he deserves a wife at all.'

'Or wants one,' Bridget said with a laugh. 'Lis, we're quite mad, sitting up till all hours discussing Martyn's future when I'm convinced he hasn't a thought further from his mind. We'll both be dog tired in the morning.'

A few minutes later, the two girls parted and were settled down for sleep. But although Bridget was soon dreaming pleasantly about riding in the car with Martyn, Luisa lay awake thinking about her friend's future. Deep in her heart, she could not really see Bridget married to Martyn. Somehow it just didn't seem to be right. She searched for reasons against it and could find none that were worth consideration. It was just – well, that they didn't give one the impression of being 'made for one another' as people so often described the perfect pair.

At last, exhausted, Luisa firmly put the whole thing from her mind and started her train of thought on the new riding school. Almost immediately she, too, was fast asleep.

Sunday was uneventful except that Luisa received firm promises of at least fifteen regular pupils and decided to go ahead with her plans for a riding stable. Jim returned to town still in a rosy haze of adoration, and Bridget spent the day composing series of letters to Bill to tell him she could never marry him now, and at last succeeded in writing and posting a short note to this effect.

Martyn spent the entire day going over papers and accounts and taking far too long about it seeing that his mind kept running round in circles about this new problem of Bridget and what he was to do about her. The day ended with very little work accomplished and still no decision made.

In fact, everyone but Jim welcomed Monday with its promise of a full day to keep them occupied. Jim, however, was quite unable to keep his mind on the lectures he was attending and flushed furiously when one of his fellow-students accused him of 'being in love'. Having given the show away he was teased mercilessly for the rest of the week and felt by the time Saturday came that he could never face Luisa again. Instead of driving straight over to the Vicarage, he mooched around his own house, kicking himself for the time he was wasting and yet unable to pluck up the necessary courage to go over and see her. At last, he could stand it no longer, and in an agony of nervousness, he telephoned.

Luisa's voice was calm and reassuringly everyday. She invited him over to see the progress she had made in clearing out the stables and to stay for tea. He tore upstairs to change into a clean shirt – totally unsuitable for helping Luisa with the stables – and drove over at a dangerously high speed to find a perfectly strange young man on the doorstep.

'Who are you?' he asked, his voice cracking a little with horrible suspicion that this was one of Luisa's admirers come to ruin his day alone with her.

'Come to that, who are you?' asked the young man.

Jim looked slightly taken aback. He studied the stranger and came to the conclusion that he looked fairly harmless. He had on a pair of rather shapeless grey flannel bags and an old tweed jacket, and his square sunburnt face was good-looking enough but not so that you'd pick him out in a crowd, Jim decided. His hair was lightish brown and more or less untidy and his blue eyes were about his only unusual feature. They were exceptionally blue and seemed to fit in very well with the description of 'sailor blue eyes'. At the moment they were regarding Jim with a mixture of annoyance and amusement.

'I'm Jim Mathers. I've come over to see Luisa,' Jim said, recovering his manners.

The blue eyes cleared suddenly and the young man held out a hand.

'Oh, I thought perhaps you were Martyn Saunders. As a matter of fact I'm Bill Smith. I've come over to see Bridget, but although I've been ringing this confounded door-bell for at least ten minutes, nobody seems to be at home.'

Seeing that this was one of Bridget's friends, Jim was more than prepared to be friendly.

'I expect they're all out the back,' he said. 'I know Luisa's in the stables. Perhaps the others are there helping her. Let's go round and see.'

Only Luisa, however, was to be found in the stables. After the necessary introductions, Luisa explained that Martyn and Bridget had gone over to the farm to dock the tails of a new litter of prize Springer pups. She surveyed Bill anxiously and decided that there would be trouble when Bridget returned. There was a very stubborn line to Bill's square jaw and he looked as if he meant business. She only hoped he wouldn't make a scene in front of Martyn who was supposed to know nothing of Bridget's personal feelings and probably had no idea even that Bill existed. She wondered how she could get in touch with Bridget and warn her. The farm wasn't on the telephone and she couldn't think of a way even if her life depended on it.

Jim, his meeting with Luisa smoothly and pleasantly accomplished without embarrassment thanks to Bill Smith's timely arrival, was feeling happy and completely content.

'Perhaps we can give you a hand until they come back?' Bill suggested, thinking how glorious Luisa looked in breeches and that yellow sweater with her red hair blowing over her face and a delightful little smudge of dirt on the tip of her nose.

Luisa was going to decline the offer but on second thoughts decided that a little strenuous work might cool off some of Bill's accumulating anger. She handed them each a pitchfork and told them to get busy on the bales of straw.

Bill worked for ten minutes and then gave it up. He was in a furious temper now and the longer Bridget was keeping him waiting while she gallivanted around the countryside, the worse was the mood he was in.

He had digested her letter with a complete numbness brought on by shock. It had been brief and very much to the point. In fact she hadn't taken the trouble to soften the blow at all.

Dear Bill, she had written,

I'm more than sorry to have to write this but the sooner you realize the truth the better. I can never marry you now. I'm in love with Martyn Saunders and even if he never marries me I shall always love him and so it's best you should know and find some other girl.

I really am sorry, Bill,

As ever,

Bridget.

When the numbness wore off, he had been desperately angry with her and swore he'd not only decline to answer her letter, but that he'd never see her again as long as he lived.

But a day later his mood had changed again and he was desperately unhappy and wretchedly puzzled. He and Bridget had known each other since they were kids. He'd loved her ever since he'd been old enough to know the meaning of the word. There never had been and never would be another girl. At first it had been all right. When Bridget had left school, she had been glad to go to dances and parties and picnics with him. Everyone had recognized their friendship and one was seldom asked without the other. If it had happened that Bridget had been asked without him, she was miserable and had even refused to go.

Then the war had come and he'd gone away. At first, when he came home for leaves, everything had been wonderful. Bridget had at last seemed as if she were really beginning to care for him. He knew now that this was only a natural reaction brought on by the excitement and romantic side of war, but he hadn't known then and had asked Bridget to marry him. Bridget had agreed but made him promise to keep the engagement secret for a while.

'We're both awfully young, Bill, and I know Mother and Father wouldn't agree to my getting married until I'm twenty. Especially as it's war-time.'

He'd argued that the war was one good reason why they should get married, but

Bridget had been sensible and practical and stuck to her point.

Then he'd had two years overseas and he'd known before he arrived back, by her letters, that she had changed. It was inevitable that she had met other chaps while he was away. For the first time in her life she had been to parties and dances without him. It had all been new and exciting, and when the Americans came over Bridget had been much in demand. It wasn't that she had fallen in love with any of them. But just that she was managing to enjoy life without him. It puzzled her and she began to wonder if she did want to settle down and marry him after all. Was she really in love with him, if she could be happy without him? she wrote one time.

Bill had no answer and agreed to wait until she was sure. It had seemed ironic and a little hard to him that now she was old enough to marry him, she no longer wanted to. But deep in his heart, he knew Bridget belonged to him. He loved her deeply and sincerely and with all his heart. There would and could be no other wife for him. He was, therefore, prepared to wait until she got over this adolescent stage and was willing to settle down.

The war over, everyday life had returned to normal. Bridget, too, had calmed down and although she did occasionally go to odd dances and parties with other chaps, Bill was once more the 'regular' date. He was, she assured him, the only man she allowed to kiss her on the way home. She was fonder of him than anyone she knew. But she wanted a little more time to decide.

Receiving her letter, Bill cursed himself for allowing her that time. Perhaps if he'd been a little more masterful and persuasive, Bridget would have married him and this whole stupid business of Martyn Saunders would never have arisen.

But it was too late, he realized, to think about what he should have done. The question was, what should he do now? Leave her alone and let this other fellow marry her? Or go down and put up a fight for her?

By the week-end, Bill knew that go down to see Bridget he must and would. He'd reason with her, talk everything over with her. It couldn't be so very serious. She'd only known the man a month. He'd make her see sense.

Filled with these intentions, Bill was immensely put out when he arrived to find Bridget departed. He hadn't warned her of his arrival but that still didn't alter the fact that it was more than annoying to find her away. And with this man, Martyn Saunders. Once or twice he caught Luisa looking at him anxiously and wondered just how much she knew. If it hadn't been for that incredible-looking bespectacled young man who was hanging around her like a love-sick young puppy, he might have been able to talk to Luisa and find out just what was going on.

This put him into an even worse temper – Bill, who was the best-natured of people and so seldom wrought up – was naturally the worse when he did get worked up. When at last Bridget arrived back with Martyn, it was all he could do to appear even mildly civil.

Bridget blushed a furious red when she saw Bill and wished herself a thousand miles away. Luisa tactfully made the introductions and Martyn held out his hand.

Bill ignored it, and looking straight at Bridget said:

'If you could spare me a minute, Bridget, I'd like to see you alone.'

'Martyn, perhaps you'd take Bill's pitchfork and give me a hand,' Luisa said quickly. 'I know you're busy, but I'm sure the exercise would do you good and we do need help, don't we Jim?'

Jim nodded his head gloomily. It seemed as if Fate were conspiring that he should not have a moment alone with Luisa.

Martyn, sensing the somewhat tense atmosphere, decided to accept Luisa's suggestion. Bridget, still without saying a word, took Bill into the house.

'What's up with that young man?' Martyn asked, as soon as they were out of earshot.

'That's one of Bridget's ex-boy-friends,' Luisa said. 'I imagine he doesn't approve of being an "ex".'

'I don't wonder she's finished with him,' Martyn said irritably. 'He certainly seems a very rude young man.'

'Oh, I don't think he is particularly. At least, he wasn't rude to us, was he, Jim?' Luisa said innocently.

Jim shook his head.

'Well, he ignored my hand obviously enough. Don't try and tell me it wasn't intentional.'

'Perhaps you inspire rudeness in other people,' Luisa said, her tone light but her words pointed.

'Perhaps I do,' Martyn replied angrily. 'Some people get me that way.'

Suddenly Luisa laughed.

'Honestly, Martyn, you do jump at a fly. For goodness sake don't let's quarrel. I fancy there's enough atmosphere knocking around without us starting. I'm sorry for what I just said, and I do appreciate your helping like this.'

Mollified by her change of mood, Martyn's scowl disappeared.

'Well, admit he did ignore my hand,' he said.

'I admit it,' said Luisa with a smile. 'I

fancy the young man is jealous, Martyn.'

'Jealous! Of me?' Martin asked. 'Of all the damn silly ... look here, Luisa, I'll go in and tell him. I haven't the slightest intention of stealing his girl-friend. If Bridget is in love with him, then she can marry him to-morrow. I'm not stopping her.'

'Perhaps she isn't in love with him,' Luisa said. 'Personally I think it would be a very good thing if she did marry him. After all, there isn't much future for her here, or is there?'

'What exactly do you mean by that remark?' Martyn asked.

'Well, there aren't many eligible young men around the neighbourhood, present company excluded, of course,' she said with a friendly smile at Jim who was gazing at her miserably. His face broke into a smile.

'Perhaps Bridget isn't interested in marriage and that sort of thing,' Martyn suggested without conviction.

'Perhaps, on the other hand, she is,' said Luisa. 'A girl usually does want to get married sooner or later, Martyn. Especially when she falls in love.'

Martyn could not possibly misinterpret Luisa's meaning and he knew, too, that this was no jibe. Last time Luisa had suggested such a thing, he'd taken it as a feminine retort to hurt him. But he had his own suspicions about Bridget and still had come to no conclusions.

He threw down his pitchfork and went moodily back to the house, and into the surgery. He had had no intention of eavesdropping, but his window was open and the sitting-room window next door was also open. Bridget's and Bill's voices came clearly to him.'

'It's no good, Bill,' Bridget was saying. 'I've made up my mind and I'll never change it. What's the good of your waiting?'

'Perhaps there's no good at all,' Bill said. 'On the other hand there might be. I can't believe you mean to go through with this. You've said yourself you don't think he cares two twopenny damns for you. What makes you think he ever will?'

'I don't think he will and I don't care if he doesn't,' came Bridget's voice, near to tears. 'The fact still remains that I love him whether he loves me or not. So I can't marry you, can I?'

There was a moment's silence, then the sound of a struggle and Bridget's voice saying:

'Let me go, Bill. If you dare to kiss me again...'

Martyn jumped to his feet and flung open the sitting-room door. Bill had his arms round Bridget and was trying to kiss her – clearly against her will. Perhaps if he had succeeded, Bill might have won the day. But

Martyn's voice cut across the room like a knife.

'I suggest as you're clearly not very welcome, that you leave the house immediately,' he said.

Bill, flushed and dishevelled, his temper now quite out of control, turned furiously to Bridget and said:

'Very well, I will. And I'm damned if I'll come back – even when he has turned you down. And as for you, Martyn Saunders, you're the most despicable cad I ever knew.'

And he flung himself out of the house to find Luisa and Jim setting off for the village to get some cakes for tea.

'Aren't you staying?' Luisa asked.

'No, I'm not,' said Bill. 'And if you're going to the village, I'd like a lift to the station.'

At the station, Luisa contrived to send Jim for the cakes while she saw Bill to his train.

'If there is anything I can do,' she said kindly, seeing the misery in his face now that his temper had cooled off a little.

'Thanks!' said Bill wretchedly. 'But I don't think there is. You see, I'm beginning to believe she is serious after all. Do you think he will marry her?'

Luisa shook her head helplessly.

'I don't know, Bill. I hope not. I don't feel inside me they are suited. Look, leave me your address. If ever Bridget's in trouble, or if this whole thing should blow over, then I could contact you, couldn't I?'

Bill's face lit up for a moment.

'That's awfully nice of you. Of course, I blew up in there in such a state, I said the most unforgivable things. I don't suppose she'll ever want to see me again. Still, perhaps she might need me. Anyway, here's my address. And ... look after her, won't you? She's terribly young still in lots of ways. She wants taking care of. She seems sophisticated and that sort of thing, but she isn't really. Don't let him hurt her.'

Deeply touched, Luisa could find nothing to say, except to repeat that she'd get in touch with him if there were any need.

Then he climbed into the train and was lost to view.

Back in the Vicarage, Martyn held a sobbing Bridget in his arm and was trying to comfort her. He was profoundly embarrassed and felt very tender and protective towards her.

'Bridget, don't, my dear. Please don't cry. There's nothing to upset yourself about. That chap had no right to behave like that. He's just a brute.'

'It – it isn't that,' Bridget choked.

'Then you do care for him?' Martyn asked. 'Because if you do, we'll go right down to the station and fetch him back.'

'No ... I ... I don't want him back, Martyn.

I'm not in love with him…'

'Look at me, Bridget!' Martyn said, raising her tear-stained face to his. 'Is it – that you care for someone else – for me?'

She shook her head in denial but he knew that it was true and he, who had been so harshly and remorselessly treated by Betty, felt deeply touched and flattered.

'Bridget, I don't deserve your love, and I don't deserve a girl like you. But if you think you can bear with me and understand that – that I can't give you a great deal in return, I'd be very happy if would marry me.'

And as she put her arms around him and lifted her face for his kiss, he knew nothing but a profound relief that at last the problem was solved. He bent his head to kiss her, but at that moment the door opened and Luisa walked in.

CHAPTER VI

Almost guiltily, Martyn immediately released Bridget.

'I'm terribly sorry for intruding,' Luisa said. 'I didn't realize... I'm so sorry.'

'There's no need to apologize, Lis,' Bridget broke in. 'As a matter of fact, I'm glad you came. You see, Martyn has just asked me to marry him.'

Luisa looked from one to the other, hardly able to accept this so unexpected remark. Such a lot seemed to have happened to-day and all of it without warning. She looked at Martyn as if for confirmation.

'I – we – aren't you going to congratulate us?' Martyn asked awkwardly. For some reason, Luisa's entrance had had the effect of bursting the bubble of elation. It was as if just by her presence she cast a cloud over things.

'Of course. I'm just a bit surprised. It's so unexpected. I do congratulate you. When will you be married.'

'We really hadn't discussed it,' Bridget said. 'I expect not for some time. We'll have to get used to being engaged first. It *is* rather sudden. I'm still hardly able to believe it myself.'

And she, too, looked at Martyn.

There was something in the appeal in Bridget's face that made Luisa profoundly embarrassed. It was like opening someone's private diary.

'I'll leave you two to get over the shock together,' she said with forced lightness. And closed the door quickly behind her.

Jim ran into her in the hall and nearly bowled her over.

'I say, I am a clumsy idiot, Luisa. I'm afraid I've not got my glasses on. Are we going to have tea?'

Luisa nodded her head, her mind still whirling with the news.

'Where are the other two?' Jim asked.

'In the sitting-room. They won't be in to tea, I don't think. They've – they've just got engaged.'

'I say, that's wonderful!' said Jim, his outlook quite changed with his new attitude to the wonders of being in love.

'Yes, I – I suppose it is,' said Luisa quietly.

'You don't sound frightfully pleased,' said Jim.

Luisa went through into the dining-room and poured out the tea in silence. Jim peered at her short-sightedly, wondering what was up. At last he said:

'Aren't you pleased, Luisa?'

Luisa looked up and away again quickly.

'I really don't see that it concerns me, Jim.

I suppose I am pleased for Bridget. She's been in love with Martyn practically ever since she arrived. I just can't get used to the idea. I never imagined Martyn felt the same way. It doesn't seem possible. Anyway, he doesn't deserve her. I only hope he makes her happy.'

'Why on earth shouldn't he?' Jim enquired. 'Bridget's a perfectly ordinary girl and he's quite a nice fellow, when he isn't being moody, isn't he?'

'Yes, I suppose so. It's just – well, I think Bill was so much nicer – so much more right for Bridget. He'll be terribly upset. I think he loves her very much.'

'Well, it is bad luck, but all's fair in love and war,' announced Jim complacently. 'You know, Luisa, I can't altogether understand this fellow, Martyn. I mean, how he could fall for Bridget when you're around, I just don't know.'

Luisa smiled suddenly.

'Thank you, Jim,' she laughed. 'All the same, you must be biased. Martyn dislikes me.'

'I don't believe it!' said Jim stoutly. 'Nobody could. I think you're wonderful, Luisa. I think you're perfectly beautiful, too. In fact, I'm terribly in love with you.'

Luisa felt an instant's desire to laugh, but she quickly rejected it. Jim's voice was so intense, and he was now looking so acutely shy and nervous, she felt she was on thin ice and must not, on any account, hurt his feelings. She said lightly:

'Jim, that's a very nice compliment, but it's also a lot of nonsense. 'Why, we only met last week-end.'

'Oh, I know,' said Jim fervently. 'But love happens like that, Luisa. One minute you're heart-free and the next you're head over heels in love. I knew it last Sunday when you came over on the bicycle.'

'Jim, you're a dear, but I won't allow you to say these things. You know very well you're only saying them because you want to believe them. Have you ever been in love before?'

'No!' Jim admitted.

'Then how can you know you're in love now?' Luisa asked.

'Have you ever been in love, Luisa?' Jim asked.

Luisa shook her head.

'Then how do you know I'm not in love with you?'

This time Luisa did laugh.

'Well, I suppose that's fair enough,' she said. 'Let's put it this way, Jim. I hope what you say isn't true because I like being friends with you the way we are friends now and I should hate anything to change it. If you were really serious, we'd have to stop seeing each other and that would be most unpleasant. Why, you're the only friend I've got.'

Jim's face was a picture of conflicting emotions. To be Luisa's friend and to know that she valued that friendship was wonderful and unbelievable. But to stop loving her – that would be frightful.

'Of course, I know you couldn't ever care for me,' he said. 'I don't expect it, Luisa. I only want to be able to go on loving you quietly in my own way. I shan't ask anything of you except your friendship which is my most treasured possession.'

He was terribly in earnest and Luisa felt more like a mother than a girl friend. Jim had obviously been reading too many love stories. Why, she was four years older than he and the whole thing was fantastic. It would be funny if Jim weren't so ardent – so serious and so nice.

'Jim, let's get this straight right away,' Luisa said. 'You are not to go on thinking you are in love with me and I shall pretend you never mentioned it. Then, when we've been friends for years and years, we'll look back on this afternoon and laugh about it. You'll be happily married to some nice girl who'll make a good doctor's wife and I'll probably be an old spinster still running a riding school.'

'I shall always adore you, Luisa,' Jim said. 'And I shall never marry.'

'Nor, most probably, shall I!' said Luisa

firmly and with conviction. 'Now, Jim, tell me you're agreed that we shall forget this and be good friends. Please!'

'Luisa, I'll do anything for you – even try to fall out of love with you and be your friend,' said Jim.

Luisa smiled.

'Then have a piece of cake, Jim, and after tea we'll go for a long ride and fix up something nice to do to-morrow.'

Jim's face cleared and his face broke into a beaming smile.

'You mean, you'll spend all to-morrow with me, Luisa?'

'Of course!' said Luisa. 'With whom, if not with you. I've no doubt the two new love-birds will wish to be alone.'

'Oh, them!' said Jim ungrammatically. 'I'd forgotten about them. Tell me more about it, Luisa. When will they get married?'

But Luisa did not wish to re-open the subject. She must have time first to sort everything out in her own mind.

'Come on, Jim, hurry up with that cake or the light will be gone before we even start our ride.'

And for an hour or two she forgot about Martyn and Bridget and gave herself up to the wind and the rhythm and joy of riding – even if her mount was just an old hack. At least there were no worries in the open air.

In the sitting-room, Martyn and Bridget were sitting on the sofa discussing their future. After the first flush of bewildered joy that had swept over Bridget when Martyn had asked her to marry him, an odd sort of reaction had set in which she could not restrain.

'You see, Martyn, I don't want to go through with this unless you are absolutely sure that you want to,' she said. 'I mean, it was all so – so sudden, wasn't it? I don't believe you'd thought about it until that moment when you walked in on Bill and me.'

'As a matter of fact, I had been thinking about it,' Martyn said, lighting his pipe. 'I suppose I hadn't made up my mind what to do about it until then. I suppose seeing Bill what's his name worrying you like that made me see red. Anyway I did mean it and I've no intention of letting you back out of it.'

Bridget sat beside him, wondering whether at such moments it was right to feel an absurd desire to laugh and cry and an equally absurd feeling of doubt as to whether one was doing the right thing. It wasn't that she doubted her own feelings. Bill's arrival and the scene they had had this afternoon had thoroughly upset her and if anything could have made her feel more sure than ever that she loved Martyn, it was having Bill try to make love to her like that. Of course, she was sorry she'd had to hurt him. But then he'd behaved abominably and said the most unforgivable things about Martyn. He'd come down to make a scene and he'd certainly succeeded, but if he'd imagined that was going to get her back, he couldn't have been more wrong. Well, he'd said he never wanted to see her again so that was that. Bill didn't count any more. Only Martyn. And Martyn was the problem. Did he really love her? Could he possibly love her? He'd said: "If you can understand that I can't give you much in return". What did he mean by that? That he still cared for Betty? If that were so, she wouldn't mind. In time, Betty's memory would wear thin and she could wait. But suppose he had not meant Betty?

'Martyn,' she asked suddenly, 'are you still in love with Betty?'

He shook his head.

'No, strangely enough I'm not,' he said. 'I've thought it all out. I was afraid to think of her before. That's one of the good things you've done for me, Bridget. But now I can think of her and only with relief that things happened the way they did.'

'Then, Martyn, forgive me for asking but I feel we should get things straight, what did you mean when you said you wouldn't be able to give me much in return?'

Martyn took Bridget's hand in his and held it for a moment. It was the first intimate contact they had had except for that one moment he had held her in his arm before Luisa broke in.

'I'll try to explain,' he said. 'I don't know if I can. I don't altogether understand it. I suppose it has to do with Betty and the way I felt about her. But I loved her passionately and – I worshipped the very ground she trod on. I couldn't think, dream, eat, sleep – none of these things without Betty's image being there with me. I gave her my heart, my soul, all of myself. And she threw it back in my face. I think that did something to me. It sealed up the fount of feeling, if I can put it that way. I just don't seem able to feel things the same way again. I try all the time to keep out anything that threatens to touch me too deeply. And I'm incapable of feeling – or should I say loving – the same way again.

'What I think I'm trying to say, Bridget, is that I just can't love anybody or anything as I did love Betty. I'm afraid I shall be a very poor sort of lover. I'll suspect you of deeper motives when you say something nice. I'll probably be beastly when you're being your kindest. I'll probably be undemonstrative and unkind. In fact I'm horribly afraid I've absolutely nothing to offer you, Bridget. You're so awfully nice. I'm terribly fond of you and I don't see why I should subject you to a lot of suffering. It doesn't seem fair. After all, what will you get out of it?'

'Everything!' said Bridget confidently. 'You see, I love you, Martyn. Just to be with you and near you is enough for me. As long as I know you care for me, I shan't want anything else. The rest will come and even if it doesn't, I shan't mind. Let's not worry about it now. We'll have a long engagement and get to know one another properly. Oh, Martyn, I can hardly believe this is true. I can't see why you should want to marry me. I'm such a dull, ordinary sort of person.'

'You're not. You're exceptional, Bridget,' Martyn said warmly. 'You're kind and big-hearted and understanding and honest and a wonderful companion. You're everything I needed to restore my faith in your sex. Come here and let me kiss you.'

But although Bridget was made deliriously happy by that short tender embrace, for Martyn it was without passion and strangely lacking in something he could not name. He pushed the thought from him, recalling bitterly that he did not wish to be reminded of those mad, rapturous, passionate kisses that he had given Betty, only to find that they had stirred her cheap little body but never touched her soul.

Once more Jim was working in London and Luisa was busy with her riding school. She had bought another pony at the market and Jim had left his mare with her on Sunday night after their ride. She had her first pupils – two small boys – coming for a ride on Wednesday afternoon. On Wednesday morning, the announcement of Martyn's engagement to Bridget had appeared in the local newspaper, and after some discussion that evening, it was decided that Bridget could safely go home for two days to see her mother without the village scandal starting with Martyn and Luisa left alone. The engagement was publicly known and so no one would consider it odd if the future groom and Luisa, who now held the place of chaperone, were alone for a couple of nights.

Bridget departed radiantly happy and for the first time since her arrival home, or for that matter in their lives, Luisa dined alone with Martyn.

Since the engagement, there had been a noticeable lack of scenes between Martyn and Luisa. In some strange way it had altered everything. Or perhaps it was just that there had been no cause for disagreement. At any rate, they sat opposite one another in comparative friendliness.

Martyn asked Luisa about her first pupils and Luisa enquired politely about Martyn's work. It was not until Louisa had cleared away the coffee cups that the subject became personal.

111

'I – I'm glad we've got this chance for discussing things alone,' Luisa said, bringing up the subject that was on her mind. 'It's about you – and Bridget. About when you're married, I mean. You see, things will be a bit different, won't they?'

'Will they?' Martyn asked, not seeing her point. He tapped out his pipe against his shoes and listened while he refilled it.

'Well, you won't want me as a third man, will you?' Luisa said, more as a statement than a question. 'I – I mean, I feel I ought to get out and leave the house to you.'

'Well, that's absurd!' Martyn said. 'It's your house. We're the ones who must go.'

'What about your practice?'

'Yes, that is a problem,' Martyn admitted. 'Still, I can quite see you won't want us knocking around. We'll just have to try and find another house in the neighbourhood.'

'It isn't that *I* mind,' Luisa said awkwardly. 'But you and Bridget will naturally want a house of your own.'

'I suppose we will. Still, there's no hurry, you know. We aren't intending to get married yet awhile. After all, we don't know each other very well. It's funny, isn't it, to think we none of us knew each other – you and Bridget did of course – a couple of months ago! It seems so very much longer than that.'

Luisa remained silent. In a way, it did seem

112

impossible that a month ago she had never met Martyn. So much seemed to have happened and yet nothing really had occurred that touched her personally. Her friendship with Jim. The riding stables. But nothing relating to her personal feelings. Whereas Bridget and Martyn had fallen in love and were going to be married. It was a huge upheaval for them. Or so one imagined marriage must be to two people. Oddly enough, they were both taking it very calmly. They still worked together as before and there were no noticeable signs of a change in their relationship. Luisa imagined there must be some and supposed they became more intimate when they were alone. She had contrived whenever possible to keep out of their way.

'Is that fellow Jim Mathers in love with you?' Martyn asked suddenly.

Luisa came out of her reverie with a start. She felt the colour rush to her cheeks and was furious about it. How silly and childish to blush over Jim Mathers.

'I ... well, he thinks he is,' she replied shortly. 'It's a sort of calf love, I think. He'll get over it.'

'He seems very smitten,' said Martyn with a smile. 'In fact, it's quite embarrassing to be in the same room with him. He never takes his eyes off you.'

Luisa laughed and then checked herself.

'It's not fair to make fun of him but he's terribly short-sighted. That probably accounts for the fact that he thinks I'm the most beautiful thing he ever saw.'

'I don't think that's the reason. You *are* very beautiful. What surprises me is that I'm beginning to believe you don't know it.'

Surprise robbed Luisa of speech. Such a comment from Martyn was unbelievable.

'You know, you're rather a surprising person, Luisa,' Martyn went on. 'Sometimes you seem so sophisticated and worldly wise, and then you blush because I mention Jim Mathers' name.'

'Aren't you being rather personal?' Luisa asked, unable to think of anything else to say to cover her confusion.

'I'm sorry. I suppose I am. I do apologize,' Martyn said quickly.

An awkward silence fell between them and the rather pleasant easy companionship which they were not accustomed to feeling towards each other, was now broken. Luisa knew it was her fault and tried to remedy it.

'About Jim Mathers,' she said. 'You don't think it's unfair of me to continue seeing him? I mean, I told him quite clearly that I couldn't possibly look on him in the same way. He's agreed to be – just a friend. I don't believe he thinks deep down he could ever be anything else.'

'How can you be so sure?' Martyn asked.

Luisa looked at him in surprise.

'Why, I don't love him.'

'But you might fall in love with him,' Martyn argued.

'That's impossible,' Luisa said firmly. 'I just know it. When I fall in love, I shall know it without a doubt.'

'Then you believe in a sort of thunderbolt that shoots out of the blue and hits you thump! and then you're in love?'

Luisa smiled.

'Perhaps not quite like a thunderbolt. But I do think it happens suddenly – just like that. One minute you're just sitting talking to someone and then suddenly something happens to make you see them in a different light.'

'Then you don't believe love can grow from a steady companionship and under-standing and that sort of thing?'

'I suppose it can grow from those things. But that's a different sort of love. I mean, friendship grows from those things, doesn't it? One would love a person in the same way as one loved a friend. Perhaps marriages based on that kind of feeling are built on firmer foundations. But I'm sure that somewhere in this world there is one man who is meant for one woman and although sometimes they may go nearly a lifetime without crossing paths, sooner or later they will meet each other. Perhaps then it's too late, or they don't realize it. But I do think there's a perfect complement for every human being.'

Martyn was silent for a moment, lost in thought. Then he said:

'I thought I was in love – in that way – with Betty. But I suppose I wasn't. I think it was probably based on physical attraction. At least the way I feel about Bridget has nothing to do with that.'

It occurred then to Luisa that Martyn was probing her thoughts for his own ends. He wasn't altogether happy about his engagement to Bridget. He wanted to be convinced, to convince himself that he was in love with her. And if he wanted convincing, then he obviously wasn't in love. In Luisa's mind one did not have any doubts. One just knew. She gazed at him in perplexity. He looked surprisingly young and uncertain. His arm, resting on the side of the chair, supported his face as he sat, deep in thought. Luisa looked at the other arm, the arm that wasn't there, and thought of his past unhappiness caused by that wretched girl Betty whom he had loved so much.

Quite suddenly, she was filled with compassion for him – compassion mixed with a protective tenderness that was almost maternal. At this moment, Martyn seemed as young and vulnerable as Jim Mathers. She felt an uncontrollable longing to go to

116

him and put her arms round him and tell him not to worry so much; not to let life hurt him so deeply; to reassure him that it must all come right in the end.

The impulse was so strong that she even rose slightly from her chair, taking a step towards him and then suddenly, she sat down again, the colour flaring into her cheeks, her heart thudding in swift, painful jerks. Realization had come to her in that one single instant that it wasn't pity or sympathy or protectiveness she felt for Martyn. It was neither a maternal emotion nor a sisterly one. It was quite purely, quite simply, love.

A moment later, Martyn looked up and met her unguarded gaze. For one long minute, his brown eyes never left her green ones and in them he read the truth. Then she was on her feet and out of the room before he could speak.

Martyn leant back in his chair, seeing without seeing his hand trembling. So it could happen after all! It could happen suddenly the way Luisa said. "One minute you are sitting talking to someone and then suddenly you see them in a different light." So it had been just now for him – and for her. And he had thought he hated her.

'Oh, Luisa, Luisa!' he whispered brokenly. 'What have I done?'

CHAPTER VII

Luisa lay on her bed in the dark, her hands clenched at her side, her eyes closed.

'I'm quite crazy!' she told herself fiercely. 'I'm imagining the whole thing. Of course he doesn't know how I feel. I don't love him, anyway. I've hated him. How can I love him now? Martyn hasn't changed. I haven't changed.'

And yet she knew she had. Nothing she could tell herself could still the swift beating of her heart and the sure knowledge that lay there that she loved Martyn with every fibre of her being. And it did make sense. People said love was akin to hate. It explained so much of their odd relationship – that starting off on the wrong footing, they had struggled against the subconscious knowledge that they were in each other's power. At least, Luisa was in Martyn's power. He alone could light the flame that no other man had had the power to do. He alone could bring her perfect and utter happiness and peace and he was engaged to her best friend, Bridget.

Struggling with her emotions, Luisa knew that Martyn did not love Bridget as she herself recognized the meaning of the word. But she was no longer sure that she had read correctly the look he had given her before she ran from the room and from him. For that single brief instant, she had thought she saw an answering look in his eyes, a dawning of realization of the truth. But she could so easily have imagined it. He may merely have been wondering why she was staring at him so steadfastly. She must have misinterpreted it. But deep in her heart, Luisa cried out for recognition of his love. She wanted to believe he loved her and yet the whole thing was so improbable – and utterly impossible. Martyn was engaged to Bridget. Bridget loved him and he was going to marry her. She, Luisa, had no place in his life. She had realized her own feelings too late. If only she had known from the first – then how different things might have been. But she had avoided Martyn whenever possible; had been curt and on many occasions rude and so her true feelings had become confused in their dislike of one another.

Had Martyn, too, been confused, or did he still dislike her? One could not change so suddenly – without rhyme or reason. And yet she, herself, had changed in that brief instant. Perhaps Martyn, too, had seen her in a different light. He, too, had been putting a barrier against life and the hurt that life can bring one. Bridget in her quiet, friendly, impersonal way had come closer to him than Luisa, who could never be mediocre. It was part of her nature that she must love or hate passionately and without reservation. Martyn had sensed it and avoided it, knowing that Luisa had the power to hurt him where Bridget had not.

For hour upon hour, Luisa lay awake, questioning, probing, wondering, never able to decide if she had given away her feelings to Martyn; if his look had been one of response or merely surprise. Whatever this past evening had meant to them both, one thing alone was clear. It could go no further. Luisa would never try to find her own happiness at Bridget's expense. Bridget came first and she would honour her friend's engagement, whatever it might cost her. Her own feelings she would bury firmly and for ever and neither Bridget nor Martyn should ever glimpse the truth.

But Martyn had already seen the truth and was, in his turn, trying to discover whether he had been imagining such things. Like Luisa, he wanted to believe she loved him. Like Luisa, he knew that it would be the worst thing for both of them since he had become involved with Bridget and could not go back on the bargain.

Try as he would, he knew that he could never again imagine he loved Bridget. Clearly he had allowed himself to confuse fondness, companionship, protectiveness with the real thing. He had never been convinced of his love for Bridget and it was only his hasty action in rushing in on her and Bill that had brought things to a head. He had committed himself in that one unguarded moment and there was no way out.

Perhaps if it had been anyone else but Luisa, Bridget's closest friend, he might have explained to Bridget and asked for his release. Selfish though this might be, in the end it must be best for her since he could give her so little in return for her love. But to throw her over and then ask Luisa to marry him – no! he could not do that to anyone, far less to a kind, decent person like Bridget. He would never be able to cause a human being the same extent of suffering that Betty had caused him. His own happiness could not be bought at such a price on his conscience.

There was, too, Luisa to be considered. If he had read her face aright, then she, too, would have to suffer. And yet, he could not be sure in the least that she loved him. How could any girl love him after the way he had treated poor Luisa? He had been rude and boorish from the start, seeing in her vices that were Betty's and never her own. Luisa was, in her way, as unsophisticated as Bridget. But her beauty had confused him and he had immediately supposed her to be another cheap little flirt with shallow emotions and no worth-while qualities.

How wrong he had been! How blind he had been not to see Luisa as she really was. Bridget had tried to point the truth to him on more than one occasion, and Bridget would hardly have for a best friend a girl such as he had made Luisa out to be. Jim Mathers, too, thought she was wonderful and wanted to marry her. And years ago, before he had ever set eyes on Luisa, Mrs Jennings had spoken of her as a 'dear, nice, kind child'. Only he had seen unpleasantness in her where there was none. And he had imagined such things because he had been afraid to face the truth. He had put up barriers against life after Betty's betrayal and because subconsciously he must have known Luisa could penetrate those barriers, he had looked only for the worst and blinded himself to all that was lovable and wonderful about her.

He, too, sat far into the night, struggling with his feelings. He, too, reached only one definite conclusion – that Bridget must come first and he must do what he could to make her happy.

In the morning when he came downstairs to breakfast, his heart beating at double pace as he wondered how he could possibly behave normally with Luisa, he learned with some relief and a contrary disappointment that she had breakfasted early and was out in the stables.

He left his breakfast untouched, drinking some black coffee, and went to the surgery to prepare for possible patients. But he could not put his mind to his work and his eyes felt hot and tired from sleeplessness.

'I must pull myself together,' he said with an effort. 'I'm bound to see her at lunch.'

But Luisa, unable to face Martyn with the control she felt was imperative, contrived to lunch early on the excuse that she had to get one of the ponies shod before her pupils arrived. It was far worse for both of them that their first meeting that day should be delayed in such a way. As the afternoon wore on, the situation became steadily more taut as each felt their nerves strung to breaking-point. Sooner or later they must see each other. Every minute that passed bringing supper nearer, each became more excited, more nervous.

When Mrs Jennings rang the supper gong, Luisa was still messing around in the stables and could not bring herself to go in. Martyn, waiting to start the meal, felt that things could not go on like this. Luisa was all too clearly avoiding him and although he felt exhilarated at the obvious conclusion to be drawn from her actions, he knew that sooner or later they would be bound to run into each other. He sent Mrs Jennings to find her.

Mrs Jennings came back after a few minutes, saying:

'Miss Luisa says she's very busy and will have something cold when she's finished.'

'Thank you,' said Martyn. And as soon as Mrs Jennings had left the room, he jumped up and went out to the stables.

Luisa, not in the least busy, was lying on a bale of straw, feeling utterly wretched and knowing herself for a hopeless coward. It never crossed her mind that Martyn would come out to find her and when she heard footsteps, she thought it was Mrs Jennings. His voice, calling her name, startled her dreadfully. The colour rushed to her face and she felt like a trapped animal. It was too late for her to climb down and busy herself with a saddle or pitchfork. She could do nothing but bury herself deeper into the bales and hope he didn't find her. How could she possibly explain such ridiculous behaviour? He'd think her crazy.

'Luisa, will you please come in to supper,' Martyn said.

She could think of nothing to say and so remained silent. But, at that minute, Boot chose to amble into the stables and made straight for her. Two seconds later, Martyn was beside her. They stared at one another, faces white, hearts beating nervously.

'Luisa! You must come in to supper. You –

I – you can't stay out here all night, you know.'

'Yes! I'm sorry. I was just...' her voice trailed into silence and her face looked up at him, her features almost indistinguishable in the gloom. She looked very white and tired and distressed and quite suddenly Martyn lost his all too insecure control. He pulled Luisa towards him and with surprising gentleness kissed her hair, her eyes and lastly, with growing passion, her lips.

'Oh, Luisa, Luisa, I love you. I love you, darling Luisa,' he whispered.

With no strength left to fight him and with every fibre of her being crying out to respond, Luisa lifted her arms and held them behind his head.

'Martyn, I love you too. I've tried all day to believe this hasn't happened. But it's only got worse and worse. I love you Martyn, desperately, with every part of me.'

'Oh, Luisa!' Martyn said brokenly, straining her to him. 'What are we going to do? What can I say? Only one thing makes any sense at all – that I love you ... that you say you love me. Say it again, Luisa. Tell me again that you mean it.'

But shy now, Luisa could only draw his face down to hers and kiss him again.

When at last they drew from each other's arms, each felt that the situation had become intolerable. There could be no avoiding the issue now. The truth was spoken and each knew that nothing could ever alter their love. Nothing, either, could ever spoil it. Deep in their hearts, each knew too that these last few moments had been stolen from time and that it might never happen again. But neither wished those moments untaken. They were there, for ever, miraculous, wonderful, revealing, to be treasured for as long as they lived.

'Luisa, we'll have to talk this thing out,' Martyn forced himself to speak calmly. 'Let's go back into the house. We'll make some excuse to Mrs Jennings. Oh, darling, you look so white and ill. I'll say one of the ponies kicked you, or something. We'll have some coffee and talk afterwards.'

Luisa nodded assent and turned to go, but Martyn pulled her to him again and she could not resist.

'Oh, my dearest, dearest love. Kiss me again and tell me that you'll forgive me for the way I've treated you. I love you so very much.'

She kissed him tenderly and smiled at him, running her fingers down the side of his face as if just to touch him so were sheer joy.

'There's nothing to forgive, Martyn. It had to happen this way. We ought to have realized sooner that hating each other, we were really very close to love. We could never have

127

been indifferent to one another. Now, Martyn dearest, let's go in before we begin to be sorry for this disloyalty to Bridget.'

Back in the dining-room, Mrs Jennings fussed around Luisa, saying she ought to have a doctor, and was there a bruise. Martyn assured her it was only a slight knock and would Mrs Jennings bring the coffee quickly as Miss Luisa still felt a little faint.

Both hated this deception but knew that it was necessary. At last Mrs Jennings came with the coffee and announced that she was finished for the night and would be off.

Then, at last, they were alone. Martyn reached across the table and took Luisa's hand.

'Don't take it away,' he said gently, as she tried to withdraw her hand. 'I understand how you feel about Bridget and I, too, feel the same. But we have so little time left to us, Luisa. To-morrow Bridget returns and we shall have to go on as if none of this had ever happened. For this evening, let us imagine that there are only ourselves in the world and make it ours.'

'Oh, Martyn!' Luisa whispered brokenly. 'If only...'

'Yes, if only we'd found out in time,' Martyn broke in gently. 'Then we would have had that lifetime together, Luisa. Now we must crowd into a few hours enough to last us a lifetime. Darling heart, come into the sitting-room and let's talk the whole thing out.'

She followed him into the other room and sat down in the arm-chair. Martyn threw himself down at her feet and leant his head against her knees. She let her hand run through his hair and he pressed closer against her. For a moment, neither spoke. Then Luisa said:

'Martyn, I'm afraid. I can't imagine life without you now. How can I be strong enough to keep this from Bridget? I'm not by nature a dissembler. I shall have to go away.'

'No!' Martyn said sharply, and then more slowly and softly: 'You see, I, too, can barely face the thought of a life without you. Perhaps it would be best if you go, Luisa, for a week or two. If I suggested going away, Bridget would think it so odd. But it's all terribly awkward. What about your riding school? Who's to chaperone Bridget and myself?'

She smiled then, for the first time, and he caught hold of her hand and held it tightly in his own.

'You – chaperoning me!' Martyn said with an answering smile. 'Oh, darling, I wish you and I were the only people in the whole wide world. I cannot really believe you love me. I don't deserve it. I've been so despicable to you.'

'That shows how much I love you if I could still do so after that!' Luisa smiled at him. Then the smile left her face and she said again: 'What are we going to do?'

'Luisa, tell me what you think. I feel I couldn't bear to hurt Bridget. I couldn't let her down now. She's thrown Bill out of her life because of me and she trusts me. But if you say so, I'll ask her to release me from our engagement.'

'No,' Luisa broke in. 'No, I couldn't take my happiness at her expense, Martyn. I think in her way Bridget loves you very much. She must do if she could turn down the faithful Bill after all these years. They've been practically engaged since their childhood. But it does seem odd the way life works. There is Bill, eating his heart out for Bridget, and you and I... Oh, Martyn, darling, how shall I be strong enough to let you go? I shall have to go away. Bridget would be bound to see the change in us both. She was always so worried because we quarrelled. She looks for chances to make us better friends. And, loving you, she'll be the first to sense anything odd in your behaviour. Martyn, I wonder if Bridget would bring her mother to stay. I could go away. I haven't had a holiday. I can make some excuse about not being able to start the riding school because Jim's horse has gone lame – any excuse like that. You and

Jim would bear me out. I'll go away for a month and perhaps when I come back we shall be able to behave more normally.'

'But where will you go, Luisa?'

She shook her head.

'I don't know, Martyn. Jim said something about his mother wanting a holiday in Cornwall, but that he didn't want to go with her and lose the summer here with me. Perhaps it could be arranged that I go with them.'

'I shall be wretchedly jealous,' Martyn said. 'What a lucky fellow Jim will be.'

'And I shall be jealous of you and Bridget. I'd give the world to be in her place, Martyn.'

With a little cry, he drew her towards him again and they held one another close without speaking. Each tried hard to keep a rein on their feelings, but each was passionate by nature and they were young and very deeply in love. Soon Louisa knew that they must release one another before they quite lost control. But it was hard for her to find the strength to break away from him. She had never been in love before – never kissed anyone or been kissed as Martyn was now doing. All the delights of newly-awakened womanhood were discovered through Martyn and he was gentle and tender and yet masterful. He knew from his experience with Betty that Luisa was utterly innocent and that she had only her instinct to guide her. He felt profoundly tender towards her and tried to subdue his own violent emotions for her sake.

He knew now that his whole affair with Betty had been on a horribly low level. He had believed he loved her because, with all her experience, she knew so well how to rouse him to fever pitch. For her it had been a game of sex. With Luisa it was a sacred giving and taking of tokens of love. Every kiss was an expression of real depth of feeling. Every embrace was fraught with tenderness and reverence. Now and only now did he realize what true loving could mean.

'Oh, Luisa, my dearest one,' he whispered against her hair, 'how can it be right for us to part? Are we sure we are doing the right thing? How can I ever make Bridget happy? The man she marries should love her as I love you. I have so very little to offer her. Surely she must know in the end that it is not enough. I shall not even be able to give her as much as I thought I could before I realized I loved you. Luisa, dearest, don't think I'm weakening, but deep in my heart, I feel it is wrong. Only this is right.'

Luisa struggled with her own conflicting emotions. In one way she could not but agree with Martyn. And then she remembered the radiant Bridget who had departed to see her mother and tell the family the exciting news of her engagement. She was so happy and thrilled. It was beyond her, Luisa's, power to spoil that.

'Martyn, you must try,' she said. 'We must both make every possible effort. If in the end Bridget should change her mind, then we can think again. But she must not change her mind through knowledge of our feelings – only of her own. You must try to make her happy. You've agreed to a long engagement. There will be time to forget me and to find some other form of happiness through Bridget. She's such a wonderful person and so kind.'

'But Luisa, it's you I love!' Martyn broke in. 'I shall be leading a life of deception. I cannot kiss her without feeling disloyal to you. I cannot hold her in my arms knowing all the time it is you I want. I cannot live a lie.'

'Then you must try not to let it be a lie,' Luisa said desperately. 'When I've gone, Martyn, everything may be different. You'll remember me as you have thought of me until now. You hated me, remember? Think only of the things about me you've disliked.'

'Luisa! How can you ask the impossible? I love you. I shall always love you. Whatever you do, however you may treat me, or if I should never see you again, I shall always love you.'

'Oh, Martyn, don't please,' Luisa begged. 'You must help me to do what is right.

Perhaps after all we are just imagining all this. It's happened so suddenly and without any reason. I can't think how it *could* have happened. Last night we were at dinner talking distinctly and meaninglessly like two polite strangers, and an hour later I saw you in that chair and knew I loved you. How could I know? How could you turn your head and look at me and know you loved me? Perhaps it was just a trick of light and we were suddenly attracted to each other in – in a physical sense and romantically told ourselves we were in love.'

'Do you really believe that?' Martyn asked almost inaudibly.

Luisa slipped down beside him and wound her arms round his neck.

'Martyn, don't look so hurt. You know I don't believe it. I love you. I love you, darling. I'm only trying not to believe it for both our sakes. But you aren't helping me.'

'How can I let you destroy with words the most beautiful and sacred moment of my life!' Martyn replied, and drew her to him, close against his heart. 'Oh, Luisa, I'm sorry, my dearest. To-morrow I will be as strong as I can. I will try then to think as you are doing – that this is just a dream. But not now. Not to-night. Nothing must spoil this. I couldn't bear it. Luisa, do you remember the first moment we met?'

She leant against him, fighting no longer,

and nodded.

'Yes!' she murmured. 'You nearly ran over Boot. And then you were cross with me because you thought I was staring at your poor lost arm.'

'Luisa, doesn't it worry you at all?'

'Martyn, dearest, how could it? I love you. The fact that you lost an arm fighting for your country could only make me love you more – never less.'

'Then you've never minded?'

'Only because it seemed to bother you.'

'Luisa, I still cannot believe you love me. You're so very beautiful.' He touched her hair and looked deeply into her green eyes. 'You've a beautiful body and a beautiful soul, Luisa, my only love,' he said softly. 'And I'm such a moody, boorish, stupid sort of fellow. I'm not worthy of your friendship, let alone your love.'

Luisa put a finger gently across his lips.

'Don't say those things, Martyn. You know we were meant for one another. To me you, too, are beautiful. You are all I've ever wanted or ever could want.'

They leaned back against the chair, arm in arm, cheek against cheek. The emotional crisis they had been through had exhausted them both and now they were too tired to do anything except sit close to one another.

Presently Martyn looked at his watch and gave a little sigh.

'It's past midnight,' he said. 'You'll be so dreadfully tired in the morning, my dearest. Kiss me once again and then go quickly for soon I shall not have the strength to let you go at all.'

'Oh, Martyn, beloved!' Luisa whispered, and bent her head to his.

CHAPTER VIII

In the morning, Luisa awoke to a moment's brief happiness as she remembered last evening. And then reaction set in with a cold violence and she lay still, unable to face the day and with it, the truth that she and Martyn had agreed never to kiss one another again, never to show the least sign to the other how they were feeling, never to talk of their love or themselves unless the latter were necessary.

"I can't do it," Luisa thought desperately. Last night, she had been so utterly content just with the knowledge that Martyn loved her, of the wonder of her own love answering his touch, his kiss, his look. This morning, she knew with a horrible certainty that it was not enough. She wanted to be able to run downstairs into his arms, to hear his voice whispering soft endearments and to know that the day was theirs and every day to come.

'Oh, Martyn, Martyn!' she cried softly. 'How has this happened to us!'

For one moment, she felt temptation returning. Engagements had been broken before. Martyn had told her she had only to say the word and he would ask Bridget for his release. Then the future would be everything they both desired. It was so easy – so very easy – and yet so utterly impossible. To-day Bridget returned. To-day, she would come back, eager to receive Martyn's welcoming embrace; eager to tell him how happy her family were to know of the engagement; full of plans for her future with him and how happy she intended to make him.

'No!' Luisa told herself fiercely. 'I can't do it – not hurt Bridget as I should be hurt if it were myself in the same position.'

And yet, temptation whispered in her ear, supposing it were such that she were the one engaged to Martyn and it was Bridget he loved, she would want his happiness before her own. It would be a dreadful, terrible sacrifice, but one she would and could make for the man she loved. She could not bear to tie him to her, knowing he loved someone else.

But, said reason, Bridget does not know he loves me – and must never know. I must go away – soon. To-day, if possible.

Wearily, she climbed out of bed and dressed. The white, tired face that stared at her from her mirror, did not seem to bear any resemblance to the flushed Luisa with the brilliant eyes that had been reflected last night as she combed her flaming gold-red hair. She looked perfectly ghastly, she decided. And with a wry smile, she wondered if seeing her like this, Martyn might decide she was not as beautiful as he had thought her when he held her in his arms for their long good-night kiss.

Mrs Jennings rang the gong and this time Luisa did not try to avoid Martyn. She felt she must see him. She needed a little of his courage this morning to help her get through the day.

'My, you do look awful, Miss Luisa,' Mrs Jennings greeted her. 'That must have been a really nasty kick you got. Don't you think you ought to see the doctor?'

'No, I'm all right – really,' Luisa said. 'It was just a bit of a shock. I shall be all right.'

Luisa went into the dining-room and Martyn could not have heard her soft footfall for he did not look up and continued reading the morning newspaper, his breakfast lying untouched before him. She felt an almost ungovernable longing to run to him and put her arms around him. He, too, looked white and tired. She knew for a certainty that he was feeling just as low, just as miserable as she was.

'Hullo, Martyn!' she said, and went quickly to her place at the table.

He looked up quickly, a smile hurrying into his face only to be replaced by a look of anxiety.

'Luisa, you aren't well!' he said. 'You look ghastly!'

She smiled then, and Martyn, catching her meaning, said quickly:

'No, darling, you could never look anything but beautiful. I mean you look terribly ill.'

At the sound of the endearment, Luisa felt near to tears. She could not trust herself to speak and was glad that at that moment Mrs Jennings came in with her breakfast.

But she could not touch it.

'Martyn, you must eat something. At least I have an excuse with my imaginary kick from the horse. But if we both turn down all Mrs Jennings gives us, she'll start to wonder.'

'I'll try!' said Martyn, but he was not hungry. He wanted nothing but release from the strain of controlling his emotions. The sight of Luisa's white face and the deep shadows under her eyes, was slowly sapping his resolve of the night before. He longed desperately to go to her and tell her not to worry. But they had promised one another that this would not be so.

'Martyn, I'm going to telephone Jim's mother and see about this holiday. I can't stay here. I couldn't face Bridget when she returns this evening. To-morrow is Saturday and Jim is home for two weeks. It could easily be arranged if I could only make some excuse that would explain such a sudden desire to get away. If only I could tell Mrs Mathers the truth – take her into my confidence.'

Martyn said nothing. The desolating thought that Luisa might go away to-morrow struck him into a miserable silence.

Luisa, however, was feeling a little better. Her own words had given her an idea. Mrs Mathers was a charming woman, sensible, worldly, understanding. They had liked one another and felt a link between them that had nothing to do with Jim. If only she could go to Mrs Mathers, ask her help and advice...

'Martyn. I'm going over to see Mrs Mathers,' she said. 'I'll talk things over with her and see what she says. Could you telephone Bridget and suggest she asks her mother to come and stay for a week or two. I think it would be a good plan in any case, even if I don't go away. It would at least mean we shan't be a threesome.'

'All right, Luisa. Would you like the car? I shan't be needing it until after surgery hours.'

'No, I think I'll ride over,' Luisa said. 'I need the fresh air to wake me up. I'll be back for lunch, Martyn.'

He nodded and reached out a hand and held Luisa's for a brief moment. Then dropped it quickly as if he were afraid to hold it longer, and hurried out of the room.

Fifteen minutes later, Luisa was on her way over to Jim's house. Mrs Mathers had been delighted to hear over the telephone that Luisa was paying her a visit, and Luisa had now quite made up her mind to pour out the whole story to the older woman.

Mrs Mathers was in the library when Luisa came in. She was struck again by the girl's beauty as she walked through the door in riding kit, her lovely hair windswept and framing the delicate oval face. But in that swift glance, she knew something was wrong. Gone were the roses from the girl's cheeks. She looked white and ill.

'Come and sit, my dear,' she said. 'I've ordered a cup of chocolate. It's a change from coffee, I think, and reminds me of Switzerland. After it has come, we must have a long talk. Last time you were here, we didn't have a real opportunity to get to know one another and I felt I wanted to know you better. I took a great fancy to you, child. You're so unusual.'

Luisa smiled a little shyly.

'I think I'm really rather ordinary,' she said. 'But I – I felt, too, that I would like to know you better. You see, I've so few friends. And I think I miss my mother. I could always talk to her and she understood...' Her voice trailed away into silence. Mrs Mathers knew then for certain that something was wrong.

The child needed her help.

'Luisa, dear, you must let me try to take your mother's place. You know, I never had a daughter and I always wanted one so badly. Of course, I adore my Jim, but boys don't confide in their mothers the same way girls do and I love exchanging confidences!'

Luisa smiled, grateful for Mrs Mathers' friendliness.

'Ah! Here's the chocolate. Now drink it up, Luisa. It's very rich, but it'll do you good.'

It was very rich, but Luisa felt a great deal better after she had finished it. Riding on an empty stomach had made her feel sick and a little faint.

'Now, let's start gossiping,' Mrs Mathers said. 'First of all, Luisa, I want to tell you how grateful I am to you for taking my Jim under your wing. You're the first girl he has ever paid the slightest attention to and you've done him a lot of good.'

'I – I'm glad you think so,' Luisa said doubtfully. 'As a matter of fact, Jim has been rather on my mind, too. You see, it's rather difficult. He … I … you…'

'You mean, he thinks he is in love with you?' Mrs Mathers asked.

Luisa nodded.

'But, my dear, that is nothing to worry about. It's only natural. If I were a young man, I'm quite sure I should be in love with you myself.'

Luisa smiled again, and then said seriously:

'But, Mrs Mathers, I don't love him. I'm afraid I never will. I'm terribly fond of him. He's rather like a young brother, except when he's being adoring.'

'Of course you're not in love with him,' Mrs Mathers said. 'Much as I adore my son, I'm not so blind as to imagine every girl thinks he's – now, how is it you modern young things put it? – the cat's whiskers.'

They both laughed, and Mrs Mathers continued.

'Luisa, Jim will fall in and out of love hundreds of times before he gets married. He's only twenty-two – and a very young twenty-two in lots of ways. It'll be three years before he qualifies as a doctor, and although he has a certain private income his father left him, he couldn't afford to marry while he is still a student. Nor ought he to marry. A wife at this stage would only distract him from his work.'

'I'm afraid he says I am distracting him from his work already,' Luisa said.

'Of course, but it won't last. At heart, Jim is more interested in medicine than in anything else in the world. It is only natural that the first time he falls in love, he can't keep his mind on his work, but it'll wear off. It's an attack of calf love, Luisa, and nothing

144

for you to worry about. I'm just extremely thankful that Jim should be adoring a nice girl like yourself who will have to hurt him a little, but in such a kind way that he'll soon get over it. No, you have no need to worry about my Jim, Luisa. Just go on being friends with him. And now, my dear, don't try to tell me that it is on Jim's account you are looking so tired and pale. There is something else on your mind. It's not finance? The riding stables are not proving an impossibility after all?'

Luisa shook her head.

'Then, Luisa, I can only assume that it is an affair of the heart. You have fallen in love. Is that it, child?'

Mrs Mathers' kind voice and her understanding were too much for Luisa in her emotional state. Without warning, she burst into tears and was soon sobbing her heart out into Mrs Mathers' comfortable lap.

'Tell me who it is, Luisa,' Mrs Mathers said, gently stroking the girl's soft hair. 'It can't be so desperate. There is always a remedy for everything in the world – unless he is married?'

'No – only engaged!' Luisa choked. 'Oh, Mrs Mathers, I love him so very much. It happened so suddenly and unexpectedly. I must go away. I can't stand it otherwise. I haven't the strength of character.'

'Now, now, Luisa! Start at the beginning

and tell me first of all who this young man is.'

'It's Martyn, Martyn Saunders,' Luisa said in a small choked little voice.

'Martyn Saunders! The vet. But Luisa, Jim tells me he is so boorish and rude to you. I thought you disliked the man.'

'I thought I did, too,' Luisa said with a ghost of a smile. 'We started off on the wrong foot. You see, Martyn had been badly let down by some girl because of his arm and he was afraid of me because subconsciously he must have felt I, too, had the power to hurt him. And I – I didn't want to have anything to do with any man.' And she explained about those years with her aunt in Monte Carlo and how she had hated the young men she had been forced to entertain.

'So you see,' she ended, 'Martyn and I rubbed each other up the wrong way when all the time we loved each other and wouldn't admit it even to ourselves. Now it's too late.'

Mrs Mathers was silent for a moment. When she spoke her voice was calm and soothing.

'Luisa, I think both you and this Martyn of yours are a couple of heroic young fools. This is no occasion to ruin both your lives – and possibly Bridget's, too – just because you are afraid to cause the girl a little unhappiness. She'll get over it. I think she ought to be told the truth.'

'But Mrs Mathers, she's in love with Martyn. It's not just imagination. Ever since she first met him, she's been trying to hide the fact that she loved him from all of us. I think if I were in Bridget's shoes and she were to take Martyn from me, I should think most dreadfully of her. Bridget and I are friends. As you know, we were at school together. She's one of the kindest, most decent people I know. I couldn't hurt her as I know I should be hurt if I were in her shoes.'

'And so you intend to hurt your Martyn instead by forcing him to go through with his engagement, marry a girl he doesn't love and go through the rest of his life living a lie? No, Luisa, it doesn't make sense.'

Luisa passed a hand wearily across her forehead.

'I know. I can't think what is best to be done. But I do think it would help if I could only get away from Martyn – give things a trial. He may find he can be happy with Bridget when I'm not there. I can think it out more clearly when I haven't to see him day after day. Besides, I couldn't pretend in front of Bridget. She is so used to seeing us quarrelling. She will be bound to suspect.'

'Then, Luisa, if you are determined not to come out in the open and tell Bridget, I think it would be a very good idea for you to go away. It will show you how impossible it is for you to live apart from him. It will show him, too, that he cannot live a lie. Then, maybe, you will both come to your senses and tell Bridget the truth and ask her to release him from this engagement. Is it possible to arrange a holiday? Can someone look after this riding school for you? If so, then you shall come to Devonshire with Jim and me and we will make arrangements to go next week.'

'Oh, Mrs Mathers, how can I thank you? I had come to ask you if I might go with you. Of course, I shall pay my own way. I insist on that. But it will help so much.'

'Luisa, you shall be my guest and there is to be no more arguing about it. I shall consider it a favour. My dear child, I have plenty of money and I know very well that you have not. Now if you are to become my adopted daughter – since clearly you will never become my daughter-in-law! – then you must do as I say.'

'Mrs Mathers, you are much too kind. Jim is very lucky to have such a wonderful mother.'

'And these riding stables of yours?'

'I think Bridget will look after the horses for me. Martyn will arrange to give her sufficient time off. The children will be going on holiday next week in any case. The riding school isn't really open and won't be until next term. I have only taken one or two pupils to try it out.'

Having promised Martyn she would return to lunch, Luisa refused Mrs Mathers' invitation to stay, and having arranged to telephone her later to hear what plans she had made for to-morrow, Luisa kissed her good-bye and set off for the Vicarage. Martyn was at the door to meet her after she had stabled Jumbo. He had a telegram in his hand. He looked at Luisa with a queer provocative expression.

'A bit of news for you,' he said.

She walked into the sitting-room beside him. Her muscles ached after the long ride. Her head ached, too. She was surprised at her ebbing vitality. The long talk with Mrs Mathers had uplifted her morale and yet the moment she was with Martyn again, back came that feeling of weakness and feverish restlessness born of unassuaged passionate love. She tried to make her voice sound casual and to remember all Mrs Mathers' advice as she said:

'Oh? What is it?'

'Bridget isn't coming back until the day after to-morrow. Her mother's brother had just arrived from a business trip to America and Bridget particularly wanted to see him as it was a favourite uncle.'

Luisa raised her eyes to Martyn. She had not altogether understood the expression in

149

his eyes. She did not understand it now. His gaze unnerved her a little – yet excited her in a curious way. She bit hard on her lower lip and tapped her riding-boot with the crop which she was still holding.

'Let's have a cigarette, Martyn,' she said with an effort to maintain the casual attitude.

He ignored the request and took the pipe from his lips and tapped it out against the mantelpiece.

'What did Mrs Mathers say to you?' he asked abruptly.

'Lots of things!'

'She knows about – us?'

'Yes!'

'She thinks that we are doing right to say good-bye?'

Luisa was silent a moment. Her heart was beginning to race. She knew that she dared not tell him that Mrs Mathers had denounced their act of renunciation as quixotic and even absurd. She was still determined to do the right thing by Bridget. Nothing would induce her to encourage Martyn to break his engagement. But her silence told Martyn what he wanted to know.

'She thinks I ought to break my engagement, doesn't she? Most people would think so. Engagements were made for that purpose.'

Luisa turned on him like a little fury.

'Don't be so damnably cynical ... just because somebody was disloyal to you, why should you hurt Bridget in the way that you were hurt?'

He gave her a deep, adoring look.

'Oh, my darling, I may be cynical but you are damnably loyal to your friend,' he said under his breath.

Setting her lips in a thin line, Luisa turned from him and kicked one foot against the fender. How tired she was! It wasn't the physical exertion of riding, to which she was well used. It was the mental strain – of taut nerves, the terrific effort to put someone else's happiness before her own.

'For goodness' sake, try and help me, Martyn. I'm not all that strong,' she whispered.

He went on looking at her. She had been flushed when she first came in but now she was white. He saw the faint golden sprinkle of freckles – which he found so endearing – across the bridge of her small nose. He saw the way her upper lip quivered, and the gleam of tears on the long silken lashes. He knew that he loved her better than life, better than honour, more that anything in the whole world. His hand closed convulsively over Bridget's telegram as he screwed it into a ball. He said:

'All right! Go on trying to be strong. And I'm a rotter because I want to make you otherwise and because I find it so hard to do the right thing by Bridget. But I'm going to ask you one thing ... I'm going to ask you to give me just one day of your life – just one whole day to myself.'

A little startled, Luisa glanced up at him.

'What do you mean?'

'I mean that as Bridget is not coming back until the day after to-morrow, I want you to come up to London with me, spend the day with me there. Let us do some of the things together that we might have done if we had had the right to be together – a lunch, a dinner, a show – the sort of gay evening I used to have before the war – before disaster overtook us all. I used to love my London then. I used to love to dance. I've still got one arm...' he gave a short laugh. 'I can put that around you. You'd be lovely to dance with, Luisa. Let's pretend that we're engaged, married, anything you like, only let us be close together for one day ... one heavenly evening. It's not much to ask. *One moment in annihilation's waste.* Didn't some poet call it that?'

She could not answer for a moment. His voice, his expression held her enthralled. It was a Martyn she did not know until this moment. Martyn, the lover – passionate, impetuous, eager as a boy, offering her the very essence of life in an outstretched hand. *One day* he had said. *One evening.* Yes, that

152

wasn't very much in a lifetime, and Bridget could have all the rest.

Martyn saw the colour flaming into Luisa's face and the answering flame in her eyes. Now he caught her roughly against him and she could feel the strong beating of his heart against her breast.

'Say yes!' His voice was urgent against her ear.

All her good resolutions were shattered. Her whole being was dissolved into one surge of longing for him. She drew in her breath.

'Yes, I'll come, Martyn. But after that it's got to end, it must ... for all our sakes.'

His lips crushed hers for a brief urgent moment. Then she drew away. She was trembling violently. To be strong-minded away from Martyn was one thing. And quite another in such close physical proximity.

She began to walk quickly away from him. He called after her:

'Promise you'll come – that you won't change your mind!'

She felt as though some strong Fate drove her – impelled her against her own will and conscience as she flung a quick, ardent look at him from the great green eyes which he found so irresistible.

'I promise I'll come!' she said under her breath and then was gone.

Martyn, in a blind unseeing way, picked

up his pipe again and gripped it between his teeth. He was a fool, he told himself. A fool, as crazy with passion and longing for this girl as though this were a first love. Yet he had never begun to love Betty this way. Losing her had been bad – but the thought of losing Luisa was like the thought of death. The pain that accompanied it was worse than the pain he had felt when he lost his arm. To lose a limb – what was that in comparison with losing your soul? For Luisa, without doubt, was his affinity. And the dreadful part of it was that he had not realized all this, but instead had tied himself up to Bridget. He could almost hate Bridget at this moment for standing between him and his desire. Yet none of this was her fault, so why should she suffer?

'Oh, what a mess!' he said aloud, and leaning his arm on the mantelpiece, he laid his head on it and shut his eyes as though to shut out the agonizing prospect of the future with all its implications.

CHAPTER IX

They went up to London together by a morning train like two truant children who had run away from school. Martyn had abandoned his work for the day, having finished his early surgery before they left. In some curious kind of way Luisa was not guilt-conscious as she made that journey. Sitting opposite Martyn in a crowded carriage, she felt happy and excited. It was a relief to have left the vicarage behind them and everybody that they knew. She could see from the calmness of his smile that he, too, was feeling relief and they enjoyed the shared memory of intimacy, of their love for each other as they met one another's eyes over the edge of their papers.

Now and again she looked at the passing scenery – the russet red of autumn leaves, the misty grey of a cloudy morning. It had turned cold last night. She wore a thick suit. When she had come down to breakfast wearing it, Martyn had looked at her and said:

'I like you in grey!'

That had been enough to make her absurdly happy, and she could smile this morning at the remembrance of late last night when she had tried on one thing after another and had finally chosen the beautifully cut suit which her aunt had given her and which she had so carefully transformed into the newest fashion. She was glad now that she had had that good cashmere jumper, green as her eyes, and with it she wore Aunt Ellen's double row of pearls, and pearls in her ears, and a demure grey felt on the back of that red gold head. Martyn could not tear his gaze from her. Gone was the windswept girl whom he met so often in country surroundings. This was a new, sophisticated Luisa with a chic, a loveliness which took a man's breath away, and he, himself, was a much smarter Martyn in that dark London suit which so seldom came out of the wardrobe these days.

They were a little strange to one another and extraordinarily exciting in such new guise.

Once at Waterloo and out of the train, Martyn tucked his arm through hers and walked down the crowded platform towards the taxi queue.

'Everything to-day shall be done regardless,' he said, dark eyes smiling down at her. 'And our first stop shall be at a florist. You must have some flowers to pin on your coat. Then let us chose a show. What would you like to see?'

She gave a sharp sigh.

'Oh, I don't know. Martyn, how little we know about each other. We seem to share the same tastes in the country, but in London...'

He pressed her arm against his side.

'We don't really like London any more. We prefer the country, but we come up to town for celebrations.'

'I'd hardly call this a day of celebration,' she said with a wry smile.

'No bitterness,' he chided her. 'We're neither of us to refer to the fact that it's all a kind of "good-bye". It's *our day* and we must make it a marvellous one.'

She sighed again but her eyes looked up at the brown lean face with a love which she had no wish to-day to conceal.

'It is marvellous – just being alone with you like this,' she said.

He gave the sudden laugh which always delighted her when she heard it, for it made her realize the sense of humour that lurked within him and which had been hidden for so long. Martyn must have been such fun before life dealt him that double blow – the loss of his arm and the loss of his love. And now it seemed so terrible that she must be the unwilling instrument of hurting him all over again.

'Marvellous being with me even in a taxi queue?' he bent down to whisper in her ear, and her eyes shone like stars as she whispered back:

'Yes, darling – even in a queue!'

It was a grey, sombre morning in London and they could see the mist over the river as they drove across Waterloo bridge. Luisa sat back in the taxi, one hand clasped tightly in Martyn's, and looked dreamily at the splendid silhouette of Westminster Abbey and the Houses of Parliament. The roar of London traffic was in her ears. She had not been in town for some time. It seemed strange after the quiet of the country. She looked at the hundreds of people hurrying down the streets and at a long line of cars, vans and buses hung up at a traffic stop. So vast a city! So many people! Yet she was alone with Martyn in that strange and faintly terrifying isolation which a woman can feel when she is with the man she loves, even in a crowd.

She felt a strange apathy as though she were giving herself up completely to him and his will. Whatever he wished she would do. She would never be with him again like this. He would ride in other taxis in this same London but it would be with Bridget – not with her. Bridget would have the happiness of sitting beside him like this, listening to his voice and feeling the strong grip of his lean fingers. Perhaps, she thought, she would be forgiven for the purely feline hope that he would not hold Bridget's hand as he held hers; would not know that same wild hunger and ecstasy which was as much of the mind as of the body.

Martyn organized everything. In his meticulous fashion he had worked out what he thought she would like. He stopped the taxi at a big florist. And to the girl who came forward to serve them, he said:

'A shoulder spray – something that will go with my...' he stopped and added a little lamely ... 'her coat.'

Luisa stifled a desire to laugh. But it was Martyn in the end who chose the flower. He had just seen a wonderful purple blue orchid. It was much too exotic for the neat grey tailor-made, and neither would it go well with the little grey coat which she held over her arm. But he said that it matched her eyes. He paid a huge sum for it without blanching and despite Luisa's protest.

Following a whim, he took her across the park to Church Street, Kensington. They would walk here among the many fascinating little shops and look at lovely things together. It used to be his hunting-ground. Martyn had once loved collecting fine glass and china, and in his student days had lodged near Campden Hill and he knew the district inside out. To Luisa it was all new and intriguing. And as they walked arm-in-arm from one shop window to another, she discovered a Martyn she had not dreamed was there – a man with artistic tastes and some knowledge of old and valuable things.

He insisted upon buying her a little cameo brooch which she admired. Coming out of the shop with it, he suddenly said:

'Oh, Luisa, what fun we could have had choosing things for our home, and what a thrill for me looking for very special treasures that would suit you.'

She looked up at him sadly.

'Yes, it would all have been so wonderful…'

His gaze travelled from the charming face to the long, slender line of throat.

'I would like to see you looking like a Victorian miniature with a velvet ribbon around that neck and the cameo pinned to it.'

'I have a painting of my mother with that very thing,' Luisa said.

'Let's go and buy the ribbon,' he smiled, 'and bring the miniature to life.'

So they bought a length of violet-blue velvet ribbon, and it was as they walked out of a big shop in the High Street that Martyn suddenly stopped and exclaimed:

'I've got a wonderful idea.'

'You're so full of ideas to-day that I can't keep pace with you. What is it this time?'

'To-night,' he said. 'What about to-night? I wanted to dance with you and you haven't a dress.'

'We're supposed to be catching a not-too-late train home again,' she reminded him.

'Then we shall do nothing of the sort! We shall buy you a dress and stay in London.'

'What – stay the night?'

He made a rapid mental calculation.

'We'll dance all night and take the milk train back,' he said.

She caught her breath, dazzled and intrigued by the suggestion, although it seemed quite crazy. But her whole world was crazy to-day. She said:

'Oh, what fun that would be! Won't you be tired to-morrow with surgery in front of you?'

'I've a lifetime in which to make up lost rest,' he said. 'And only to-day with you.'

She was capturing his reckless mood, fast and furiously.

'I'll do anything you say.'

'You're a darling, Luisa, and I love you!'

'I love you, Martyn.'

And there they stood, outside John Barker's in High Street, Kensington, with the milling crowd of shoppers around them, and were lost to the world as they looked into each other's eyes, making that sweet despairing avowal.

Now Martyn had another idea. They could choose to dine and dance in a place where he might wear a dark lounge suit but she must have a dinner dress – a new one and they would choose it together, and with it she should wear the velvet ribbon and her cameo brooch.

This time Luisa expostulated, laughing.

'Honestly, darling … I'd have to have shoes, everything…'

'Too easy! We'll buy them now. Anything – everything you want.'

'You really are a little mad!' she whispered, loving him for it.

'And only one day to be mad in. If you were my wife, I would want to give you a present because … well, let's pretend it's an anniversary – our silver wedding if you like!'

She pouted, her eyes dancing at him.

'That makes me too old and you'd be a staid old husband and you'd cancel our theatre because the farmer's prize cow was calving.'

He roared with laughter.

'That sounds unromantic. Very well … it's our first anniversary. We've been married one glorious year and I'm still insanely in love with you.'

She felt her heart-beats shaking her whole body. And with her pleasure a terrible grief that it must all be make-believe. But she went on smiling and playing the game of pretence with him. She would not damp his spirits for anything in the world. He passed from one delightfully mad suggestion to another. They would go, he said, to a studio flat at the top of Campden Hill where lived an artist friend of his, Peter Morrell. Peter was a bachelor. He had made some money as a black and white artist. Luisa had, in fact, heard the name. Morrell had been in the army with Martyn.

'He lost a leg and I lost an arm,' said Martyn. 'And thank God it wasn't the other way round for both our sakes.'

They would go along to the studio and see Peter and ask if Luisa might change there before dinner.

'He would like to see you. You are so beautiful. He does those quick pencil sketches. He might do one to give me.'

'Darling, you do take a girl's breath away,' she said, shaking her head. And with a mischievous smile, she added: 'And to think you used to hate the sight of me!'

'I think I always admitted you were beautiful!' he laughed back.

They walked on, arm-in-arm. In due course the crazy suggestions were all carried out. Luisa did not want Martyn to spend so much money on her but he refused to take 'no' for an answer. They found the very dress for her in one of the smaller shops. Luisa was so exquisitely slim – it was not hard to find a dress to suit her. And the Autumn sales were on, so Luisa cleverly saw to it that the cheque Martyn wrote out so grandly, was not too ridiculously big. And the fates were with them. The dress was perfect. When she came from one of the fitting rooms to show Martyn, who sat smoking his pipe, waiting for her, he felt his heart turn over at the sight of so much loveliness. The radiant slenderness poured as though into a mould of dove-grey chiffon, slipping a little off creamy shoulders, sewn at the line of slight bosom with gleaming sequins, and with a beautiful design of sequins glittering around the tiny waist. It was full skirted and 'ballet' length and there was a sequin bolero with long tight sleeves which covered the décolletage.

Luisa moved shyly towards him, gold-red head tilted with innocent pride in her own perfection. He swallowed hard, took pipe from mouth and said:

'I've never seen anything more beautiful … that is the one we shall have. We've made one mistake. The violet ribbon. We'll go and find a black velvet for your cameo. That will complete the picture. Peter Morrell will be crazy to paint you.'

'I don't mind what *he* thinks,' she said, and her eyes told Martyn what she felt about *his* opinion.

They came out of the shop with the heavenly dress in a box. Luisa sighed blissfully.

'I haven't had a dress like this for ages.'

'Now what shoes? Silver sandals, did the woman say?'

'Yes. That will do.'

'Will the coat spoil the whole effect?'

'Definitely. But I shall only wear it to get to the restaurant,' she reminded him.

They found the silver sandals. Martyn watched the man buckle a strap around Luisa's small ankle. Somehow he felt profoundly moved by the sight of the little slender foot and a gleam of polished nails showing through the transparent nylon stocking. This sweet intimacy of shopping with Luisa was almost too much to be borne. And time was rushing by. Already it was nearing lunch-time. Then would come the afternoon ... then the one short evening. Oh, God, he thought, if one could put back the clock ... or make time stand still.

Before lunch they called at Morrell's studio. They met the artist on his way out of the front door with a large portfolio under his arm. He greeted Martyn enthusiastically.

'My dear chap – how nice! You're a stranger. Where've you been? Buried in this veterinary job of yours, I suppose...'

He paused, a professional eye raking the lovely red-headed girl at Martyn's side.

'This is Luisa...,' Martyn said.

Peter Morrell smiled:

'Why should you bring anything so dazzling to my studio on the very day that I must catch a train to Manchester and stay there, Martyn you old son of a gun?'

He talked at great length without giving Martyn time to explain … apologizing that he must absent himself … that he could not pause even for an hour to reproduce Luisa's loveliness on a canvas, for Martyn. His business in Manchester was urgent – connected with a black and white job he was doing for a big advertising firm. He had to catch the next train. Martyn and Luisa wanted somewhere in which to rest and change? Then the studio was at their disposal. Morrell tossed a latch-key into Martyn's hand. Use the place as his own … throw the key through the letter-box when he left … Morrell had another. He'd find milk in the ice-box. Bread, sausages … anything they could see, they could take if they had no wish to go out. He must fly. He kissed Luisa's hand. He clapped Martyn on the back. He limped down the street, hailing a taxi as he went. Luisa and Martyn looked after the tall, rather ungainly figure with the untidy hair, and drew breath.

'That's that,' said Martyn. 'Typical of old Peter.'

'He's nice,' murmured Luisa.

'So is this…' said Martyn, glancing at the latch-key in his hand.

Luisa's teeth bit into her lower lip.

'Ought we to…?'

'It's a heaven-sent opportunity just to be alone. We shall get tired tramping the streets, my sweet.'

She surrendered to Fate once again. Five minutes later she found herself sitting in the untidiest, but most charming, room she had ever seen, Peter's studio – typical of an artist who lived alone – untidy, dusty, but full of secret beauty. One or two fine pieces of furniture. Curtains of splendid colour and design, torn silk but still lovely, framing the dusty window-panes. A half-finished sketch on a block thrown on a wooden table which was littered with papers and scribblings. A grand piano at one end of the room. One perfect Persian rug on a rough wooden floor. And other rugs in tatters. A glimpse through an open doorway of a tiny kitchen with a hastily left breakfast on the table; a small grey kitten playing with a strip of coloured paper on the floor.

Luisa, drawing off her gloves and shaking back her hair, looked at the walls on which there hung one or two fine paintings by contemporary artists.

'This is an experience for me, Martyn. I've never been in an artist's studio before.'

Martyn, hand in his pocket, walked around the room looking at this picture and that.

'He has one or two new once since I've been here. What money he makes he spends on good paintings. But as you can see the rest of the place goes to rack and ruin.'

'I thought he was delightful. And no wife? Or girl friend?'

Martyn brooded.

'There was a girl once. One of his models when he was very young. She did him about as much good as Betty did me and left him a cynic about women. I doubt if Peter will ever marry.'

The name Betty jarred suddenly on Luisa. She did not want to think about Martyn's old love any more than she wished to remember Bridget. At the moment she felt that it could not be possible that there should have been any other woman in Martyn's life but herself. With deliberation she thrust away these thoughts. For this once she would be all egoist and grasp every moment, every hour with greedy hands.

Suddenly she went towards him and with a completely natural unembarrassed gesture, curved an arm around his neck and pulled his dark head down to hers.

'Oh, I love you so much,' she said brokenly.

That one sound arm of Martyn's went around her fiercely, pulling her closer. The pliancy and sweetness of her went a little to his head. He kissed her hungrily, desperately, and then drew away from her with a haunted look, shaking his head.

'Oh, Luisa, if you knew how much I loved you, Luisa, Luisa…!'

He drew his hand across his eyes as though he could no longer see and was trying to get back some kind of vision.

She sat down rather unsteadily on a deep-cushioned sofa at right angles to the big stone fireplace in which there were the charred logs of last night's burning. Her pulses were racing and on fire for him after those desperate kisses.

For both their sakes, she must keep a tight rein on herself, she thought, wildly. And she sought for defence in a purely practical suggestion.

'Darling, what about lunch? You didn't eat much breakfast and neither did I. Let's go out and eat and then come back here and I'll make you some coffee. There's sure to be some milk.'

Automatically he fell in with her suggestion although body and soul demanded that he should take her back into his arms again. Carefully she took the dress out of its folds of tissue paper, found a coat-hanger in the bedroom next door and hung up the lovely thing of chiffon and sequins, then rejoined Martyn in the studio.

Lunch was a little stilted as though both were distrait. Laughter and jokes were forced and however hungry they were, neither seemed to eat very much. As they came out of the restaurant, Martyn gave a grim laugh and said:

'It cannot be said that the prisoners ate a hearty meal!'

'Prisoners?' she echoed.

'We are condemned, aren't we? To spend the rest of our lives apart.'

'Who forbade me to be bitter in that taxi-queue at Waterloo?' she reminded him.

He hugged her arm to his side and his brow cleared a little. Perhaps she did not know quite what a strain this day was going to be for him, he thought. Perhaps he, himself, had not suspected it. And perhaps the entrée to Peter's studio spelled danger. The latch-key was a symbol of that very danger and he touched it uneasily. In almost a rough voice, he said:

'I don't know about you but I don't want to spend the whole afternoon in Peter's place.'

Her cheeks burned with sudden recognition of what lay in his thoughts. Had it not been in her own – the sweet, white-hot danger of aloneness – shut away with him from the rest of the world and that insidious recurrence of the thought *'for the last time'*. They must not spoil their day. Whatever happened they must not spoil it.

'How about a matinée as we're going to dance to-night?' he added.

'I think that would be marvellous,' Luisa agreed with forced enthusiasm.

'We'll go into a theatre-ticket office and

choose a play. Shall it be musical, farce, variety or straight drama?'

'Anything but drama,' said Luisa hurriedly. 'Let's go to something very gay and bright. We never get enough music at home. I used to play. I noticed Peter's piano.'

'I'd no idea that you were a musician, my Luisa. What else are you? There are so many entrancing things about you!'

She tossed her head.

'I've no technique but I can play by ear and pick out tunes. Take me to a musical comedy and I'll play you extracts from it afterwards.'

'Done!' said Martyn with a smile.

They found that they had come on the right day for the matinée of one of the most popular musical comedies of the moment. There were two seats just returned, and Martyn took them.

They sat through two and a half hours of gay frothy dialogue, tuneful melodies, laughter and dancing. Their hands entwined, they sat close, watching, listening, and turning now and then to look deep into each other's eyes. It was a pleasant show and under normal circumstances it would have pleased them both. But they came away from it as dissatisfied as they had gone in – with their hearts full of that dread of ultimate loss, and the unappeased hunger of two deeply emotional beings.

After the show, tea, and then back to the studio to change, before going on to a cocktail bar and dinner and dancing. He had booked a table at one of the new restaurants where they could eat and see a floor show later on.

Now it had begun to rain and the Autumn evening was sad and full of that strange melancholy which can be found more easily in a great city than in the country where the rain seems friendly, and darkness falls like a benison. They were both conscious of the sudden gloom as they walked into Peter's studio. The little kitten sprang at Luisa mewing and she picked it up, and stroked it.

'Poor lonely little thing!'

Martyn stared at her and wondered whether this evening was to be a drawn-out agony instead of the happy celebration he had planned. He said:

'Let's light the fire!'

Luisa set down the little cat.

'I must say all your ideas are good, Martyn,' she said.

They knelt together in front of the big open grate and rekindled the fire, watching the wood ignite until the sparks flew up the chimney and a delicious smell of wood-smoke filled the studio. Now the curtains were drawn and the gloom dispelled, contentment crept back into their hearts for a little while. They sat together on the sofa –

she in the crook of his arm while she listened to his low voice telling her many things that she wanted to know – about his early boyhood and later his training in the veterinary college and his deep love of animals.

Luisa took his hand, stroking his long sensitive fingers, thoughtfully.

'You were bound to do something like that. You have healing hands.'

'I *had!*' he said.

'I never think of you as having lost the other one. You do so much with this,' and she raised the one hand to her lips and kissed it gently.

There was a strained, hard lump in his throat and a fierce longing for the might-have-been. Bridget assumed suddenly the proportions of a monstrous barrier between this sweet and unutterably desirable woman and himself. For a moment all loyalties and heroics were swept away. They were Luisa's loyalties rather than his own. He had no wish for renunciation and sorry though he was for Bridget who was the innocent victim of this three-cornered disaster, he felt that there was no logical reason why they should suffer like this. To feel this way about Luisa and yet be married to Bridget – what hell! Life was too short for such sacrifice. He could not, and would not, go through with it – as much on Bridget's behalf as on theirs. Luisa had forced the decision on him but when he had brought her up here for this 'good-bye', had he not hoped in the depths of his heart that she might weaken and capitulate?

He voiced his thoughts suddenly, harshly, with Luisa held tightly against him.

'We can't go on like this for the rest of our lives. It would be inhuman. We must tell Bridget how we feel!'

At once Luisa was on her feet, tearing herself away from him, mentally as well as physically, eyes dilated in a white, determined young face.

'I won't listen to you. We've been through all this. I would never have come if I'd known you were going to try and alter my decision. I tell you I won't – *I won't*. Bridget is my friend. To take a friend's lover away ... why, I'd never be able to live with myself if I did it. I'd feel so low. So would you in the end. Oh, Martyn, so would you!'

He looked up at her shaking his head, his own eyes smouldering.

'No, my dear. I never have been quixotic like you. I want to do the right thing, but I'm not convinced that your way is the right one. And whether you walk out on me or not, I don't know if I could find it possible now to make Bridget my wife.'

She gave a shocked exclamation.

'But you must! If you don't I shall still feel responsible even though I go a thousand miles away from you.'

'Then don't go. Stay with me and let us both tell Bridget the truth.'

She put her hands to her mouth, trembling.

'Martyn, Martyn, this wasn't in the bargain. We were to have a glorious day together. But it was to be good-bye. Don't try and alter my mind for me. I love you and you could, I suppose, break me down in the end. But I think I'd hate you for it afterwards. Bridget would always be between us. Oh, Martyn, help me!'

She burst into tears and flung herself down on the sofa, buried her face on the curved arm and wept inconsolably. Nothing he could say or do now would comfort her. Her choked sobs rent his heart and left him devitalized and no longer in the mood to try and storm his way back into her heart. At last he sat silent, stroking the bowed lovely head, his eyes full of hopelessness. He said:

'This is dreadful – that you should cry like this and that I should be the cause of it. My poor darling, I'm sorry. But I just thought there might be a chance for us. It isn't that I want to hurt Bridget. You know I'm not callous about her. I'm very fond of her and always will be. But I don't want to marry her any longer.'

Luisa raised her head. Her face looked devastated but she had stopped crying and was composed again. In a muffled voice, handkerchief pressed to her lips, she said:

'I understand, and I want you just as much as you want me, but I could never get over this feeling that I mustn't betray my friend.'

Martyn stood up and kicked back a log that threatened to fall out of the grate. He felt suddenly tired, flattened and bruised in spirit.

'So be it! I suppose we had better think about preparing for the evening, or would you rather go straight home?'

Now the colour flamed back into her white, strained face. She sprang up and with a gesture which he found infinitely touching, laid her cheek against the empty sleeve of his coat.

'No, darling, I couldn't bear to go back just now, but please don't be angry with me, or hurt. Try and understand how I feel about Bridget.'

He sighed with a bitterness which he could not altogether control.

'My darling, I do understand in a way, but I wish you weren't so brave and that you were a little more self-seeking. However, I've almost wrecked our evening. We must pull ourselves together and think about a drink and then our dinner.'

'I expect I look a sight now,' she said forlornly.

'You are the most beautiful woman in the world and always will be to me, my Luisa!'

She fought back the inclination to cry again.

'Do you think I could have a bath?'

'Yes! There's a geyser in the bathroom, I'll light it for you. Then I'll take a walk while you dress. I need some fresh air. I've had enough of this.'

She had never felt more miserable. He spoke harshly because he was so hurt and knowing it, Luisa did not hold it against him. It would be so easy to surrender and wipe Bridget off the map and say: *Take me, I am yours!* And yet it was so impossible. She knew that she must go on swimming against the tide or sink and be forever lost in ignominy. Yet hurting Martyn was far more awful than any hurt that she could give herself.

She was almost glad when he was gone and she had the studio to herself. She got into her bath, relaxed a moment in the hot soapy water and shut her eyes. She was exhausted. Afterwards she made up her face until she felt that she had recovered its freshness, and brushed her shining hair until it was a nimbus about her small head.

When Martyn came back, she was dressed and waiting for him in front of the studio fire. Now he saw her again as the radiant lovely Luisa who had come forward to him for his inspection at the dress shop, glowing in her chiffon and sequins, and with his cameo pinning the little velvet ribbon around her long, white throat. He, himself, had regained some of his good spirits after a sharp walk through the autumnal evening. It had stopped raining and the air was fresher.

He came forward, took Luisa's hand and touched his cheek with it.

'So beautiful you are, my love, that I feel a shabby old vet, who has no right to take you out. You should be dancing to-night with some marvellous fellow who...'

'Martyn!' Luisa broke in swiftly, her voice deepening in its sincerity, 'there is no one in the whole world with whom I would rather be going out to-night other than you. And to me you always look handsome.'

Afraid of the emotion which had risen so swiftly at her words – afraid of the passionate longing to draw her towards him and crush her slim body against his own – Martyn gave a deep sigh, and then, with an effort, smiled down at the girl who stood with her face raised so appealingly to his.

'Come, my darling, to-night we shall make the happiest and most treasured in our lives.'

In the softly-lit restaurant with its shaded lamps and gently beating band, Martyn and Luisa danced. They were oblivious to the many glances cast in their direction. Many a woman's eyes were cast admiringly at the tall handsome dark man with the one arm who had, himself, eyes for no one but the beautiful young red-headed girl in the circle of his arm. They envied her the love which shone so unmistakably from his eyes, the complete isolation with which he surrounded her so adoringly, the eagerness with which he bent his head a little to catch a whispered word, the gentle abandon with which he laid his cheek to hers and drew her yet a little closer against him. To be loved by such a romantic man! they thought, and how could she be blamed for returning such a love? Where had he lost his arm – in the war? But what did that matter now he had come back to her, adoring her in that way every woman longs to be loved!

They had no notion of the bitter-sweetness of Martyn's thoughts, no idea of the impending parting for these two – that this was just one night stolen from a thousand others which must be suffered apart in vain longings and loneliness. How *could* they know – when the girl, slim, young, fascinatingly beautiful in her lovely grey chiffon dress and the flaming hair framing her white face, smiled so trustingly and happily into the dark eyes above her? There was no thought of the past or the future in that pale yet glowing face – only a blissful unconditioned happiness in the present. How wonderful to love and be loved in such a way. How happy these two must be!

Perhaps a little of their imaginings found their way into Martyn's thoughts.

'Happy, my darling?' he asked Luisa, bending his head to hers.

'So terribly happy, Martyn!' she whispered to him, 'Oh, darling, I love you so very much!'

'You're so beautiful!' Martyn whispered back.

She closed her eyes and Martyn's grip around her waist tightened a little so that their two bodies were moving in perfect unison. From the moment when they had taken those first steps, Luisa had realized that Martyn was a wonderful dancer; that their steps matched to perfection as surely their whole bodies and souls, too, must match. There was no awkward struggling to adjust themselves to each other's styles, no difficulty in following Martyn's lead. Their feet moved as one, and for Luisa it had a strange fascinating and dream-like effect on her mind and body. The dance-floor, the other couples, the table where lay their half-eaten dinner, faded into the background and her whole being seemed to float in perfect unison with Martyn's. She had no other thought but of his nearness, heard no other sound but their two hearts beating in time to the music and in tune with each other. To-morrow, too, was forgotten and there remained only this moment of most wonderful perfection of indescribable happiness.

And for Martyn, too, these few hours were the happiest in his whole life. He knew now more certainly than he had ever known before, that Luisa belonged to him; that she loved him as greatly as he loved her, in the same way that was both spiritual and physical. Her mind read his unspoken thoughts as he could read hers, and there was little need for words. Understanding, tenderness, passion flowed from one to another. They were hours of perfect union and he was happy even while, unlike Luisa, a memory of to-morrow would fill his heart in sudden pain that was nearly unbearable. Then he would hold her closer, feeling the slim lithe young body against his own, bend his head so that his cheek lay against the white softness of hers, and forget again his love and longing for her.

They did not cease dancing until the band retired and the waiters, suddenly wide awake, went round the tables, clearing away, hurrying lingering couples so that they, too, might go wearily to bed. Then only did Luisa go for her coat while Martyn paid the bill.

Outside, the sky was inky black although it was nearly two o'clock and soon the dawn would break. An occasional taxi sped swiftly by beneath the myriad street lamps that found their reflection in the wet pavements. The roar of London had died down to a gentle murmur – to an occasional horn hooting in the distance, to footsteps going hurriedly homewards echoing in the sharp cold of the night.

'No stars!' Luisa said softly, a strange sadness stealing over her, a melancholy which was part tiredness, part because fantasy was turning slowly to reality again.

'Two!' said Martyn, gazing deep into her eyes, and was rewarded by her swift returning smile.

They hailed a taxi and were carried quickly through the empty streets to Peter's flat. Martyn did not try to kiss her but sat holding her hand tightly in his own. Neither had spoken.

In the studio, the big log fire had burned low and there was a warm red glow from the hearth. Luisa went quickly towards it and sat warming her hands, while Martyn paid the taxi and came more slowly up the stairs. Without a word, he went to her in the soft red light, lifted her to her feet and removed the grey coat.

'Dance with me again, Luisa – one more dance!' he pleaded.

But as his arm closed around her, neither moved, only their faces as they searched and found each other's lips.

All the longing, all the passion, all the glory of that evening were in that one long kiss. Their two bodies were pressed closer and closer until Luisa felt the strength draining from her. So this was love – perfect love as she had always known deep in her heart it must be – this uncontrollable desire to surrender one's whole self in complete abandon. She was frightened and yet too lost in the stirring emotions that swept through her whole body; her heart was beating with such great breath-taking speed that it seemed as if she were lost in it – that she could never find words again.

'Oh, Luisa, Luisa!' Martyn cried as if the words were torn from him. 'I love you so, I love you so, *I love you so...*'

Perhaps in that moment, hearing the pain, the longing, the torment in his voice, Luisa might have lost her last vestige of control. Maybe then, she, who had planned to be so strong, was the weaker of the two. But Martyn released her suddenly and taking an almost inhuman grip on himself, forced himself to lead Luisa gently to the sofa where she sat down obediently beside him, her face white, strained, raised questioningly and helplessly towards him.

He knew then, looking deep into her eyes, that he could dissuade her from her loyal intentions; persuade her to his will, no matter what he desired of her. She was, in this one minute, his – all his to do with as he wished. No matter what lay in the future for either of them, her surrender could never be more complete than when she sat silently waiting for him to state his will. It was her very weakness that gave him strength; her lack of control that gave him back his own. For he knew as sanity returned, that this was not the way he wanted Luisa to be his. Nothing but perfection in all things could do justice to their love. There could be no regrettings later, no conscience, no single thought at the back of either of their minds that what they were doing was wrong. His love for her was capable of any sacrifice, for it had now a quality of protectiveness that surpassed his own desires.

His voice was gentle and warm with tenderness as he said:

'It will soon be time to go, my dearest.'

She flung herself towards him then, her face tragic in its unhappiness.

'No, Martyn. No – not yet. It can't be time. This can't be good-bye. Oh, Martyn, help me, for I can no longer help myself.'

'I know, darling, I know,' he murmured, stroking her head with those long sensitive fingers. 'And that is why it must soon be time to go. To-morrow – or rather to-day – you will have time to think about this more reasonably. The decision is in your hands, my dearest Luisa, and you will know, when you can think more clearly, what is the right thing to do. So you see, this might not, after all, be good-bye for us. And Luisa – even if you decide it should be – I cannot believe that we shall not be together again like this some time, some place in the future – perhaps in another world. We belong to one another and even should we live at other ends of the earth, nothing can really separate us, for my heart lies in yours and yours in mine.'

The tears were coursing down her cheeks now and he let her cry, knowing that for her this would be some measure of emotional relief. For him there could be none and he never loved her more than when he suffered so for her without her fully realizing it.

In the train going home, she slept against his shoulder, the shadows of fatigue violet beneath the closed eyes. He held her tenderly with a suffocating pain in his heart, feeling that in giving way to her tiredness and drifting into dreams of her own, she had already eluded him as if this were but a warning from Fate of things to come.

He was almost glad when the train drew into the station and he could busy himself with more practical things, collecting the car from the car park, tucking Luisa into it with a rug around her knees and driving swiftly up the lane in the misty grey light of the new day, so putting an end to that torturous yet wonderful night.

By the time Martyn had washed and shaved and had breakfast, the first callers had arrived at the surgery, so he had no time to sleep. But he had insisted that Luisa go straight to bed, and she had obeyed him with a meekness that showed him only too clearly how tired and completely worn out she was. Wearily he turned his mind to work and, as always, he found in it escape from his own thoughts, a certain exhilaration and pleasure, so that for the time his tiredness vanished and the girl he imagined lost in sleep up in one of the rooms above him was forgotten.

Indeed, Luisa did sleep, but only for a few hours. When she woke, her head ached and her eyes were hot and heavy with fatigue. But try as she would, she could not sleep again. Even reliving every perfect moment of that day now past, could not banish the dreadful hopelessness that seemed to hold her in its grip. Last night she had been ready to forget everything but her love for Martyn and his for her – their need of each other. But to-day Bridget was returning and she knew, somewhere deep within her – that all they had been through – she and Martyn – could not alter her convictions. Weaken them, perhaps! For could she ever give herself to any other man now as she expected

Martyn to give himself to Bridget? Could he make Bridget happy – just through friendliness and kindness? It would not be enough for her – not now! And yet was that not the very answer? Bridget had never been in love – had never known what it meant to be loved by Martyn. She would not know what was missing from her life and even a word, a smile, the right to call herself Martyn's wife, must give her tremendous happiness. And what right had she, Luisa, to destroy that future? For Bridget, of all people, who had been such a true and wonderful friend to her.

'Perhaps it would have been best if Martyn had not come into our lives!' Luisa tormented herself. 'Best for the three of us!'

And yet how to imagine a world now in which Martyn did not exist?

With a sudden effort, Luisa sprang out of bed. She could not bear these thoughts – could not bear to know that down in the surgery was the man she loved – perhaps waiting for her to come to him, longing herself to go to him and say 'I'm yours, Martyn, take me, take me!' But not having the right.

She dressed hurriedly, and without stopping for breakfast went to the stables to harness Jumbo, who whinnied with delight at her coming. She had left a note on the hall table to say she had gone for a ride and would be back for lunch, but as she mounted

Jumbo's quivering back, she wondered now if she would not ride for the whole day. With the wind in her hair, the cold frosty air against her cheeks, the motion of Jumbo's long strides beneath her, she could forget everything and become part of nature itself.

She dug her heels into Jumbo's sides and her heart rose as he sprang obediently into a gallop, head up, eyes alight with understanding of the reckless mood of his mistress astride his back.

How many hours Luisa galloped she did not know. Jumbo tired first and his slowing gait brought her back to reality. He was blowing hard, and she realized suddenly that they had kept up a fearful pace for some time.

And then, without warning, she noticed Jumbo had lost a shoe and was lame. Luisa dismounted and stood beside him, weariness now sweeping over her again, and with it the realization that she had been mad to ride off in such a way when she was so tired; and although Jumbo had made his own pace, she felt responsible for his lameness and his tiredness, too.

'Nothing for it but to find our way home,' she said, patting the steaming neck. She turned Jumbo's head back the way they had come.

Jumbo, was very slow. Luisa let him amble homewards and lost herself in her own thoughts. She was so far away in her dreams that when Jumbo shied suddenly at a piece of paper in the lane, she was too late to do anything about it. She fell with a sickening thud and felt a blinding pain at the back of her head.

For a moment or two she lay quite still, unable to think at all coherently. Then Jumbo, pushing his soft muzzle against her face, brought her back to her senses. She sat up and saw the lane revolving about her and the sky seeming to turn upside down. She felt dreadfully sick. Then the scenery steadied and the sickness wore off. She felt the back of her head and saw a thin warm trickle of blood on her hand.

'I'd better get home!' she thought. 'It may need a stitch.'

She stood up dizzily, holding on to Jumbo's saddle for support. The cut from the back of her head was bleeding more profusely now and she could feel it trickling slowly down her neck. Shakily, she tied her thin silk scarf round her head but she had not the strength to knot it. She pulled it off again and closed her eyes until she felt better.

With a great effort she pulled herself on to Jumbo's back and he ambled forward again. The reins hung loose as Luisa clung to the saddle with both hands, but fortunately Jumbo knew his way home. After an eternity, they reached the Vicarage and Luisa slid down from the saddle, knowing that she must find strength to walk indoors and find Martyn. With each step she became a little fainter, a little muzzier, and it was only by an enormous effort of will power that she was able to reach the dining-room door.

She opened it and stood there, wondering why although her lips framed Martyn's name, no sound came from them. Then she felt his arm round her, heard his voice very far away, and slipped into a painless oblivion.

Martyn had waited ten minutes for lunch, hoping that Luisa would still be coming.

Suddenly the door opened, and he looked up and had the biggest shock of his life. Luisa was deathly white and a horrible red smear of blood was across one cheek. She was swaying on her feet, and although her lips moved no words came from them. Instantly, he jumped to his feet and his arm was round her as she fainted. Cursing the absence of his other arm, he shouted for Mrs Jennings to come and help him.

Together they lifted her on to the sofa in the dining-room, and Martyn sent Mrs Jennings to telephone for the doctor immediately. Meantime, he smoothed the hair from Luisa's forehead and found the jagged cut at the back of her head. Very gently he staunched the flow with his handkerchief, his eyes never leaving her face.

'Luisa, Luisa, my dearest. Oh, Luisa!' He said her name over and over again. When Mrs Jennings returned to say the doctor was on his way, it was all he could do to conceal his frightful agitation and anxiety.

'She should never have gone riding that horse, her not being well after that day in London,' Mrs Jennings said. 'Never touched her breakfast. You didn't ought to have let her go, Mr Saunders, sir.'

'No, you're right! I should have insisted she took the car. It's my fault. It's all my fault,' he cried, filled with remorse.

Mrs Jennings assumed that he and Miss Luisa had had words again. She had been all too well aware that they didn't get along well in the past, and once she had heard Mr Martyn's voice raised in anger. No doubt poor Miss Luisa had rushed out of the house upset-like, and got thrown from the horse. Well, no wonder, Mr Martyn looked so upset. If anything happened to Miss Luisa, he'd be to blame.

Martyn's anxiety grew when despite Mrs Jennings' effort with cold water, Luisa did not come round from her faint. He paced up and down the room, cursing the doctor for being so slow and no longer caring if Mrs Jennings saw his feelings. Had he known she misinterpreted them, he wouldn't have cared. All he could think of was that Luisa, his darling love, was terribly hurt – that she might even die.

Seeing his expression, the doctor turned Martyn out of the room as soon as he arrived. Mrs Jennings gave him her account of what she thought must have happened, and the doctor examined Luisa carefully.

'Concussion!' he said without hesitation. 'It would be best not to move her. Can she stay here?'

'I can make a bed up on the sofa easy,' said Mrs Jennings.

'Then do so and we'll get her into bed right away. Get a hot bottle – two if you have them.'

'Is it serious, Doctor?' Mrs Jennings asked from the door as she went to do his bidding.

'Very!' he replied briefly.

When at last he had finished ministering to Luisa and left the room, he found Martyn pacing up and down outside. Martyn immediately asked the same question.

'I'm afraid she has concussion,' the doctor told him. 'I can't say how long she will remain unconscious. She must be watched constantly. Is there anybody here who can nurse her?'

Martyn explained that Bridget and her mother were arriving at tea-time; that, meanwhile, he and Mrs Jennings would act as nurses.

'Doctor – you don't think – it isn't

possible that she's going to die?'

'I hope not, young man, for all our sakes,' said the doctor pointedly, remembering Mrs Jennings' accusations that it was Mr Saunders' fault. But the stricken look on Martyn's face softened him a little.

'Now don't you get ill worrying,' he said more gently. 'Better have a drink and steady up. You'll need your wits about you. I must be telephoned immediately she shows signs of coming round. I'll be back at tea-time in any case. Here are the telephone numbers where I shall be between now and then and instructions what to do.'

After the doctor had gone, Martyn went into the sitting-room and sat down beside Luisa's bed. She looked touchingly young with her head tied up in bandages, her lashes lying softly on her cheeks. Martyn's heart smote him with an agony of love for her and a dreadful haunting remorse. It was his fault. If she hadn't been tired and distressed after their London party, this would never have happened. Luisa was a wonderful rider and Jumbo the slowest and quietest of animals. Even a child could manage him. And yet Luisa must have been thrown.

Recalling Jumbo, he sent Mrs Jennings to put him in his stable and rub him down as best she could. Then, when she returned, he gave her his chair and went to telephone Mrs Mathers in case she could throw any light on the matter. But the maid told him she had gone down to the village and wouldn't be back until tea-time.

Knowing there was nothing more he could do, he went back into the room where Luisa still lay, so still and quiet, with only her slow, deep breathing to reassure him that she was still alive.

Mrs Jennings departed to make them all 'a nice cup of tea', and Martyn sat down again, his hand holding Luisa's as if in this way he could bring her back to him. And for the first time for many years, he prayed.

CHAPTER X

At tea-time, Bridget and her mother had arrived by taxi from the station. It had been arranged that should Martyn not be there with the car to meet them, they must assume he had been called out to a case and make their own way to the house.

She was totally unprepared, therefore, for the news with which Mrs Jennings greeted her.

'Ever so bad, she is, poor Miss Luisa. Mr Saunders is in with her and Doctor's coming again any moment. She hasn't shown no sign of life since – except her breathing.'

Bridget gave one look at her mother and together they went inside.

Bridget's mother was a rather plump, pleasant little woman in her early fifties. She would really have been called plain but for her cheerful homeliness and kind smile. Mrs Jennings, sizing her up, decided that Miss Bridget would look just the same when she was her mother's age.

'It seems a good thing I came, Bridget,' she said to her daughter. 'If anyone is a good nurse I am!'

Bridget helped her out of her coat and gave her mother a grateful look.

'Yes, mother, you're a two-fold blessing when there's illness about. I'll go and see Martyn and try and find out more about it. I expect you'd like a cup of tea.'

'I've a kettle boiling,' said Mrs Jennings. 'I'll bring a tray into the dining-room. They've put Miss Luisa in the sitting-room. She can't be moved, Doctor says, until she's better.'

Realizing that Mrs Jennings' gloomy mood was worrying her daughter even more than was probably necessary, Bridget's mother hurried her away to the kitchen to get the tray.

Bridget opened the sitting-room door and went quickly across to the sofa. Martyn looked up and gave her a quick glance. His worried expression so concerned her that she had no time to wonder why he had not kissed her. Her eyes went swiftly to the bed and back to Martyn.

'Is she – very bad?' she asked.

Martyn nodded.

'Concussion. She's been out three hours. I wish the doctor would come. Oh, Bridget, I am glad you are here. I've been off my head with worry.'

She pulled a chair up beside him and took his hand. It was terribly cold. Something more than Luisa's accident must have

196

occurred to put Martyn in such a state.

'Martyn,' she said softly, 'tell me what has happened?'

He missed the personal significance of her question or else he might have told her the whole wretched truth there and then. But he took her question to be a general one.

'It's all my darned fault,' he said. 'I feel entirely responsible. You see, Luisa was up in town yesterday and was very tired.' (There was no need, surely, to add that he, too, had gone?) 'This morning she left a note to say she had taken Jumbo and would be back to lunch. If only I hadn't let her go.'

Bridget, like Mrs Jennings, concluded immediately that Martyn and Luisa had been having words again and that Luisa had rushed angrily out of the house and ridden recklessly – for she was always reckless when she was angry – and so had had this fall. She, too, took Martyn's concern to be one of remorse because he felt the quarrel had been his fault. And Bridget, knowing how in the past Martyn had been curt and even rude without provocation, could imagine that more than likely, it had been his fault. She felt terribly sorry for him.

'I'm sure there's no need to worry so, Martyn,' she said. 'I'll see the doctor myself when he comes. Everything possible will be done, and my mother, who is the best nurse in the world, will take care of her. She's having a cup of tea now and then she will take over. You look dog-tired. You've been overworking, I suppose, as well as worrying.'

Martyn gave a wan smile.

'I'm afraid I've done no work at all. Mrs Jennings answered all calls this afternoon and said I was out. But your mother will be tired, Bridget, and needing a rest herself. I'll stay with Luisa. You go and have tea.'

Believing that Martyn's conscience was bothering him to such an extent that he felt he must see this through himself, Bridget did not try further to persuade him to leave Luisa's side.

She bent and kissed the top of Martyn's head, but he did not look up.

'I'll go and show Mother her room. She's looking forward to meeting you, Martyn, and is very happy about the engagement,' she said, and left him.

Strictly speaking, Mrs Castle was not very happy about the engagement. She had always imagined that Bridget would one day marry Bill, of whom she was inordinately fond. When Bridget had come home with the surprising news that she was engaged to the young veterinary surgeon whom she had known barely a month, she could hardly believe her daughter was serious.

But Bridget had finally convinced her that she meant to go through with it and when Martyn telephoned suggesting Bridget should take her along for a week or two as Luisa might be going on a holiday, she welcomed the opportunity so that she might see Bridget's future husband, and if all did not seem well, perhaps prevent this sudden engagement from going further. Deep in her heart, she believed that Bill was right for her daughter in every way. But she was open-minded enough to realize that love does not always strike in the right direction.

The doctor called again and showed extreme concern when he heard Luisa had still not recovered consciousness. He would not take the risk of having her moved to hospital – the nearest one being ten miles away, and it was arranged that Bridget, Martyn and her mother should do four-hourly watches through the night, and he must be called immediately her condition showed signs of changing.

Unable to insist on remaining at Luisa's side, Martyn said a few brief words to Mrs Castle, and knowing himself to be desperately in need of sleep, for he had had none for nearly forty-eight hours now, he went to bed. Here he set his alarm clock for one a.m. when it would be his turn to watch, and knowing that it might endanger Luisa's life if he happened to fall asleep during his watch, he forced himself to close his eyes. Before very long he was in a deep sleep of complete physical and nervous exhaustion.

When his alarm rang, he awoke suddenly and with a horrible premonition of disaster. But when he had flung on some clothes and hurried downstairs to the sitting-room, it was to find Mrs Castle, knitting calmly and reassuringly.

'No change?' Martin asked, seeing Luisa, her eyes still closed, her breathing still deep and regular.

'No, I'm afraid not. Just once, she moaned a little and moved a hand, but nothing more.'

Mrs Castle pointed to a tray on the table.

'Bridget filled the thermos with coffee before she went to bed and left some sandwiches. You must eat something, Mr Saunders. You missed your dinner, you know.'

Martyn nodded.

'Thank you. I will. Now you go off to bed, Mrs Castle. You must be tired out, sitting up like this after a long train journey.'

She said good-night to him and Martyn poured himself a cup of coffee, mentally thanking Bridget for her thoughtfulness. He ate a sandwich, and then sat down by Luisa's bed. Very gently he took her hand in his and remained so for an hour, watching for any movement and at the same time memorising every line of her beloved face – the way her nose turned ever so slightly upwards at the tip, the long graceful line of her white throat which only last night had been pulsating against his lips.

'Luisa! Luisa!' he murmured.

Suddenly she moaned and her hand stirred in his. He sat rigidly, waiting for some further movement. Then he called her softly and slowly her eyes opened.

'Luisa!' he said again. 'Luisa!'

Her eyes moved round the room and focused on his but without recognition. He thought she was still only semi-conscious but she said suddenly:

'My head hurts. I'm thirsty. Who are you?'

Thanking God for this miracle, Martyn reached quickly for the glass of water the doctor had left with a sedative in case she came to and was feverish. Luisa sipped a little and then lay back on her pillow staring up at him. One hand went to the bandages round her head.

'You had a slight accident, my darling,' Martyn told her. 'But you'll soon be well again.'

'Are you the doctor?' Luisa said suddenly.

'Luisa, it's Martyn. Darling...' suspicion ugly and threatening... 'you can see me, can't you?'

'Of course I can,' Luisa answered. 'But if you aren't the doctor, who are you, and where's Mother? I would like to see Mother. I don't feel very well.'

Horrified, Martyn stared down at her. He knew he must go and telephone the doctor, but he could not bear to leave her. Either she was talking in a delirium or else there was something terribly wrong. Could she have forgotten her mother was dead?

No sooner was this thought in his mind when Martyn realized with sickening certainty the truth. Luisa had lost her memory. It happened so often after a fall.

'Lie still and try not to worry,' he said. 'I'm going to leave you for a moment or two. I'll call Bridget.'

'Is Bridget here? How nice!' Luisa said. 'I haven't seen her since we left school last year. Oh, my head does ache. Please ask Bridget to come.'

Martyn hurried from the room and ran up the stairs to Bridget's room and knocked on the door.

Bridget came on to the landing in her dressing-gown.

'What is it? What's happened?' she asked, seeing Martyn's distraught face and fearing the worst.

'It's Luisa. She's speaking but... Bridget, she seems to have lost her memory. She asked for her mother and she didn't recognize me at all. I mentioned your name and she said she hadn't seen you since last term at school. You'd better go to her. I'll telephone the doctor.'

Bridget hurried downstairs and went into Luisa's room. Common sense told her that it would be best not to worry Luisa in any way at all. She leant over the bed and said gently:

'Hullo, Lis. It's Bridget. Remember me?'

Luisa opened her eyes and stared at Bridget in a puzzled way.

'Why, it's Bridget. Goodness, you have grown up since you left school. I hardly recognized you. Bridget, tell me what's been happening. I've been ill I suppose. I think I fell out of the hay loft, didn't I? You know, when I woke up just now there was a strange one-armed man sitting by the bed. Who was he? I don't think I liked him very much. He seemed rather frightening.'

'Luisa, you mustn't talk so much. Just lie quiet and listen. You have had an accident and cut your head. But you're getting better now. That man in here was Martyn Saunders. He's my fiancé. You see, I'm down here to look after you, and Mother is here, too, so we had Martyn as well for company. I'm sorry he frightened you. I expect it was seeing a strange face.'

Luisa was silent as she took all this in. Then she said:

'Bridget, where's mother and father? Are they asleep?'

Afraid to tell her the truth, Bridget said quickly:

'Don't you remember, Lis, they went to Switzerland for a holiday? Your mother wasn't very well. That's why I'm looking after you.'

'Oh, I see!' said Luisa. 'I suppose I must have been very ill to have forgotten all these things. Bridget, you never wrote and told me you were engaged. What about poor old Bill?'

'Luisa, you mustn't talk any more. The doctor will be here in a minute and he'll be dreadfully cross if he finds out I've been letting you talk like this. He said you were to lie quiet and rest. Now tell me if there is anything I can get you.'

'I'd like another drink,' said Luisa. 'I feel very sleepy.'

After what seemed an eternity, the doctor arrived. Bridget hurried out to meet him and told him exactly what had happened.

'I didn't dare tell her her mother and father were dead so I said they were abroad. She doesn't recognize Martyn at all. I explained he was my fiancé and was down here to help me look after her. Doctor, how long will this go on?'

He shook his head.

'I don't know, Miss Castle. It all depends. Loss of memory is usually a fairly short business but it could go on indefinitely. Usually complete recovery of health will restore the brain. Whatever happens, she must not be worried. Make up any story you like but don't let anyone shock her with the truth. Warn everyone. Another shock might have very serious mental consequences. I'll go and see her. Fortunately I've treated the family for years so she'll know me. Keep strangers out of her way. Better take over Mr Saunders' watch yourself. By to-morrow she may be well enough to do without a night nurse. We'll see.'

Luisa was, without doubt, very much better in the morning. But the fact remained that the past seven years of her life were completely and utterly forgotten. Martyn was a stranger to her and when he looked in after breakfast, she felt again that she didn't like him; that in some strange way she was frightened of him and wanted to get away. He looked terribly ill and strange. His eyes stared at her and made her feel uncomfortable.

Her reaction to him was painfully clear to Martyn. The blow of knowing that she had lost her memory was bad enough in itself, but to be treated as a stranger by her ... see her withdraw a little when he came into the room as if she disliked him ... it was almost more than he could bear. But he could say nothing to anyone and because he must bottle it all up within himself, he suffered dreadfully.

When Mrs Mathers called round that afternoon to see Luisa for a brief instant, she could not help but wonder what this must mean to Martyn Saunders, and on a sudden impulse she went to find him.

He was in the surgery sitting by the window, his head in his hands. He jumped up when he saw her and tried to appear normal and calm.

Mrs Mathers introduced herself and pulled up a chair beside him. She was moved by his stricken, tired, exhausted face, and knew that there was a job for her here – to help him if she could.

'Martyn!' she said, 'for I take the privilege of dispensing with formalities seeing I am many years older than you. Firstly, I want to tell you how very sorry I am. Secondly, to tell you that you must not let this affect you so deeply. Luisa may recover her memory any day.'

Martyn turned to her appealingly.

'Mrs Mathers, you know?'

'Yes, my dear boy, Luisa told me everything yesterday. I advised her to have the whole thing out with Bridget and then marry you. But although I think, maybe, my words had made some impression for she saw clearly that for you to marry Bridget might ruin three lives instead of one, she could still not bring herself to be the one to hurt her friend. She decided to give the thing time to work itself out and was coming to Devonshire with me. No doubt she would have told you all this but for the dreadful accident. I have, of course, cancelled the trip. Jim is arriving this afternoon and will not hear of going away without Luisa, let alone while she is so ill.'

'Jim – is very fond of her, too, isn't he?' Martyn said, more as a statement than a question.

Mrs Mathers nodded.

'Yes! He fancies himself in love with her. But Luisa isn't for him. I knew that the first day I met her. When Luisa told me about you yesterday, Martyn, I knew I should like you; I'm glad I have had this opportunity of meeting you for I am deeply attached to Luisa and now I know that she has given her heart into the keeping of the right man.'

'But, Mrs Mathers, much as I appreciate all you say, don't you understand that I have no right to Luisa's love – or to give her mine? And now, far worse, she doesn't know me – doesn't remember anything that has happened, and even turns from me when I go near her. It seems in her subconscious mind she is afraid of me and hates me.'

'Martyn, do not distress yourself on that account. You must surely see that this is, indeed, a reaction from her subconscious mind. The moment before her accident, she had but one thought in her mind – to get away from you – for Bridget's sake. That her fear of being too near you is quite simply that of any woman who loves a man and knows she has no right to show her love.'

Martyn shook his head wearily.

'Perhaps you are right. I do not under-stand these things. The subconscious mind is out of my line – so is psychology. I'd like to believe that Luisa – as she is now in her own mind – a young girl just left school – would still recognize me as the man she was destined to love.'

'But, Martyn, you cannot ask the impos-sible. As she really is, it has taken her a month to discover her love for you and yours for her.'

'I suppose that is true. But what is to happen now? Give me your advice, Mrs Mathers. Should I tell Bridget the truth or would that be betraying the trust Luisa has in me? If only I knew what to do.'

Mrs Mathers was silent for a few minutes, and then she said gently:

'Martyn, I could not take the respons-ibility of making such a decision for you. It is your life. You must do what you think best. You left the decision in Luisa's hands, that is true. But it might be for the best for you to take the initiative. You are engaged to a girl you do not love and yet the girl you do love may – forgive me for putting this so brutally – never love you again. I cannot decide this thing for you, Martyn. But if I can help in any way, ever...'

'Thank you. You are very kind,' Martyn

said. 'Pray God that Luisa will soon recover her memory. I will do whatever she thinks best – even go through with my engagement if she asks me. I think that until she herself can decide this matter, I must keep the last promise I made her. It is the only thing I can do. For the time being, at least, I will say nothing to Bridget. It could do no good in any case, and I would not wish to hurt her for no reason.'

Mrs Mathers rose to go, and said she would be over to-morrow with some eggs for Luisa, and maybe bring Jim with her. He might possibly help to restore her memory. The doctor had said the sight of familiar faces as long as they did not distress her, could do no harm and might have some result.

'Yes!' agreed Martyn. 'I am the only one she cannot bear to see and therefore the only one who can do her no good. Life is very hard!'

There was nothing she could say to comfort him and so she left him and went home to tell her son the news.

Bridget was worried about Martyn. He seemed to have taken this whole thing very much to heart and nothing she could say changed the haunted look on his face. Luisa had been very obviously distressed when Martyn had looked in to say goodnight to her, and of course Martyn had noticed it.

Bridget felt that Martyn was certain Luisa blamed him for the accident.

She had spoken to Luisa again about Martyn, saying:

'Luisa, why don't you like Martyn? After all, we're friends, so you can speak out to me. I'm going to marry him and so if you have anything against him, please tell me.'

Luisa looked worried.

'I don't know what it is, Bridget. So much that is strange worries me. I can't think why I should have forgotten so many little things. I mean, mother and father going abroad. Have you told them I'm ill? They haven't written or wired.'

'We thought you would rather not worry them as your Mother wasn't very well,' said Bridget.

Luisa nodded.

'Yes, of course. I understand. But Bridget, I do remember falling out of the hay-loft. Why did the doctor say something this afternoon about riding?'

'I think he was referring to another case like yours where a girl had hurt herself in the same way falling off a horse,' Bridget improvised quickly, making a mental note that she must tell the doctor about the hay-loft.

'Oh!' said Luisa. And then: 'I like your mother, Bridget. Is she pleased about your engagement?'

'Yes, very!' said Bridget. 'She likes Martyn.'

'Are you sure you do love him, Bridget?' Luisa asked next. 'Somehow it seems all wrong to me.'

'Wrong?' asked Bridget. 'Why?'

'I don't know. I think you should be marrying Bill.'

'But I'm in love with Martyn, Lis.'

'Yes, of course. I'm sorry to be so silly about him. He's just strange to me, I expect. And he looks at me so oddly. How did he lose his arm?'

'In the war,' Bridget said unguardedly. And added hastily: 'He's always in the wars. Car accident, you know. He is lucky to be alive.'

'He doesn't look very lucky, does he?' Luisa said. 'I mean, he looks so unhappy. Does he love you, Bridget?'

'I think so, Luisa. But he's an odd sort of person. He doesn't show his feelings much. You see, he had an unhappy love affair and now he's afraid to show his feelings.'

'I don't want to fall in love – ever,' said Luisa. 'It's funny, but I used to think at school it would be fun to have a husband and a home and babies. But now I don't want to. I shan't ever get married.'

Bridge changed the subject and told Luisa that to-morrow a school friend of her mother was coming to tea and bringing her son, Jim, who was an awfully nice boy.

'How old is he?' Luisa asked.

'Twenty-two!'

'Oh, a year older than I am,' said Luisa. 'That'll be fun.'

Bridget smiled.

'I thought you were never going to fall in love, Lis, and here you are getting excited at the thought of a possible young man to take you out.'

Luisa smiled.

'I shan't fall in love,' she repeated. 'But it'll be fun to have someone young around the place, won't it? Tell me more about him.'

Yes, Bridget told herself with a worried frown, Luisa was happy enough talking about anybody or anything, seeing anyone just so long as it wasn't Martyn. So he wasn't going to get that chance to make amends.

'Poor Martyn!' she said softly to him that evening. 'If only you and Luisa had been able to make friends before this happened.'

But he only turned his head away, remembering all too clearly that glorious evening before the accident when they had discovered their love, and the night when they had declared it so unreservedly. Even then it had been too late.

CHAPTER XI

Luisa was feeling much better when Jim arrived next day to see her. She was still a little worried and perplexed by the effect of her accident. It seemed she had forgotten so many silly little things – nothing important, of course, things like her mother and father going abroad. She could not, however hard she tried, recall her mother's illness, nor their decision to spend a week or two in Switzerland.

Another thing that puzzled her was Bridget being here. She supposed if her mother and father were going on holiday she must have made arrangements for Bridget to come and stay for company, but she couldn't remember writing to ask her.

And there was Mrs Jennings who said she was now living in the village because her aged mother was an invalid and had to be looked after at night. Before the accident, Luisa could remember that Mrs Jennings lived in and her aged mother hadn't been an invalid at all. She supposed something had happened suddenly to her – a heart attack, that had made her bed-ridden. But she couldn't remember.

The doctor had told her not to worry about these little things. As soon as she was well again, he told her, it would all come back to her. Meanwhile she must keep quiet and try not to tax her mind too much. She had had a nasty dose of concussion and she must keep quiet. Luisa, whose head ached horribly whenever she struggled to sort things out, was only too ready to obey him and let everything slide for the time being.

At first she was a little shy with Jim. But he seemed quite at his ease with her and soon they were talking like two old friends. He told her about his studies and the hopes he had of becoming a great surgeon one day and Luisa had a pleasant afternoon with no time for those little niggling thoughts to bother her.

'As soon as you are better, mother wants you to come on a long holiday to Devonshire with us,' Jim told her. 'It would do you so much good, Luisa. You see, I'm acting like a doctor already and doctor's orders must be obeyed!'

She laughed with him and told him she loved a holiday by the sea but did not feel she should go until her mother and father returned from Switzerland and she could discuss the financial question with them.

'You see, Jim, I think they may be rather hard up if mother has been ill, too. There will be my doctor's bills as well.'

'I'm sure it could be arranged, Luisa,' Jim said, having been warned by his mother that Luisa still imagined her parents to be alive. 'Don't worry about that side of it, Luisa. Just leave everything to us. We're going to take care of you, you know. Mother never had a daughter and she wants to adopt you – for the time being, of course.'

Luisa smiled.

'You're very kind, Jim. I like your mother, too. Somehow you make me feel safe. You know since my accident such a lot of silly little things have worried me. Nothing seems to be quite the same as it was before I fell out of that loft. It's rather hard to explain.'

'Would it be like going back to a place you were fond of as a child and finding it different when you were grown up?'

'Yes, that's it exactly,' Luisa said. 'I suppose it's customary after concussion, doctor?' And she smiled at him.

'Of course! Anyway, you haven't a thing to worry about, Luisa. A week or two at the sea and you'll be as fit as ever again, and then it will all slip back into its right perspective.'

Jim, primed in advance, did not mention Martyn's name, but Luisa brought it up of her own accord.

'Have you met Bridget's fiancé?' she asked him.

He nodded his head.

'How do you like him as one man to

another?' Luisa asked.

'I think he's very nice – a bit moody, but really quite a nice chap,' Jim said carefully.

'I suppose he is,' Luisa said doubtfully. 'But there's something about him which frightens me, Jim. The doctor says it's just because when I came round after the accident, his was the first face I saw and a strange one, so naturally I was frightened. But I don't think it's altogether that. I do hope Bridget will be happy with him.'

'I expect she will be,' Jim said. 'But I don't think they will be getting married just yet. Bridget says they are having a long engagement. You see, she hasn't known him more than a couple of months.'

'I always thought she would marry that childhood sweetheart we used to tease her about at school,' said Luisa. 'Bill someone or other. I never met him but he sounded awfully nice. Are you engaged to anyone, Jim?'

He shook his head.

'No, but … I'd like to be,' he said lightly.

'Then you're in love,' Luisa teased him. 'Tell me about her.'

'Well, she's a beautiful red-head – just like you, Luisa. And she has lovely green eyes, like yours, and strangely enough she just had an accident, too, and has her head all done up in bandages.'

Luisa laughed outright.

'Jim, you are a flirt!' she said. 'We've known each other ten minutes exactly.'

'Half an hour!' said Jim. 'When it's an hour, I shall propose to you properly.'

'And I shall refuse you,' said Luisa. 'I'm never going to get married.'

'You're breaking my heart, Luisa, when you say such a thing. At least give me some hope for the future.'

She laughed again, not taking him seriously but enjoying the banter.

'Well, if I marry anyone, it'll be you, Jim, since for one thing I like you, and for another, I think I might enjoy being a doctor's wife. And lastly, if you're going to be the greatest surgeon and live in Harley Street, you'll be very rich and I shall be able to buy a lot of horses.'

'And ride them down Oxford Street?' Jim asked. 'I withdraw my proposal, Luisa. I will not be married for the money I might one day have.'

When the doctor came that evening, Jim was still with Luisa and they were playing two-handed whist. Luisa was sitting up and laughing and after a quick examination, the doctor told her he was very pleased with her progress, and said she might get up for an hour the following afternoon.

Outside Luisa's room, he drew Jim aside and said:

'Young man, you seem to have a very

beneficial effect on Luisa. I've been worrying about her because she seemed morose and inclined to brood and wonder about the things she has forgotten. Whatever happens, I wanted to avoid that. It could lead to brain fever, perhaps, or even worse. You've acted as a tonic. I don't know why and it doesn't matter. But if you're fond of the girl, then spend all the time you can with her. She seems to like your company.'

Jim looked radiant.

'I'd do anything in the world for her, doctor. And I am only too willing to spend all my time with her. Fortunately I'm on holiday for the next two weeks. Doctor, tell me honestly, what chances has she of complete recovery?'

'I can't say, young man. When the superficial wound has healed and she is fit enough, I'd like her to see a brain specialist. I am only a G.P. you know and her condition is a bit beyond my powers. But it'll have to be very carefully arranged. Whatever happens, she mustn't be allowed to guess that there is anything seriously wrong. She must meet the specialist on a social footing.'

'Perhaps I could arrange that,' Jim said. 'There's a very brilliant man I study under at the hospital. I could tell him about Luisa and I think he would be interested enough to come down to stay with me for a weekend and we could ask Luisa over. She wouldn't suspect anything as I am a medical student. He could be a friend of my mother, interested in my career.'

'A brilliant idea,' said the doctor, shaking Jim's hand. 'See if it can be arranged. I think by next week-end she should be fit enough to risk a drive to your house. Well, I must be off. I'll look in to-morrow morning.'

Luisa's condition improved physically, but her memory showed no sign at all of returning. Martyn kept as much out of her way as possible, unable to bear the sight of a smile dying from her face when he entered her room or the queer haunted expression that came over her when he spoke to her. He could hear from the surgery Luisa's laughter when Jim was with her and he suffered terribly from hurt and jealousy but there was absolutely nothing he could do about it.

His relations with Bridget were naturally affected. He could not bring himself to show any signs of affection for her other than those of a friend. She, in her turn, made no demands on him, but she, too, was hurt by his attitude, even while she imagined she understood the cause. But it naturally did not make sense to her that because Martyn was blaming himself so bitterly for Luisa's condition, he must necessarily exclude her from his life. She wanted so much to help and comfort him. To tell him that no one but himself could possibly blame Luisa's fall on one quarrel.

"If only," she thought with a sigh, "he would break down that iron reserve and let me get a little closer to him."

But she had patience and tact and except for the moment before she went to bed when she would go to him and kiss him good-night as one might kiss a child, she made no visible effort to invade his privacy.

His work was suffering, partly his own fault and partly because Bridget had to spend a certain amount of time in the sick room and his papers and accounts were all behind hand. Bridget felt relieved that Luisa would soon be out of bed and leave her more time to give Martyn the help he needed. He was up until all hours at night and refused to allow her to stay with him to help. She needed sleep if she was to do her share of nursing, he told her. And she could not persuade him to let her remain.

Actually, Martin did not work late. He sat up in the surgery, bent over his papers, until the dawn crept through the windows. But he was not working. He was simply unable to sleep, and so he remained downstairs, thinking, worrying, pacing up and down, longing to go into Luisa's room and lean his head against her and cry like a child. It was the effort of keeping away from her that wore him down so terribly. If only he could see her, and yet he knew it wasn't possible.

Either Bridget or her mother slept in Luisa's room, taking it in turns. She was never alone. And in the day-time, she would be awake and would not want to see him. It was as though those sweet, bitter, tempestuous hours together in London had never been!

Once he moved his chair over to the open window and sat there trying to comfort himself with the thought that no more than a foot away was the window of the sitting-room. Inside that window, Luisa lay asleep but although he strained his ears, he could not hear her breathing. He remembered the hours he had sat by her bedside immediately after the accident when he had been afraid she would die. God had spared him this but in a way Luisa was now as surely dead to him as she could ever be. The last seven years had been erased from her memory and his love for her and hers for him with them. In her mind she was eighteen again, and he had no part in her world, except that he alone, of them all, she did not feel happy to have around. She feared him – he who loved her best in the world and would have died to spare her suffering.

Lying awake in her own room, Bridget had seen the reflection of the surgery light on her ceiling and had known that Martyn was still up and as she believed, working. She had put on a dressing-gown and gone down to him. As she opened the door, he had looked up suddenly, not seeming to recognize her, and then he had buried his head on his arms again, hiding his face from her.

She had gone to him and not knowing what to do, had stood beside him quietly, running a hand lightly over his hair. Presently he had taken her hand in his strong grasp and said in a muffled voice:

'Bridget, help me. Tell me you believe there is a God. Tell me that everything must come right in the end.'

She had not understood his meaning, only that he needed comfort.

'There is a God, Martyn, and although His ways are sometimes hard to understand, they are always for the best. Everything will come right, darling. Don't worry so.'

He had not spoken again, and after a moment or two she had left him, feeling herself worried and uncertain. If only she could get closer to Martyn – mentally closer to his mind. But she did not know him well enough and her love did not seem to provide her with that intuition she needed to show her what to do that was best for him – and for her. She felt lost and lonely and distressed as she went back to bed. It was by no means as simple as she had thought it would be for Martyn and herself to grow nearer and dearer to one another. He had told her that he was afraid he could offer her little in return for her love but she had been confident that in time Martyn would find it easier to show his feelings, to express himself in words and gestures. But in a sudden moment of revelation, Bridget knew that if anything they were greater strangers than they had ever been.

"It will be better once we are working together again," she comforted herself. She said the same thing to her mother who had not failed to notice Martyn's queer behaviour.

'It seems such a peculiar way to love anyone,' Mrs Castle had remarked to her daughter. 'I mean, he never calls you "darling" or holds your hand.'

'He seldom kisses me either, Mother,' Bridget had admitted. 'But Martyn is different, Mother. You see, he has a sort of complex.' And she explained about Betty.

'Then you think he is still in love with her?' Mrs Castle asked anxiously.

'No, I'm sure he isn't. It's just that it is taking him time to get over the hurt.'

'I wish you could have fallen in love with someone more simple,' Mrs Castle had said, patting her daughter's hand. 'I know you are worried about him, Bridget. I would have liked your marriage to be a happy untroubled affair, full of laughter and gaiety and sunshine.'

'I should have liked it that way, too, Mother,' Bridget said with a smile. 'But I came into Martyn's life too late. It will be that way soon. You'll see. He's worried and moody now because he feels responsible for Luisa's accident. He's taken it to heart in a way I should never have believed. You see, he and Luisa never really liked one another. He doesn't speak about it but, I understand from Mrs Jennings that they quarrelled that day at lunch time. Of course, it wasn't really Martyn's fault she fell from her horse. He's taking the whole thing too seriously. But at heart Martyn is a kind, loving person. I don't think he ever hated anyone or anything in his life until that other girl hurt him so dreadfully. Luisa always reminded him of her. I think he was just beginning to realize that Luisa and Betty weren't in the least alike, but I suppose one cannot stop disliking someone overnight, and so there was another scene and now this. Martyn will come round as soon as Luisa's health improves.'

'I hope you're right, Bridget. You know, my dear, I still find it hard to accustom myself to the idea that you are going to marry someone other than Bill. You know how fond I always was of him. When the war was over, your father and I hoped very much that you two would settle down. But it just hasn't worked out that way.'

'No, I'm afraid not,' said Bridget. 'You know, Bill came down here, Mother, when I wrote and told him I was in love with Martyn. He made a dreadful scene. Of course it ended up with both of us saying we never wanted to see one another again. I'm sorry in a way we had to end so many years of friendship like that, but I suppose a clean break is the best. I'm afraid he was very hurt.'

'Poor Bill! Well, perhaps by now he'll have met some other girl,' said Mrs Castle.

And the conversation was closed.

By the end of the week, Luisa was allowed up and Jim had gone ahead with his plans and invited Mr Simkin, the brain specialist, to his home. He told Luisa that he had a most important medical friend of his mother's to stay and that he wanted Luisa along to be very nice to him.

'If you make a good impression and say all sorts of nice things about me, it may help me in my career, Luisa,' he had told her.

Unsuspecting of the truth, Luisa had readily agreed to go over, and was only too pleased to be allowed out for a short drive and a change of scenery. These last few days the Vicarage had started to depress her. She was worried, too, because her mother and father had still not written. Even allowing for the fact that they knew nothing of her accident, she felt sure they would have sent her a postcard to tell her when they would be home. Bridget told her they would be away for a fortnight, and it was already ten days since her accident. So she welcomed the opportunity to get out and away with Jim, whom she liked immensely and who was always cheerful and amusing and affectionate. Bridget seemed to smile so seldom nowadays, and although Mrs Castle was a dear, she was not Luisa's contemporary. And Martyn, of course, she never saw and did not wish to see.

'You know, Jim,' she said as he drove her very slowly and carefully towards his home, 'I am going to prove to you that I am the soul of tact and discretion. I shall flirt just a little with your old medical friend to make him feel young again, and I shall talk intelligently about your career, and he will think we are going to be married and because he will like me immensely, he will do everything in his power to help you, so that we can live happily ever after. I'm sure the romantic approach is the best one!'

She laughed, but for once there was no answering smile on Jim's face. He did not take his eyes from the road, but he took one hand off the wheel and felt for hers.

'You know, Luisa, I wish it were true. I wish you were really going to marry me as soon as I qualified. I wish you loved me.'

Luisa gave his hand a quick squeeze.

'Jim, you know I'm terribly fond of you.

226

But you mustn't be so serious. You know you're only flirting with me just for fun.'

'It has been fun, but I'm serious, Luisa, about loving you.'

He would not have said more had Luisa showed the slightest signs of distress. But she seemed almost pleased as she replied:

'You know, Jim, I think in a way I love you more than anyone else I know. You're such fun to be with. I feel happier with you than with anyone else. Perhaps it is because I always feel that I'm safe with you. You know, since my fall, such a lot of things seem strange and peculiar. Jim, you don't think my fall did anything to – to my mind, do you? I mean, I don't seem to be able to remember things very clearly.'

He hastened to reassure her.

'Of course not, Luisa. I told you before it was just a natural consequence of con- cussion. You've nothing to be afraid of. Nothing is going to hurt you. Luisa, let me take care of you. I'll look after you always and love you as long as I live. We'll have lots of fun together and you shall make me the greatest surgeon in the world and I will tell everyone that my beautiful wife is alone responsible for my brilliant success.'

She smiled, then her face became serious again.

'Jim, tell me honestly,' she said. 'I trust you. I don't trust the others. I think they are keeping something from me. It's about mother and father. Why don't they write? I don't remember them going away.'

'What do you remember, Luisa?'

'It's been coming back to me slowly,' Luisa said, more to herself than to him. 'I know I was in the hay-loft because something had upset me. Something awful. I always go there when I'm upset. As a very little girl I used to hide up there when I'd been naughty. I was crying when the bale of straw slipped and I toppled over. I can't remember why, though. I'm sure it had something to do with mother and father.'

Jim thought quickly, and put two and two together. In her mind, Luisa was confusing the two accidents. Mrs Jennings had told him that when Luisa heard her mother and father had been killed, she had hidden in the loft for a whole day before her Aunt Ellen had arrived. That evening she had fallen out of the loft and been badly shaken, but not seriously hurt in any way. She had been ill, but that was from grief, and she had recovered in time. He wondered desperately whether he dared tell her the truth about her parents. Sooner or later she would be bound to find out.

'Luisa,' he said gently. 'Try to remember the reason you were crying. You are right when you say it has something to do with your mother and father. That's why you've been so ill, you know. You're forgetting because you don't want to remember in your subconscious mind.'

He pulled up the car and turned to the girl at his side. He could see that she was struggling to recall what had happened, and that it was coming back to her. He prayed desperately that there would be no serious consequences.

'I – I think I do remember. I had a telegram. Mrs Jennings brought it to me. It had dreadful news in it – about mother and father ... oh, Jim!'

She turned to him with an agonized look on her face, and very gently, he put his arms round her, and was relieved when she sobbed violently against his shoulder. As long as she could cry, all would be well.

'Luisa, darling, don't cry. Please, Luisa. You'll make yourself ill again. You mustn't do that. Remember you have to impress my Mr Simkin for me? Darling, don't distress yourself. I will take care of you. You need never feel lost and alone.'

She cried softly, knowing that she had lost the two people dearest to her in the world. But somehow, deep-rooted as was her grief, it did not seem terribly close to her. It was as if it had happened so long ago that part of her sorrow had worn away with time. She put it down to her illness, and slowly her sobs quietened, and only her tears fell.

Very gently, Jim wiped them away with his handkerchief, and his arms around her felt strong and comforting.

'Thank you for telling me the truth, Jim,' she said, at last in a choked voice. 'I knew I could count on you. I knew I couldn't trust the others. I suppose they were trying to spare me. But I feel better now I know the truth. It was worrying me terribly. You're very kind, Jim.'

'I'm sorry to have to spoil the afternoon for you, Luisa, dear,' he said. 'I wanted this to be such a happy day for you. Try and smile for me, will you, Luisa?'

She did smile at him then, through her tears.

'Meeting Mr Simkin will give me something to think about, Jim,' she said, with courage. 'I'll powder my nose and pull myself together to make this good impression for you. You know, Jim, I don't know what I should do without you. You won't leave me, will you?'

'Never as long as you need me,' Jim said, fervently. 'You see, I meant it when I said I loved you, Luisa.'

'Perhaps I'm a little in love with you, too,' Luisa said. 'I know the future would seem very empty without you. When I'm better, we'll talk it all over, Jim.'

He restarted the car and drove the last mile to his home in a state of exhilaration mixed with serious trepidation. Luisa thought she loved him. She had promised to talk things over. She might even marry him, one half of his mind thought excitedly. And then the other half told him that this was a different Luisa, a girl who was ill and had lost her memory. Any day, any moment, she might recover, and who knew how she would feel about him then. Had he any right to marry her? Would it be taking advantage of her illness?

He pulled up outside the house, and re-solved to have a heart to heart talk with Mr Simkin after he had seen Luisa, and could give them some idea of her chances of complete recovery.

CHAPTER XII

Mr Simkin was not very encouraging. He was immensely interested in Luisa's case, and had tactfully led the conversation around to her accident. Of her own accord she had asked him if he would like to see the scar at the back of her head, and he had been able to examine her, although not very thoroughly.

'Really I would need to take X-rays to see if there is anything pressing on the brain. An operation may be necessary.'

'You mean she is still in some danger?' Jim asked, anxiously.

Mr Simkin shook his head.

'No, I don't think that, provided she does not receive any sudden shocks. The trouble is it may be just such a shock that would bring her back to normal. It's an unusual case, Jim. Loss of memory is usually complete. The patient cannot remember his name, his address – anything about himself. But I have known, and treated another case like this, where the patient simply forgot a number of years in his life. But it was more a psychological condition, although in this case, too, the patient had a fall which brought it on.

233

This particular man had been very worried about his domestic affairs. On top of that, his small daughter ran under his car and was killed. It was an accident, of course, and he was completely exonerated from blame. But he nevertheless blamed himself. It preyed on his mind until his whole nervous system was upset. Then he smashed himself up in his car, and when he recovered from the resulting concussion, he had forgotten the preceeding six months, during which the tragedy of his small daughter had occurred. He didn't want to remember them. Strangely enough, he did in time recover completely. For months after the accident, he had a horror of young children. He could not bear to see them around. It was his sub-conscious mind connecting a young child with his own daughter, of course. A story was concocted to explain her absence and he never made more than the slightest enquiries about her. Once again, the sub-conscious mind at work. He was afraid to ask too much for fear he would be made to recall the truth.'

'What made him remember in the end?' Jim asked, interested in the similarity between this and Luisa's case.

'He was out walking with his wife and a child ran across the road in front of a passing lorry. She wasn't hurt, but it was sufficient to shock him back to normality.'

Jim sat in silence, waiting for Mr Simkin to

continue his story.

'Of course, he might have gone on for years without remembering anything of those particular six months,' continued the specialist. 'Such may be the case with Luisa. But on the other hand, any little thing might startle her back to the truth. The difficulty here, as I see it, is whether or not to leave her alone to recover or not. The question is really a personal one. Are the forgotten seven years of her life important? If not, then maybe it would be for the best to allow her to continue as she is. The alternative is to explain to her what has happened and get her to agree to come up to London for observation and then, if necessary, I will operate. But the danger there lies in the effect of the knowledge of the truth on the girl herself. It could be a dreadful shock to her to learn that she was living exactly seven years behind time. That shock might be harmful. It is impossible to say until I've seen X-rays. We cannot know the extent of her injuries, if any, until they are taken.'

'Perhaps we could simply say that an X-ray would be a good idea just to make sure that there was nothing behind that super-ficial wound,' Jim suggested.

'Yes! It could be done. But would she suspect anything? Worry alone may harm her. Where the brain is affected, one must go gently, my boy. We have made great progress in research but there is still a lot for us to learn. Then there is the association of the brain with the nerve centres to be considered. Has the girl forgotten the last seven years because sub-consciously she wants to? Were they happy years? Has anything happened of late that has upset her – made her feel that her present life is too difficult for her to cope with?'

Jim, who knew little of Luisa's life abroad with her Aunt, and nothing of her love for Martyn, for Mrs Mathers had thought best not to betray Luisa's confidences to her son, told Mr Simkin that as far as he knew, there had been nothing in the last seven years of Luisa's life that could have affected her sufficiently to make her want to forget them.

'But then, I haven't known her very long, Mr Simkin,' he added, truthfully. 'The thing is, I'm very much in love with her. I'd like to marry her. But – well, before this accident, she just looked on me as a friend. She knew how I felt, of course, but she wouldn't take me seriously. I didn't really expect her to. I knew I could never mean much to her. She felt the differences in our ages, and I quite see I must have seemed very young and gauche to her. But she is different now. She is, I imagine, at the same age which she imagines herself to be – about eighteen. So she presumably sees me in a different light. She – she seems fond of me. When I told her

I'd like to marry her and take care of her, she really appeared to be considering it. But I don't want to tie her to me if one day she might come to herself again, and see me as she used to do. It wouldn't be fair to her.'

'No, it wouldn't,' agreed Mr Simkin. 'And that chance is a likely one. I strongly advise against this marriage, Jim. For one thing, you are far too young to marry. You have your career in front of you and you ought to be concentrating on that. Not many students of your age can afford to get married. I assume you have a private income, since you suggest it, but that of course is your affair. All the same, my boy, you ought not to think of marrying – at least until you have qualified. You show great promise, and it would be a pity to ruin your career for any girl.'

'I do understand what you're getting at, sir,' said Jim, 'but I don't think Luisa could ever be responsible for ruining my career. She'd spur me on to greater efforts. But that is not the only reason I suggested marriage. You see, she isn't very well off. She had a little capital which she planned to use to finance a riding stables. Already most of that has been spent on horses which will now have to be sold again. I imagine she will not be allowed to ride for some time. The rest of her capital has gone to pay the doctor's bills. She is now without means, and is obviously in no state of health to get a job. If she did decide to marry me, I could look after her, and she need never worry about the financial side.'

'Well, that is entirely your affair, Jim. It is your life, and although I will offer advice, I never interfere. The decision rests with you. Has the girl no relatives who could help her for a little while?'

'She has one aunt, I believe,' Jim said. 'But from what I gather, Luisa and she did not hit it off very well. Luisa said once, she hoped she would never meet her again. I'm sure she wouldn't want to accept help from her.'

'Talk it over with your mother,' said Mr Simkin. 'She may give you different advice. Of course, I'm sorry for the girl. If it is decided that she should be told the truth, I will gladly perform the necessary operations, if any, and have her under my observation free of charge. As regards your marriage to her, however, I can only repeat that I feel it is a bad thing for you at this stage of your studies, Jim.'

'I see, sir. Well, thank you for your help and your offer. I'll talk things over with my mother as regards Luisa's health, and the question of marriage. She has more or less adopted Luisa, she is so fond of her. Apart from Bridget, Miss Castle, who is taking care of her, I don't know who else there is to make the decision about her going to London for observation. But no doubt my mother will know what is best.'

Jim was even further discouraged when, after returning Luisa to the Vicarage, he went home to have things out with his mother, only to be told by her of Luisa's visit the morning of her accident.

He could scarcely believe that Luisa had been in love with Martyn and yet, when he thought it over, it was understandable. He realized then what a hopeless state of confusion they must all be in. Martyn trying to behave normally with Bridget. Luisa afraid of seeing him and avoiding him. Jim could almost feel sorry for the fellow. His was a devilishly awkward position. If he broke his engagement to Bridget, it would do no good now since Luisa showed every sign of disliking him. Bridget, of course, knew nothing of this whole business. As for himself, it made things doubly difficult to decide.

'You see, Jim, although Luisa might be quite happy for a month, maybe years, as your wife, we cannot say when she will recover. Mr Simkin said maybe never. But it would be a dreadful thing, Jim, if a day or two after your marriage, she remembered everything and wanted to go to Martyn. She would end up hating you for trapping her when she was unable to decide for herself.'

'But Mother, suppose Martyn goes through with his marriage to Bridget? Then it might be the best thing for Luisa. She would realize then that it was out of the question for her to go to Martyn.'

'Yes, there would be two fences for them to cross then, I agree. But no matter how many obstacles you put between people who love one another, it cannot prevent them from continuing to love each other. What happiness could you hope to find for yourself knowing that for the rest of your life she was yours but was always wanting to go to Martyn?'

'It's a chance, I know, but I'd take it, Mother, if I thought I could make Luisa happy and secure even for a year or two. Then if she recovered and wanted her freedom, I would give it to her. At least we would have had those years. And it might even be longer – perhaps for ever.'

Mrs Mathers sighed, unable to decide what should be done. The decision, which was really Luisa's, and hers only, could obviously not be made by the girl herself. Either she must be told the truth and risk the consequences, or else the decision must be made for her. And who was there to do it, except herself? She alone knew the whole truth – herself and now Jim. But Jim was in love with her and could not see the thing in an unbiased light. On the other hand, Jim was her son, and she wanted his happiness above everything. Was she therefore able to look at the whole affair without bias? Mr

Simkin had advised against this marriage because of Jim's career. She wanted to advise against it because of Jim's future happiness. But were either of them being fair to Jim, who loved her?

And there was, too, this question of Luisa's health. Who was to decide whether the girl should go up for observation? It was a great responsibility for anyone to take. Normally it would have been her parents to decide, or if she were married, her husband. But Mrs Mathers, although she was deeply attached to Luisa, was not a relative, and really a comparative stranger. But there was no one else. Martyn could not decide. He, too, had an axe to grind. He would want Luisa well again. And Bridget – her only hope of marriage to Martyn was for Luisa to remain as she was. No, neither of them could decide.

It seemed to Mrs Mathers after due consideration, that the ultimate responsibility must lie with Mr Simkin. They would act on his advice.

She put the whole story to him after they had dined. Jim had driven over to the Vicarage again to spend the evening playing two-handed whist with Luisa, who was back in bed, and she and Mr Simkin had the sitting-room to themselves.

'Frankly,' he said, when he had heard the whole story, 'I would say that it would clear everything up for everyone in this emotional tangle, if Luisa made a sudden recovery. I can see what difficulties could arise if she does marry Jim, and Martyn breaks his engagement, and she recovers to find him free, and herself tied. But a doctor should not really allow such personal elements to come in conflict with a purely medical outlook. My own opinion is that it is far better to let Luisa recover of her own accord. A sudden shock now could have very serious consequences, as I explained earlier to Jim. Intense worry such as would be the outcome of telling her the truth, could have the same consequences.

'Frankly, Mrs Mathers, I would rather let the matter stand. I do not think there are any complications. I think the accident which caused concussion, and the slight flesh wound, brought on this loss of memory aided by the girl's mental state at the time of the accident. I am fairly certain now that it is a nervous condition, and not due to any injury to the brain itself. What you have told me has thrown new light on it since I spoke to Jim. I would advise against X-rays or anything of the sort. That is my opinion as a medical man. As a friend, I would say that this marriage with your son should be prevented if it is at all possible, as much for his sake as for hers.'

'I'll do what I can to make Jim see reason,'

said Mrs Mathers. 'As a friend, Mr Simkin, give me your advice on another matter. Do you think it would help at all were I to tell Bridget the truth about Luisa and Martyn? With Martyn free, Jim would see the reason for waiting.'

'That seems to me to be too personal a matter. It is entirely up to this fellow, Martyn. Personally, I think it is carrying honesty, loyalty, fulfilment of obligations – call it what you will – too far, once it entails marrying a girl you don't love when there is another one you do care about. It is bound to end unhappily for himself and the girl. But I think it is up to him to decide this for himself. With all due respect, dear Mrs Mathers, it is not your business!'

She laughed with him, and then her face was serious again, as she said:

'I did advise Luisa before the accident to have it out with Bridget. Perhaps I could persuade Martyn to do so. If he realizes it may otherwise mean Jim will marry Luisa, he might consider it. But I know him very slightly indeed. I understand from Luisa that some girl let him down badly, and it is therefore understandable that he does not care to let Bridget down in his turn. However, I will do what I can. Tell me, Mr Simkin, do you think there is a chance that two weeks in Devonshire with the sea air and a complete change of scene, might possibly hasten Luisa's recovery? Could it do her good?'

'It could do her no harm, and it might well have a beneficial effect.'

'Then I will take Luisa away next week, as I had planned. I won't speak to Martyn until we return. Perhaps, by then, Luisa may show signs of recovery. I can persuade Jim not to make any definite proposals to Luisa until then, I'm sure.'

Mr Simkin agreed to this plan, and Mrs Mathers went ahead with her plans for the holiday.

Back at the Vicarage, Martyn was in his surgery which had now become his retreat, wondering how much longer he could endure this situation. He had closed his windows, unable to bear the sound of Luisa's and Jim's voices coming from the sitting-room. He had been listening all afternoon for the sound of Jim's car returning on the drive, not for any purpose but just to know that Luisa was back. He could not bear to have her out of sound as well as out of sight. And yet now she was home, he could not bear the sound of her laughter. It hurt him beyond belief to know that she could be so happy with Jim, even while unselfishly he could be glad for her sake.

He had heard her voice in the hall outside and wished that he hadn't.

'I wonder if Martyn's in his surgery,' Jim

had said, and Luisa's voice had come in a whisper:

'Don't let's stop to see, Jim, I'm tired!'

And he had known her real reason was that she didn't wish to see him.

He tried now to concentrate on his work. But it was quite hopeless. He decided to go out, and finding Boot lying outside Luisa's door, he whistled him softly to heel saying:

'Come on, old fellow. We aren't wanted. We'll take each other for a walk.'

But although the fresh air refreshed him physically, he returned later even more mentally exhausted than before. Bridget greeted him at the door and suggested he should come into the dining-room, which had now been made into a second sitting-room, to talk for a while.

Having no reason at the tip of his tongue to refuse her request, Martyn went with her.

Bridget, worried and unhappy about Martyn, and egged on by her mother, who was even less happy about her daughter's finacé, had decided to discuss everything with Martyn, and see if she could not manage to bring them closer together. They had drifted so far apart, she felt, that they were now more like two strangers than a couple about to be married.

But when she switched on the light and saw Martyn's tired white face, and the blue shadows under his eyes, and the thin lines around his mouth, she knew that she could not after all worry him with personal affairs at this moment. If Martyn continued like this, she felt sure he would be ill. His nerves were in shreds, and he looked as if he had not slept for weeks.

'Martyn, you really don't look well,' she said at last, breaking the silence between them. 'Aren't you sleeping properly?'

He shook his head.

'You're not still worrying – about Luisa?' Bridget pursued.

He looked up then – his face haggard.

'I don't think I shall have a moment's peace, Bridget, until she is well again. You don't know ... you don't realize...' he struggled to tell her the whole bitter truth, but she broke in, circumventing him.

'Martyn, I do understand that you feel responsible. But only you think that way. Luisa's accident *was* an accident. Whatever happened before could not have made her fall from that horse. You mustn't blame yourself. Luisa would be horrified if she understood. I know you think she blames you ... the way she avoids you ... and that sort of thing. But it's only because you are a stranger to her. Please, Martyn, believe me. You simply must take a grip on yourself. Why, even your work is suffering.'

'I know!' Martyn said. 'I can't concentrate. I think I'll have to go away. Staying here in the same house with her I...' Again it was on the tip of his tongue to tell her. Again she broke in.

'A holiday would do you the world of good, Martyn. But you know Luisa is going away next week with Jim and Mrs Mathers? They are having a fortnight by the sea in Devonshire. Perhaps as you say, once Luisa is out of the way, you'll feel better.'

"So she is going away – with Jim!" Martyn thought. "Oh, God in heaven what have I done to deserve all this? How will it all end? And Bridget, too. What is to happen to her? I owe her so much, and I am making her unhappy, too!"

He turned to her then, and took her hand.

'I'm so sorry, Bridget,' he said, his voice husky and almost incoherent. 'I'm treating you abominably. I'm being wretchedly selfish. I'm so sorry.'

'It's all right, Martyn, I understand,' Bridget said, although she could not truly understand his suffering. She only knew that he was suffering, and that whatever the reason, she must try to understand and sympathize and help him. 'You've no need to worry about me. I shall be happy as soon as you are happy again. It will all work out all right.'

'Will it?' he asked her. 'I wish I could believe it, Bridget. I wish I knew what to do for the best. It's all so unfair on you. But I

247

can't help it, Bridget. It's terribly selfish of me, I know, but I just don't seem to be able to decide what is for the best.'

'Don't worry about anything, Martyn. Concentrate on your work. Whatever happens, don't worry about me. You know, Mother says I have the patience of the gods,' she added in a lighter tone. 'I don't mind how long I have to wait, Martyn. It's enough for me to know I can be near you and help you in any way. Once Luisa has gone, I shall be able to help you again, as I used to do before she was ill. We shall be the same good companions and friends we used to be. Remember?'

He tried to smile at her, but her words only served to worry him more. He had wanted to tell her – to tell her everything. If necessary, ask her to release him from their engagement, since he now knew he could never love her. But how could he say those things when once again she was unselfishly offering him friendship, companionship, sympathy, and asking nothing in return but to be able to give him those things – and to be near him.

'Forgive me if I leave you now,' he said desperately. 'I think I'll go to bed. I'm very tired.'

He stood up and leaning over, kissed her gently on the forehead. It was a gesture utterly devoid of passion – a kiss such as he might have given a sister.

For a long while after he had left her, Bridget sat on the sofa, staring at Martyn's empty place beside her, thinking. She was fighting against what she felt to be a weakness in her love for him. She tried to convince herself that everything she had said to him she meant with all her heart, and yet deep down within her, a voice was crying out that she wanted more than that one fraternal kiss. She wanted more than friendship, than companionship. She wanted to be held in his arms and loved as Bill had loved her. She wanted to be kissed as a man kissed the girl he loved. She wanted to be able to laugh with him and go to occasional dances and parties and films. She wanted to be planning her trousseau and thinking happily about her forthcoming marriage. Instead of which she had none of these things, was doing none of these things. It wasn't after all so much to ask. Every girl had a right to them once in her life.

The moment of doubt and weakness passed and Bridget talked severely to herself, telling herself that these things would all come in time. Time – that was what Martyn needed. She must continue to be patient, to understand and sympathize and demand nothing. Then, in time, all these things would come to her. She closed her eyes and lay quite still, imagining that Martyn was holding her in his arms as Bill used to hold her and saying, as Bill had once said:

'Oh, Bridget, darling, darling Bridget. Say you will marry me to-morrow. Not next week, or next month, or next year, but to-morrow. I need you, darling. I love you ... more than anything else in the world.'

They were Bill's words, but she wanted to hear them on Martyn's lips. But she dared not ask herself when that day would come.

CHAPTER XIII

Luisa was thoroughly enjoying her holiday by the sea. Mrs Mathers had taken rooms in a luxurious hotel in which there was every comfort and excellent food. The weather was perfect, and Jim in the best of spirits.

After three days, Luisa felt well enough to tackle long walks along the cliff tops, and once they took a picnic lunch with them, leaving Mrs Mathers in the hotel talking to some former acquaintance she had met there.

'You know, Jim,' Luisa said, as she put away the picnic things, and lay down beside Jim on the soft green turf, 'I'm beginning to think I should like to live here for ever and ever. It's a new world to me. You see, I've never really been away from the Vicarage for long. We could not afford holidays twice a year, and mother and father always took me to Switzerland in the winter. I'm finding out now what a seaside holiday in the summer can be like.'

'I'm glad you're happy, Luisa,' Jim said, taking her hand gently in his own. 'I'm glad, too, that you are looking and feeling so much better.'

'Part of it is because I've stopped worrying, I think,' Luisa said, dreamily. 'Down here we seem to be in another world. Nothing very much seems to matter except the next meal, and making plans for the next day. It's wonderful of your mother to have me down with you, Jim. How shall I ever repay her?'

'To see you well again is all mother wants in the way of repayment,' Jim told her honestly. 'She's very fond of you, Luisa, and it's a pleasure to her to be able to do this for you. Besides, it takes me off her hands. Imagine how lonely I should have been down here without you.'

Luisa smiled at him and pressed his hand in her own.

'You are nice, Jim,' she said, softly. 'You always say the right thing. Whenever I start to worry, you always have the perfect answer to put my mind at rest. In fact, you're the perfect companion in every way.'

'Now you're saying the nice things!' Jim said, with a smile. 'We're very full of compliments this afternoon.'

'Well, what's wrong with that?' asked Luisa. 'I feel I should like to-day to be perfect – to go on being perfect. It's as if I had a premonition that something was going to happen soon to spoil it all.'

'What do you mean, Luisa?' Jim asked, his heart filling suddenly with anxiety and suspicion.

'Oh, I don't know. Perhaps it's just that "last day of the holiday" feeling, when everything is marvellous, but you know all the time at the back of your mind that tomorrow you have to go back to school.'

'But Luisa, we have another ten days here!' Jim reminded her.

'I know!' Luisa said. 'I'm just being silly, Jim. It all seems too nice to last, that's all. It's – just – unreal. Oh, I do wish we could go on like this for ever!'

Jim was silent, remembering his promise to his mother, that he would not make any proposals to Luisa until after this holiday. He longed to tell her that he would give anything in the world to be allowed to keep Luisa happy for ever – that if she would only marry him, he would take care of her, and see that every day of her life was as happy as this one. But all he could say was:

'I wish we could go on like this for ever, too, Luisa.'

She turned to him, then, and said softly:

'Jim, you remember that day in the car when – when you told me about mother and father?'

He nodded his head.

'Do you remember asking me to marry you?'

Again he nodded assent, not knowing what to say now that Luisa herself had brought up the subject.

'I wasn't sure then,' Luisa continued. 'I hadn't known you long, and I don't think I really believed that you loved me. But now I know you do, Jim. I know, too, that I am happier when I am with you than with anyone else. Perhaps that is what love means. I don't know. But if you still feel the same way, Jim, I'll marry you if you'd like me to.'

'Oh, Luisa!' Jim cried, his mind trying to accept the wonder of this statement, and at the same time, reason struggling to show him how disastrous it might be. 'Luisa, I do love you. I want to marry you more than anything else in the world. But I want to be sure that you do really love me – do really want to be my wife. Marriage is for always, Luisa, and I couldn't bear to feel you were tied to me against your will. Are you quite sure?'

'As sure as anyone can be,' Luisa replied. 'In fact, I think the way I feel about you, Jim, is the only thing I really am sure of. Everything else is cloudy and uncertain – as if it were part of a dream.'

'Luisa, you're sure that it isn't the other way round? That this is the dream and the other – reality?'

'No, Jim, I don't think so. And if this is a dream, it's a very pleasant one. Jim, are you trying to discourage me? I do believe now I've decided to marry you that you've changed your mind!'

She was teasing him but he found it hard to give her an answering smile. His position was an extremely difficult one. Given his way, he would have married Luisa to-morrow, had she wished it. But his mother had pointed out the difficulties with emphasis. She told him Mr Simkin's opinion and told him, too, that she meant to do everything she could to persuade Martyn not to go ahead with his engagement to Bridget.

'It would be utterly crazy for him to marry her now,' she said. 'Even should Luisa never recover, Bridget will be a constant living reminder of the girl he loves. And if she does recover, then Martyn must be free to go to her. So you see, Jim, your marriage to Luisa would ruin the only chance either of them have of ultimate happiness. No one can feel that Luisa will stay this way for ever. She must get better. There is every chance she will do so. I'm terribly sorry, Jim darling. It is very hard for you, I know. You love her and she seems fond enough of you. She is for the first time since you met her, within your reach. You could, no doubt, succeed, and make her your wife, but it wouldn't be fair to her, to Martyn, or to yourself … only in the case where Luisa's complete recovery was out of the question.'

'But, Mother, I've already asked her to marry me,' Jim had said.

'Then, Jim, should she bring the matter

up, you will naturally not go back on your proposal. If necessary, you can become engaged, on the private understanding that you will, of course, release her the moment she recovers. If it is a question of years, then we shall have to think again. But I have the strongest feeling that it will not be that long. I have the belief that this holiday will improve her health and make all the difference. I'm not asking you to remain engaged to Luisa indefinitely, Jim. Only that you give it time. Don't hurry things. Let them sort themselves out.'

He saw the reason in her arguments and remembered them as he heard Luisa say those words: 'I do believe now I've decided to marry you that you've changed your mind.'

'Luisa, I haven't changed my mind. I've loved you from the first day I met you. It's just that – that I can hardly believe you could wish to marry a chap like me. I'm trying to credit my own good fortune.'

Luisa leant forward and kissed him lightly on the cheek.

'There! Now do you believe it?' she asked him, her eyes smiling at him. 'You're so shy, Jim. Now we are engaged, you may kiss me, if you wish. And it may interest you to know that you will be the first man who has ever done so.'

'Oh, Luisa!' Jim cried, realizing how

completely she had forgotten Martyn, and longing to crush her in his arms and hold her there for ever. But the kiss he gave her was as innocent and gentle as the one she had given him. He did not want to remind her in any way of Martyn.

'I'm so happy, Jim,' she told him. 'I must write and tell Bridget to-night. We won't be married right away, will we? I think I'd like a nice long engagement, so that I have time to enjoy being an engaged girl first. And when I'm used to it, I can start to enjoy being a wife.'

'I think a long engagement is a good idea,' said Jim, thankfully. 'Anyway, Luisa, we are both young and there's a lifetime ahead of us. We don't have to hurry into marriage, do we?'

'No, we must have time to get to know each other even better than we do now. It's strange to think we only met two weeks ago. Somehow it seems so much longer. You know, Jim, I have the oddest idea that I've met you before, but I can't remember when. Do you feel the same way about me?'

Jim bit his lip. It was clear to him that Luisa's mind was not so completely closed to the last seven years as it had been at first. Little things were coming back – suspicions of memories.

'Perhaps we knew each other in another incarnation,' he suggested. 'Do you believe in reincarnation, Luisa?'

'I don't know,' Luisa replied. 'But I do often have that feeling that I've seen some perfect stranger before. I think I felt it with Bridget's fiancé. There was something about his face that seemed familiar. Whatever it was, I don't think we can have been very good friends in that other incarnation. I felt sort of – frightened of him. And places, too. Your house did not seem like a strange house to me. But then mother and father may have taken me there when I was a child. I think mother knew the previous owner slightly.'

The topic became general, and after a while, they walked back to the hotel to join Mrs Mathers for tea. Luisa informed her of their plan to become engaged, and soon afterwards said she was going to the writing room to send off that letter to Bridget, with the good news. Jim sat in the lounge talking to his mother and explaining how it had happened.

Mrs Mathers realized then, that there was nothing she could do about it. Jim could not have refused what amounted to Luisa's acceptance of her son's earlier proposal. She was relieved to know that they had agreed to a long engagement. But although she did not express her worries to her son, she could not help but wonder at the effect of Luisa's letter on Martyn. She could do nothing from this distance, and she was dreadfully afraid that Martyn in a reactionary mood, might rush his marriage to Bridget in sheer desperation. If only she were there to talk to him and advise him. If only she had told him before she left home that this engagement might be forthcoming.

At last she decided that she herself would write to him to-morrow. She little knew at that moment that the letter would never be written, and even if it had, it would never have reached Martyn.

Bridget received Luisa's letter next morning and opening it at the breakfast table, gave a little cry of excitement.

'Oh, Martyn, listen,' she said. 'Wonderful news. Luisa says she is feeling much better for her holiday, and is having a wonderful time. Then – and here is the big news – she says she and Jim have decided to get engaged...' She broke off hurriedly as Martyn said in a low fierce voice:

'Let me see that letter!'

Too surprised to refuse, Bridget handed it to him.

Martyn's eyes devoured the loose, rather untidy lines of Luisa's handwriting.

'...I really think I am properly in love with him, Bridget,' he read. 'He's so very kind and nice, and we are the greatest friends. This afternoon *he kissed me and I've come to the conclusion I enjoy being kissed by a man. Of course it'll be nothing new to you who have been engaged some months now! Oh, Bridget, I do feel happy and content. It's all such fun. Do you suppose we could possibly arrange a double wedding from the Vicarage? You and Martyn, and Jim and I. But we aren't going to get married for quite some time. I want a nice long engagement, and time to enjoy it, before I take on the responsibilities of a married...'*

Martyn tore the letter across, and across again, unable to read further. He knew now that this was the end. He had reached the end of his endurance and this whole farce must be terminated once and for all. Bridget was staring at him in amazement, and he felt a moment's brief compunction for her. Then he said in a cold, hard voice:

'Would you excuse Bridget, Mrs Castle? I'd like to have a word with her alone in the sitting-room.'

'Of course,' said Mrs Castle, nervously. She wondered whether Martyn had gone off his head. It wouldn't have surprised her, for he had certainly been behaving very oddly of late.

In the sitting-room, Martyn felt his control slipping away.

'Bridget, I'm sorry, but this last thing is too much for me. I can't go on like this. I must tell you that I love her. I love Luisa, do you hear? Now that she has decided to marry Jim Mathers, there is no point in my remaining here. I just couldn't stand it. I'm going away. I'm dreadfully sorry if this hurts you, but I would be grateful if you would release me from my engagement. It cannot go on...'

Bridget was stunned. She sat in silence trying to understand all that Martyn had said. For the moment anyway, she could not feel any other emotion than surprise. It dominated everything. Martyn, in love with Luisa. Martyn, going away. Martyn, breaking the engagement. And then, slowly, the pieces that had been puzzling her, fitted into their places. Martyn's behaviour since the accident. The despair and hopelessness on his face. His reactions when Luisa recovered consciousness and could not bear to have him near her.

'Martyn,' she said. 'Tell me one thing more. Did Luisa feel the same way – before her accident?'

Martyn nodded, feeling cold and empty now that it had all come out. He could no longer feel angry, tired, hopeless, despairing. There was nothing left. Nothing but a cold emptiness and a sick feeling in the pit of his stomach.

'It happened when you went home to stay with your mother,' he said. 'Don't ask me how, Bridget. It just happened! We had decided not to do anything about it – Luisa felt that it wasn't fair to you. We didn't want to hurt you, Bridget, but I'm afraid this way you have had to be hurt after all. I just cannot go on with it. You had to be told the truth.'

'Of course, Martyn. I'm glad you told me. I felt that all was not well between us. You mustn't worry about me. I suppose Luisa was worrying when she rode home – that was how the accident occurred. She was tired and worried. So all this time, I have been the one to blame and I thought you were blaming yourself.'

'I was!' Martyn interposed quickly. 'You see, she was tired and upset that morning. It was at my suggestion she went to London and stayed so late. You are in no way to blame at all, Bridget. You, more than anyone, are utterly blameless. You are the one who has been hurt and let down. Oh, Bridget, my dear, don't cry. Please, Bridget. It makes it so much harder. I'm so very fond of you, Bridget, and I hate myself for having to be the one to hurt you. Bridget, please, please don't cry. I'd have made the most awful husband for you and you know it. You should have married that nice Bill of yours. It's all been so hopelessly muddled.'

Bridget wiped her tears away with the handkerchief Martyn offered her.

'I'm not really crying for myself, Martyn,' she said, shakily. 'Only for you and Luisa and – and life. It *has* been a hopeless muddle. If only I'd known, I'd have broken the engagement, and you two could have found your happiness together. I felt from the very start that you and Luisa *ought* to be friends. I was too blind to see that you could never be anything so ordinary as friends. For you both, it would be love or hate. And now Luisa has decided to marry Jim. Martyn, you must prevent it. You must go down and stop this marriage – this engagement. After so much suffering for everyone, you cannot let Luisa tangle herself up with Jim, when any day she might come to herself again and wish herself free. Martyn, you must stop it.'

'My dear Bridget, it is typical of you that even now you are thinking only of others. But what could I do? Luisa cannot bear the sight of me. There is nothing I could say that would make sense to her. No, Bridget. It's no good. I'm going away. If at any time Luisa should recover her memory, and should she not be married to Jim, then you must send for me, if you will.'

'Of course, Martyn. But where will you go? What address shall I have to write to? What is going to happen to your work here?'

'It's nearly at a standstill in any case,' Martyn said, with a wry smile. 'I don't know where I'm going or what I'll do, Bridget. I can't think straight at the moment. But I'll write. Now I'm going to pack a few things. I must get away from here before I lose my mind.'

Seeing that he had nearly reached the end of his tether, Bridget decided not to worry him further with questions as to his future.

'I'll pack for you,' she said. 'And Martyn, don't worry. Have a long holiday, and when you are better it will seem easier to decide what is to be done.'

He turned to her then and for the first time since the day they had become engaged, he took her in his arms and held her close to him.

'Dear Bridget! At this moment when I am going away and may never see you again, I think I am only just realizing the true extent of your worth. Forgive me, Bridget, and try not to think too harshly of me. I value your respect too much to wish to lose it. Take care of yourself, my dear, and I shall pray for your ultimate happiness, for you deserve it. And lastly, I want to thank you for all you have done for me and given me since I've known you.'

She clung to him then, the tears coursing down her cheeks, knowing in her heart that this was really good-bye, and that in her own way, she would always love him. She would remember him with mixed feelings, but never without affection.

It did not occur to her that already in her mind she had put him in the past, and was looking to the future. She would not have admitted that when Martyn's car disappeared into the distance, she felt a lightening of the load that had seemed to lie heavy on her shoulders the past few weeks; but deep in her heart, she knew that although he was gone, her heart had not been broken after all.

The same morning, Luisa and Jim were on the beach, lying in the hot sun in bathing suits. Luisa's white body had taken a golden tan already and tiny freckles had appeared on her nose and arms.

'That's the penalty for having red hair, Luisa,' said Mrs Mathers, who was lounging happily in a deck chair, with a sunshade to keep her cool.

'I say, who's that over there?' said Jim, pointing across the sands to a young man in grey flannels, who was walking towards them. He shaded his hand with his eyes, and said: 'I'm sure I know that walk. Do you recognize him, Mother?'

'No, I can't say I do, dear. Wait until he comes closer.'

Jim and Luisa sat up lazily and studied the figure as it came towards them. Luisa showed no signs of recognizing him, but suddenly Jim gave a little cry, and jumped to his feet.

'Mother, it's that chap, Bill,' he said.

His words meant nothing to her, but she gathered from the worried tone of his voice, that this must be someone Luisa had known – someone who did not know that she had forgotten seven years of her life. She looked anxiously at the girl.

'Bill who?' Luisa asked.

'Don't you remember Bridget talking about him?' Jim asked, nervously.

'Oh, her childhood sweetheart!' Luisa said. 'I've never met him, of course. How do you happen to know him, Jim?'

He was spared an answer, for Bill had now reached them, and was holding out his hand to Luisa.

'Goodness, Luisa, what a wonderful surprise. Who'd have thought we'd run into each other down here?' He turned to Jim, and nodded his head. Jim introduced him quickly to his Mother, and then said:

'I suppose you recognized Luisa from the snapshots Bridget had of her at school. It's funny I never realized the Bridget I knew at the Vicarage was that girl friend of yours. We can't have met since we were at school together, Bill.'

It was a gallant attempt, but his words meant nothing at all to Bill. He stared at him anxiously.

'I say, old chap, have you got a touch of

the sun?' he asked. 'Look, here, Luisa, may I sit down? I want to hear all the news. You haven't written to me, so I assume there's no good news for me. Still, I've never stopped hoping. She hasn't married him yet, has she?'

'Who married whom?' Luisa asked slowly.

Bill wondered if after all it were he who was suffering from a touch of the sun. Jim sought desperately for something to say, but his mind was now a blank. Mrs Mathers, too, could do nothing to prevent this. She watched Luisa anxiously.

'Why, Bridget and Martyn, of course. What's the matter with you, Luisa? Have you lost your memory, or something?'

It was only a figure of speech, but it had the most disastrous effect on the whole party, so it seemed to Bill as he stood there watching them. Luisa buried her face in her hands and burst into tears. Mrs Mathers jumped up and rushed across to her. Jim stood staring back at him, saying:

'You damn fool. You idiot. If anything happens now, it'll be your fault.'

'Look here, Mathers, I'm sorry if I've spoken out of turn, but just what *is* going on? Suppose you tell me what's happening, and then I won't make another blunder.'

Jim was about to draw Bill aside to tell him the truth, when Luisa looked up, her face drenched in tears.

'Bill, sit down here. Tell me everything – everything that you know about me. You were right just now. I lost my memory. But it's coming back. It's coming back slowly. I can remember you at the house and promising to write to you. You were in love with Bridget, weren't you?'

Bill nodded, surprise robbing him of speech.

'And she is engaged to – to Martyn...' Luisa's voice trailed off into silence, and the three people, watching her, saw her turn as white as a sheet, and knew that whatever she had recalled to mind was painful to her.

'Martyn!' she whispered again, and then turning to Mrs Mathers, she said violently: 'How long have I been like this? What has really happened? Tell me everything – everything. You must help me to remember.'

'Of course,' said Mrs Mathers, gently. 'But first we will go back to the hotel. We shall not be disturbed there. Come along, Bill, you'd best come, too. You and Jim support Luisa, and I'll carry the lunch.'

And slowly the little procession moved across the sunlit beach, and up the steps to the hotel.

CHAPTER XIV

Back in the hotel, Mrs Mathers insisted that Luisa should lie down on her bed while they talked. She was worried because the girl looked so white and strained. She wanted to call a doctor, but Luisa would not hear of it until she had everything straight in her mind. Jim could think of little else to do for her but give her a couple of aspirins, which might act as a sedative.

There was no doubt about the fact that Luisa was beginning to remember all that had been totally forgotten since her accident. But things were coming back to her in haphazard disorder, and she was hopelessly confused and agitated.

'I think it might be a good idea if we do the talking, Luisa, and explain everything,' Jim said, quietly. 'Just lie quietly, and then if there is anything that still confuses you, you could ask.'

Luisa nodded. Her head ached and she was glad to be resting on her bed, even while every nerve in her body was jangling and straining to remember what had happened to her.

She stared at the three faces around her ...

Mrs Mathers's, sympathetic, anxious, worried; Jim's, wretched, and yet curiously impersonal, as if he were only concerned with her as a patient; Bill's, mystified, but his eyes kind and strangely reassuring.

'Please!' said Luisa, her voice almost inaudible. 'Tell me what happened – I fell from my horse, didn't I? From Jumbo?'

Jim took up the story, and Luisa listened quietly. The only expression on her face was rapt attention, and once, when Martyn's name was mentioned, a swift passing glory, and then her eyes closed as if this particular memory brought her both wonder and pain.

At last Jim came to the point where he and his mother had brought her here to the seaside, hoping the change of air and scenery would do her good. Then Mrs Mathers interposed quietly:

'And so, by chance, Luisa, Bill happened to be on holiday here, too. He knew nothing of your illness, and so naturally talked to you as if nothing had happened. That seemed to break the spell, and here we are.'

No one spoke for a moment, and then Jim said:

'How are you feeling, Luisa? Don't you think it might be a good thing to let me telephone for a doctor now?'

'No! Please. I'm quite all right,' Luisa said. But her face and eyes were drawn as if she were in great pain. 'Would you and Bill mind very much if I talked to Mrs Mathers – alone?' she asked.

The two men left her immediately, and Luisa turned to the older woman, saying desperately:

'Mrs Mathers, tell me quickly – what has happened to Martyn? How is he? Jim said I seemed to be upset by his company. Did I refuse to see him? Oh, how terribly he must have been hurt!'

'Luisa, don't torture yourself. Martyn knew you were ill. We all worried about you.'

'But he loved me, Mrs Mathers. And I wouldn't see him. I came away without saying good-bye...' her voice broke and tears came into her eyes, but she brushed them away quickly. 'Tell me,' she went on, 'what has happened – between Martyn and Bridget? Are they – married?'

'No, my dear, and somehow I don't think they will ever be. Things have not gone well for them. Martyn loves you, Luisa, and he is not a man who can dissimulate easily. I think if you were to go back to him now, he would want to break his engagement. I feel very strongly that it would be best for everyone – including Bridget. She cannot have been very happy. Martyn has, quite naturally, been morose and, I imagine, poor company. The last time I saw Bridget, she did not look very well – or very happy. You know, Luisa, I think if this young man of hers were to return now – Bridget might realize that she had been making a mistake. I have an idea he is still in love with her.'

'I – I'm sure Bill hasn't changed,' Luisa said. 'Oh, Mrs Mathers, I wish I could be sure what you say is true. I want nothing else but to go to Martyn and make him happy again. I love him. I shall always love him. If he cannot be happy with Bridget, then maybe after all it would be for the best if he broke his engagement. I wish I could be sure Bridget would turn to Bill. I always felt she was more suited to Bill than to Martyn, but that may simply have been because I, too, loved Martyn, and felt that he and I were meant for one another.'

'I believe you were meant for one another, Luisa,' said Mrs Mathers. 'And if Martyn is your man, Luisa, then he cannot also be Bridget's. There is some other man in the world who will make her a better husband, and I do believe that this Bill is the one.'

Luisa sighed.

'I don't think I have the strength to fight against my love for Martyn now. I need him. I'm sure he needs me, too. Mrs Mathers, when do you think I could go to him?'

Mrs Mathers tried not to think of Jim and his coming unhappiness. Luisa seemed oblivious of her engagement to her son, and she felt it would be better not to remind her now. In fact, it was best forgotten altogether.

Fortunately it had not been made public in any way. No one else knew of it except Jim, Luisa and herself, and Luisa now had forgotten it, so it seemed. But this was not true. Suddenly, the girl sat up and stared at Mrs Mathers, her eyes brilliant, her cheeks flushed.

'Mrs Mathers!' she cried. 'Jim. I'm engaged to Jim. I remember. Since I've been ill. Oh, Mrs Mathers, how could I have allowed this to happen? I don't understand. What am I going to do?'

Mrs Mathers laid a restraining hand on the girl's arm.

'Calm yourself, Luisa, child,' she said soothingly. 'Jim understands. He knew you loved Martyn. He knew, too, that marriage was impossible, for should you ever recover your memory, you would want to be free for Martyn. That time has now come, and he will, I know, treat the engagement as if it had never existed. It would be far better that way. No words. No apologies. No explanations. He will be a little upset, but it is nothing more than he expected.'

Luisa was weeping quietly, now, the tears coursing down her cheeks. There seemed nothing she could do or say. She had been forced by circumstances to hurt the two greatest friends she had – Bridget and now Jim. And Jim's mother, who should have hated her for what she must be doing to her son, instead was offering her sympathy, kindness and – freedom.

'Luisa, don't distress yourself. There is absolutely nothing to cry about now. It is going to be all right.'

'Jim! Poor Jim!' was all Luisa could say.

'Luisa, if Jim cares for you at all, and I know he is very, very fond of you, he would hate himself for the rest of his life if he thought you were crying on his behalf. He has wanted your happiness all along – and only that. If setting you free to marry Martyn can make you happy, then he will do so gladly. In any case,' she added more practically, 'he is far too young to think of marrying yet, Luisa. Mr Simkin, who is a very famous and brilliant brain specialist, has the highest regard for Jim and great hopes for his future. But his advice was that my son should not marry yet awhile. He wanted nothing to interfere with the boy's career. Looking at this whole thing purely practically, Luisa, this is the best thing that could have happened. Looking at it senti-mentally, I am sorry that Jim will be upset and disappointed; sorry, too, that I shall not have you for a daughter-in-law. But I hope, Luisa, that we shall go on seeing plenty of each other. If you and Martyn marry and settle down at the Vicarage, we shall be neighbours. I hope that we shall continue to mean more to each other than that.'

Luisa leaned over and kissed Mrs Mathers gently, still unable to check her tears.

'You are so kind – so very kind. How can I ever thank you – repay you?'

'By being happy and well, Luisa,' said Mrs Mathers, practically. She was deeply touched by Luisa's words and the warmth of her tone, but she felt that all this emotion was bad for the girl. 'Now let us make plans for to-morrow,' she said. 'We can catch the first train. Bill must be persuaded to come with us. It will be a tactical move to have him on the spot to dry Bridget's tears! Jim, too, of course, will accompany us. He is enough of a doctor now to be able to take care of you. You must keep as quiet as possible, Luisa, and try not to worry. It would be too awful if you lost your memory again, now wouldn't it?'

Luisa nodded and smiled. The first shock of surprise was wearing off now, and she felt an immense lightening of a load that had seemed to be worrying her for a long time. In its place came a slowly increasing excitement. To-morrow she would be going back to Martyn. To-morrow she would see him and he would hold her in his arm and all this – this nightmare, would seem as if it had never been. To-morrow … to-morrow.

Downstairs in the lounge, Jim and Bill were getting to know one another at the bar, and were exchanging confidences. Jim had realized that it was all up with his engagement. There was no doubt about the fact that Luisa had made a swift and complete recovery, and it was too much to expect that she had changed her real feelings for Martyn. He doubted even whether Luisa remembered her engagement to himself!

'It's certainly tough, old chap,' said Bill. 'But I suppose in a way you were prepared for it.'

Jim nodded.

'I don't think I ever really believed Luisa and I would be married. She's far too good for me, in any case. I'm a very dull, ordinary sort of fellow and medicine is about the only thing I'm any good at. Luisa is so vital and beautiful and alive. She needs a chap like Saunders, I suppose. For some strange reason, they make a good pair. Not that I particularly like the chap – but I suppose I'm biased. I'm jealous, naturally.'

'Come to that, so am I!' said Bill, with a grin. 'After all, you seem to forget he's engaged to my girl.'

Jim ordered another round of beer, and looked at Bill enviously.

'You've nothing to worry about. As soon as Martyn breaks his engagement, all you've got to do is to comfort Bridget, and there you are!'

'I'm not so sure of that,' said Bill with a frown. 'She may resent my being there –

associate me with unhappiness or something. Women are so peculiar. You never really know how they are going to take things. Take Bridget, now. She was dead keen to marry me when war broke out, but her parents wouldn't allow it as she was so young. And then, when I returned from overseas, she wasn't really keen at all. Said she wasn't ready to settle down and asked me to be patient. Well, I waited and then what happens – she falls in love with someone else. You know, Jim, it's my idea that women need a little firmness. I should have *made* her marry me.'

'What, against her will?' asked Jim.

'Well, not exactly. But sort of changed her will, if you see what I mean,' said Bill.

'That may be all right for you and Bridget, but I couldn't do that with Luisa. Of course, it's different in my case. I've known all along Luisa wasn't my girl, in the sense you mean. I suppose it is all working out for the best, but I can't help feeling pretty bad about it. Frankly, I wouldn't have minded so much if she'd married Martyn before her accident and – and our engagement. I suppose it's because I've had hopes recently that I never entertained for a second before Luisa was ill. She seemed to turn to me after the accident, and was happier with me than with Martyn. But of course, that's easily explained medically. Now I come to think of it, Mr Simkin told me about a case very similar to Luisa's. Some man forgot six months because he didn't want to remember them, and he had a horror of small children. That was because he associated them in his sub-conscious mind with the tragedy that had occurred, when he ran over his small daughter and killed her. I didn't know how Luisa felt about Martyn, then. But I can see now that she couldn't bear to have him around because sub-consciously he reminded her of unhappiness. You see, she had decided she owed it to Bridget not to let Martyn break the engagement however much she loved him. At least until Martyn had given it a fair trial. Luisa told mother everything, shortly before she had that fall from her horse.'

'A ghastly thing to have happened,' said Bill. 'Of course, I hadn't the vaguest idea when I met you all this morning, that there was anything wrong, so I just blew the gaff!'

'Perhaps it was as well,' said Jim, philosophically. 'Whichever way you look at it, you were responsible for bringing back Luisa's memory. That at all events is a good thing. What were you doing down here, Bill?'

'Just mooching around. I'd a week's holiday due, and came here because I couldn't think what else to do. In the past, I should have spent all my spare time with Bridget. I never imagined I should be lucky enough to run into Luisa, and so get news of Bridget.

Luisa promised to write were there any goods new for me. I assumed from her silence that there was none. I went over to Bridget's home last week, but they told me Mrs Castle was staying with her daughter. I must admit that piece of news made me pretty downhearted. I imagined a wedding or something. Oh, here's your mother, Jim.'

They went with her into the lounge, where she told them her plans for the morrow.

'I think it would be a good idea if you were to come with us, Mr Smith,' she suggested. 'Would it be possible?'

'Of course,' Bill said, eagerly. 'I still have five days' holiday left. I can do as I wish. I'm down here on my own.'

'Then I take it you wish to come?' Mrs Mathers asked. 'It's none of my business, but I imagine Jim has clarified the position, and I rather gathered you might wish to see Bridget?'

Bill gave a cheerful grin.

'I'll welcome the opportunity, although I can't say I feel particularly happy about the sort of welcome I'll get. She said she never wanted to see me again.'

'A woman often says things she doesn't mean, and afterwards regrets them,' said Mrs Mathers, calmly. 'Bridget will need someone to turn to. I know I should, particularly someone like yourself.'

'It's very kind of you to say so, but I doubt

whether Bridget takes quite such a complimentary view of me. I'm really rather dull and ordinary, and last time I saw her, I lost my temper and flung out of the house. She must think dreadfully badly of me now.'

'That's a chance you'll have to take,' said Mrs Mathers, with a smile. 'But I'll lay odds on you, Bill!'

When Bill had returned to his hotel to pack his bags and get ready for an early start, next day, Mrs Mathers, and her son had a long talk together. She was glad to see that he was not taking this whole affair quite as badly as she had expected. He was strangely matter-of-fact.

'It's Fate, I expect, Mother!' he said. 'And I quite see that it is best for Luisa this way.'

'And for your career, Jim,' his mother added quietly.

Jim waved his hand.

'I'm not thinking of that, Mother. Next to Luisa, it doesn't count.'

'It must count,' Mrs Mathers said, seriously. 'It's your future Jim. If Luisa marries Martyn, you will want something to think about – to concentrate on. Don't let this spoil your wonderful enthusiasm, and all the efforts you have made so far, Jim. You are doing so well.'

'I shall go on working, Mother. Don't you worry about that. But for the moment it's Luisa I'm thinking of. You don't imagine anything will go wrong now, do you? You don't think Martyn could be such an ass as to insist on continuing with his engagement to Bridget?'

'I don't think so, Jim. And even if he does, I have an odd premonition that Bill will make a difference somehow. I like that young man. I can quite understand Mrs Castle saying she was so disappointed he was not to be her son-in-law after all. Well, let's hope she may yet get her wish.'

'Everything sounds as if it is going to work out for the best,' said Jim, a little doubtfully. 'But I can't say I feel as sure as you sound, Mother.'

'Well, we'll see to-morrow,' said Mrs Mathers. 'At least we can celebrate Luisa's complete recovery. I think she will be asleep now. When I left her she was drowsy from those aspirins you gave her, and I think she is also exhausted with all that has happened to-day. When she wakes, you must go and see her, Jim. She is worrying now about you – the engagement. I told her I knew you would wish to treat it as if it had never been – which is almost true since it is unofficial, and only of one day's standing.'

'Of course, Mother. Luisa has no need to worry. I will set her mind at rest.'

'Bless you, Jim!' his mother said, softly. 'Not every woman is as lucky as I am. Few can have sons who make them so proud. You are everything I ever hoped my only son would be.'

'Thank you, Mother,' Jim said, softly. 'And you, too, are the perfect mother.'

They held hands and stayed together thus, sitting in silence and perfect harmony.

The next day dawned slowly and reluctantly with clouds of misty rain blowing against the windows of the hotel, and the sea beyond was grey and stormy.

Luisa, drawing her bedroom curtains to reveal this scene, could not feel daunted by the change in the weather. She had awakened much refreshed and filled with excitement and a wonderful anticipation. Soon – soon, she would be with Martyn! Another few hours and she could go into the surgery where he would undoubtedly be sitting and run into the safe shelter of his arm. She would see the incredulous wonder in his eyes as she told him again and again that she loved him; watch the happiness flood his face when she explained that she was well again – well, and his for ever and ever.

Only for a moment could Luisa's happiness be clouded, and that was at the memory of what she must do to hurt Bridget this day, when everything ought to be perfect. But then came the memory of Bill's face, and Mrs Mathers's reassuring words, when she had said:

'I have a feeling Bridget will end up happily after all with that nice young man.'

Perhaps this was too much to hope for, and yet deep down inside her, Luisa, too, felt that this was the right thing. It was the right ending for everyone, and all along she had felt that Bill was meant for Bridget.

Jim seemed surprisingly cheerful, and only his mother knew what the effort cost him. To have his holiday with Luisa curtailed, his engagement broken, and moreover to know that he must return the girl he loved to the man she loved – not everyone could have done this with Jim's show of bravado. But throughout the long train journey, it was Jim who kept the conversation going with cheerful witticisms and amusing banter with Bill.

Bill, too, was in wonderful form. He, like Luisa, was filled with happy anticipation, but he was nevertheless not as sure as she was, that all would end well for him this day. But optimistically he would not allow such thoughts to remain with him for long.

Mrs Mathers happily fussed round Luisa, making sure she did not over-tire herself. There would be enough excitement to tire her at the end of the day without her wearing herself out on the journey. Not that the girl looked ill to-day, she thought, for Luisa was radiant – like a bride on her wedding day. Her cheeks had regained their healthy colour and her eyes were clear and bright – those green translucent eyes which were so incredibly beautiful. She could not help but sigh a little, remembering her own lost youth and the husband she had loved with as much fervour and ardour as Luisa loved her Martyn.

Luisa's excitement and Bill's nervousness increased rapidly as they reached the station and Jim went to telephone for a taxi to take them to the Vicarage. Mrs Mathers and her son had decided to take the taxi on to their home and leave the others to sort matters out for themselves.

So it was that Luisa and Bill stood alone at the Vicarage door, which was opened by Mrs Jennings.

'Landsakes, Miss Luisa!' she cried. 'Are you home from your holiday already?'

Before Luisa could speak, another figure appeared from the back of the hall, and Bridget ran forward with a little cry.

'Luisa!' she said. 'What a wonderful surprise...' her voice trailed away as she caught sight of Bill. She looked from one to the other uncomprehendingly.

'I've brought Luisa home,' Bill said, simply. 'She recovered her memory yesterday and so we decided to come back right away. There are a number of things she wants to settle.'

Not knowing what to say to Bill, so surprised was she to see him, Bridget turned again to Luisa.

'I'm so glad, Luisa,' she said. 'We were terribly worried. It's wonderful to know you are quite well again.'

She left Mrs Jennings to close the door and took Bill and Luisa through to the sitting-room. The bed had been taken away and the room looked just as it had always done. Luisa glanced around it, memories of that evening with Martyn flooding back to her.

Bill was staring at Bridget, thinking how white and tired and wretched she looked. He felt instinctively that all was not well with her. She was avoiding meeting his eye and he did not know what to say to her. The three of them stood there in silence until at last Bridget felt she must say something.

'Did – did Martyn get in touch with you, Luisa?' she asked.

Bill and Luisa looked at her in surprise.

'No, he didn't!' Luisa said. 'Is there – any reason why he should have done so?'

Bridget bit her lip and stared at the ground.

'I just thought perhaps that was the reason you had returned. So you don't know?'

'Don't know what?' Luisa asked, her throat dry, a nameless dread filling her mind.

'That we've broken our engagement – and Martyn has gone away.'

Bill heard only the first words – Luisa only

the second. Each spoke at once and then broke off, waiting for the other to speak first.

'You go ahead, Luisa. What I have to say can wait,' said Bill, his heart singing jubilantly within him. Bridget was free again. She had broken her engagement to Martyn of her own accord. He could hardly believe his own good fortune – could hardly dare to think what this might mean to him.

'Where has Martyn gone?' Luisa asked, through dry lips.

'I don't know, Lis.' Bridget said, gently. 'You see, he's very much in love with you – he has been for a long while. He couldn't stand it here any more. Your illness was – dreadful for him,' she said, awkwardly. 'He went away last night. He said he would write in due course. But I don't know where he is now. I'm so sorry, Luisa.'

Once more the three stood in silence, each very conscious of the others' feelings, and none knowing what to say.

CHAPTER XV

Martyn sat in an armchair in his club reading the morning paper and wondering with a gloomy pessimism whether or not there would be another war. It was, of course, an appalling thought and yet in one selfish way he would have welcomed a war at this minute. It would have removed from him the responsibility of deciding what to do with his life. He could have got some work or other doing a worthwhile job for his country, in spite of his missing arm. But without a war, what incentive had he to work?

Deeply depressed, Martyn surveyed the few years since he had come out of hospital, and could see in them nothing but a waste of time.

"Oh, I've succeeded well enough as a vet,' he told himself. 'I've made enough money to live on, and I've saved a good bit, too. But for what? Now that I have a bank balance and a career, it all seems so much wasted effort. What happiness can either of them bring – without Luisa?"

So it seemed to Martyn that the future held nothing at all for him. Life without the girl he loved – a home shared with her and perhaps, in time, children – simply did not add up.

He tried to get a grip on himself – tell himself that other chaps had lost the women they loved and still found it possible to take an interest in their work – make something of their lives. But somehow the troubles of those shadowy people did not touch him closely or compare with the loneliness and hopelessness from which he was now suffering. He recalled Betty, and how impossible life had appeared when she turned him down – and yet that, too, did not seem comparable with his present emotions. He knew all too well that he had been suffering from hurt pride – pique. Luisa had gone so much deeper into his real self. His heart ached for her and he had no pride. Were it possible that to throw himself at her feet and beg her to come back to him could, in fact, bring her back, he would have done so willingly. But for some reason, just the sight of him upset her, and the doctor had made it amply clear that she must not on any account be worried.

Would she ever be well again? Martyn asked himself. Was there, after all, this much hope for his future? Or would she have married Jim by the time her memory returned? Judging by the letter Luisa had written Bridget from the sea-side, Luisa's marriage to Jim seemed fairly definite.

Martyn felt that the more he thought about it all, the more hopeless seemed the outlook.

'Hullo, Saunders! News depressed you? You look pretty gloomy, old chap!'

Martyn looked up and saw one of his acquaintances staring at him in concern. He had not met John Sheldon more than two or three times and was not very sure whether he liked him. But in his present mood he did not care very much whose company he had so long as he was not left alone to think.

John Sheldon pulled a chair alongside Martyn's and lit a cigarette.

'I don't know that it's just the news,' Martyn replied to his question. 'It's life in general.'

'Tricky business, life!' remarked his companion. 'Never know when it's going to turn round and kick you when you least expect it. Reminds me of a mare I once had. Affectionate as the devil for days on end, and then she'd get a mood on her, and the next thing she'd kick out at you.'

'One never seems prepared for it!' agreed Martyn. 'That's the trouble.'

John Sheldon eyed his companion, and noticed again the deep lines of worry around the eyes – the bitterness all too clearly marked in the expression of his mouth.

'Woman-trouble?' he asked. 'You don't have to answer that of course.'

'Yes – I – I suppose so. But I'd rather not

talk about it. I'm trying to put it out of my mind.'

'I understand!' said Sheldon, without understanding in the least. He was a simple, rather brainless man, slightly older than Martyn, and financially very well off. He had been left a large private income when he was twenty-one and had, in consequence, become something of a playboy. He never missed any of the best shows in town. He was always seen with some glamorous female, and seldom with the same one twice. He was photographed at Ascot, at Cowes, at Epsom, at social functions of all kinds. And he wintered regularly in the South of France, unless he was cruising in the Mediterranean in his private yacht.

Martyn knew these luxurious ways of his companion, but had never particularly envied him. It seemed such an empty life, gadding about from one pleasure to another. And yet now, for the first time, he envied Sheldon. Men like him never really got hurt or worried. They didn't take life seriously enough to let themselves be hurt by it. They floated along in a placid, empty, meaningless way, finding a new girl friend, or getting plastered if they were mildly depressed – hopping off to some other corner of the world if they became bored by their present existence. Yes, he could envy Sheldon in his present mood, but he never could really get close to the fellow. Their outlooks were fundamentally different. Sheldon skimmed the surface of life – Martyn lived it to its extremes. For this reason, Sheldon would never understand how he was feeling. If he told him about Luisa, no doubt Sheldon would suggest he find some other girl.

This was exactly what Sheldon was doing.

'You know, Saunders, no woman is worth getting in a state about,' he said cheerfully. 'There are plenty more fish in the sea. I know it seems bad now, but it'll blow over. What you want is a little gaiety, my boy. Don't sit around here moping. Get out and about. Get drunk if you want. Or better still, come to the party I'm giving to-night. It's to be a real slap-up affair. Lashings of lovely women to make you forget this girl of yours. How about it?'

Martyn shook his head.

'It's very kind of you, Sheldon, but I don't think I will, thanks all the same. I'm afraid I should spoil your party.'

'Nonsense!' Sheldon said. 'You're just a bit backward in coming forward, Saunders – that's your trouble. No need to be shy, you know. Besides, the girls will like you. You'll be an enormous success. You're a good-looking chap. Wish I had your interesting face instead of my own pudding. Still, the girls forget my face when they see my wallet.'

Martyn looked at Sheldon with a moment's

pity. Sheldon was in fact a very unattractive-looking fellow. He had one of those round red faces which could never even remotely be considered romantic. No doubt life had hurt him, too, since he could make that bitter remark about his popularity having to be bought with his money.

'Now, how about it Saunders?' Sheldon continued. 'I'm sure it will do you good.'

Martyn was about to refuse the invitation a second time and then, quite suddenly, he changed his mind. After all, why not go? He had nothing else to do. The alternative was sitting here alone worrying about the future and getting nowhere. He had had three nights of that, and still he had not decided what to do with himself. Perhaps a good rowdy party was just what he needed. At least he wouldn't be lonely.

'All right, Sheldon. Thanks very much. I'd like to come.'

Sheldon clapped him over the back and said:

'Capital, Saunders! I'll pick you up here at six o'clock. It's lounge suits, but I expect the women will dress. They like to show off their new frills and furbelows you know. I've got to pick up a couple of them at six-thirty, so don't be late.'

The day wore on slowly, and by evening, Martyn was more than glad that he had accepted Sheldon's invitation. It was years since he had been to a party in town. Somehow after his accident he had been afraid to face a lot of people – afraid they would talk about his arm and pity him. Bridget and Luisa had cured him of that. It no longer bothered him. And in London one saw so many disabled service men, they ceased to attract attention.

He dressed with care and was ready in the lounge when Sheldon joined him soon after six. Sheldon had hired a car for the evening, and he and Martyn drove away from the club in a luxurious Daimler to fetch Sheldon's two girl-friends.

Martyn wanted to wait in the car while Sheldon went up to their flat to collect them, but Sheldon insisted on his coming up, too.

'They always keep a bottle of Scotch up there,' he said, with a wink. 'It'll do you good to start the evening well. Get you into the party spirit.'

So Martyn went upstairs in the lift, and waited while Sheldon rang the bell.

A tall languorous young woman opened it and flung her arms round Sheldon's neck and kissed him full on the lips, looking over his shoulder at the same time at Martyn. Martyn turned his head away quickly, embarrassed as much by the public embrace, as by her scrutiny. He knew instantly that he disliked this girl. She was without doubt one of the ones who was interested only in

Sheldon's money.

'Darling!' she said, in a loud, exaggerated voice. 'How lovely to see you. And who's the friend?'

Sheldon turned and introduced Martyn.

'This is Cynthia de Large!' he said. 'Martyn Saunders.'

Martyn held out his hand, but instead of taking it, she linked her arm in his and drew him into the sitting-room, leaving Sheldon to follow behind.

'This going to be fun,' she said, shaking a mass of rather brilliant red hair over her bare shoulder, and keeping her arm linked in Martyn's. 'What to drink, Mr Saunders – or may I call you Martyn?'

'We'll both have whisky, Sweetheart,' Sheldon said, with a wink at Martyn. He seemed quite untroubled by Cynthia's obvious interest in his friend.

Martyn sat down on the arm of a chair, and hurriedly lit a cigarette. The room was permeated with the smell of perfume, and although normally he liked women to wear perfume, he could not tolerate it at this strength. He began to feel that he had made a mistake coming this evening after all. Sheldon's girl friend, pretty though she was, was nevertheless loud-voiced and rather cheap. It was not a word he cared to use in respect to women, but no other word so exactly described this Cynthia de Large.

Her hair looked dyed, and the low-cut evening frock she was wearing was almost indecent. He hoped that this was not to be his vis-à-vis this evening.

'Where's Betts?' Sheldon was asking. 'Still beautifying herself, I suppose.'

'On the contrary, I'm quite ready,' said a voice from behind them.

Martyn turned swiftly, something in the timbre of the voice seeming strangely familiar. As he turned, he knew with a swift shock that his ear had not deceived him. It was Betty's voice, Betty herself, standing there staring at him with equal surprise.

She recovered herself more quickly than Martyn and went over to him, a smile on her face.

'Well, this is an unexpected surprise, Martyn,' she said, smoothly. 'I haven't seen you in years, have I? How did you find out my address?'

'I – I, as a matter of fact, I didn't know you would be here, Betty,' Martyn said, biting his lip. 'I came along with Sheldon. He hadn't mentioned any names.'

A flicker of annoyance crossed swiftly over Betty's face, but it was only momentary. It would have suited her ego better to know that Martyn had been trying to find her again – perhaps had been trying for months – years. However, she did not intend the others to see her annoyance.

'Well, I must say, I'm surprised to see you,' she said. 'You're the last person in the world I expected.'

'You two seem to know one another,' Sheldon remarked, unnecessarily. 'That's a bit of luck, isn't it?'

Betty moved away from Martyn, and went over to the table to pour herself a whisky. Her back was turned to them as she said:

'We know each other very well, as a matter of fact. We used to be engaged, you know.'

Martyn could think of nothing to say. He was so totally unprepared for this meeting that he could not adjust himself to the fact that it had happened. Under cover of talk, he studied Betty, and came to the impersonal conclusion that she was as beautiful as ever – a little older, perhaps, but still very lovely. He knew, too, that every shred of power her beauty had once had over him, was completely absent. He noted her beauty only as an artist might see a model for a picture. Betty and his feelings for her were dead to him. It would not even hurt him now to hear her say she had thrown him over because he had been deformed in the war.

Betty, however, was no longer thinking of Martyn as a disabled ex-service man. She was noting things about him that she had never noticed before. How attractive he looked with his thin, fine-drawn features; how distinguished he looked in that blue lounge suit; how well that very slight grey at the temples suited him; how well he compared with the other young men in her life – Sheldon, for example, and those others. There was something about Martyn's quiet depth and essential masculinity.

"I could have married him," she thought. "I turned him down because I thought that arm of his would be a handicap to him – prevent him getting a decent job. I should have hated to be married to a poor man. Of course, he thought it was the arm I minded. I was a fool. He has obviously done well. I must find out. I wonder if he's married now.'

An idea was crystallizing in her mind. Since she had jilted Martyn, she had met many men – had been admired by many of them – even loved. But somehow none of them had wanted to marry her. They just had not happened to be the marrying sort. Martyn didn't know it, but she was three years older than he. Now she was in her thirties, and a girl didn't want to wait too long to get a husband. She was beginning to look her age, too. Parties, drink, late nights, no exercise – all were helping to bring those wrinkles and lines quicker than they should have done. She still had her figure, at least, but underneath the skilful make-up, her face was no longer beautiful, and she knew it.

Besides this, she had to consider her rapidly dwindling wealth. When her mother and father had died, leaving her quite a considerable sum of money invested so that she should be able to live on the interest from it, she had thought herself wealthy enough. But her tastes were such that five pounds a week was not sufficient to live on after all – it barely paid her drink bills. And so she had drawn on her capital, until there was frighteningly little left. She knew it was time to get married. She had thought for a few months that she might be able to hook poor Sheldon. She didn't care for him in the least – was even repulsed by his ugly face. But he had money. Sheldon, however, showed no signs of coming up to scratch. That was the trouble with him. He was fine for a party, a cruise, lavished money on his girl friends, but he was never so blind as to marry them. Cynthia had warned her, and she was beginning to realise it was the truth.

And now Martyn had come into her life again. He had adored her for years – loved her passionately as none of her recent boyfriends had been capable of loving her. And Martyn was attractive. It seemed, too, that he had been getting on all right in spite of his missing arm. Well, if he wasn't married, this was her chance. The cards were all on her side. To-night she would remind him sentimentally of those good times they had had. Sheldon's parties usually lent themselves to a good deal of sentiment, particularly in the early hours of the morning when the lights were low and the music dreamy, and couples paired off and sat in dark corners, and consumed quantities of drink.

These thoughts flashed through Betty's scheming little mind while at the same time she back-chatted with Cynthia and Sheldon. She wanted to give Martyn time to recover from his surprise, and realize how lovely she still was – how much he still loved her. Then she would turn her attention to him.

Sheldon soon suggested it was time they were on their way, and Betty drew Cynthia aside while they were getting their coats.

'Look, here, be a dear, Cynthia, and keep Martyn back if you can for a few minutes. I want a word with John alone.'

'Only too delighted!' Cynthia said with a pointed smile. 'I think he's terribly attractive. Where did you meet him before and what possessed you to break your engagement to him – or did *he* break it?'

'Don't be catty!' said Betty. 'And mind your own business. I broke the engagement because I wanted to. And lay off him. He's mine this evening. See?'

Cynthia shrugged her shoulders, but said nothing. She knew only too well that but for Betty, she would never have been leading this life. Betty had met her when she was a mannequin with five pounds a week, returning every night to her little suburban house.

Betty had taken an interest in her for some reason of her own, and after several more meetings, suggested Cynthia should leave home and share her flat. It was Betty who had taught her how to treat men – to flatter them and get things from them. She had already had a good grounding through her job – which had taught her how to dress – make-up, and a graceful poise. It was some months before she realized that Betty had been using her for her own ends.

Cynthia was able to get model clothes at low prices from the salon. Naturally, when Betty wanted anything, Cynthia would buy it in her own name and Betty would then be paying half prices. And then, too, they had taken recently to borrowing clothes from the salon. It was easy enough for Cynthia to pack a dress away one evening, wear it that night and take it back next day. Only once had this nearly resulted in a tragedy, when Betty had spilt a glass of whisky down one of the 'borrowed' dresses, and then discovery had been averted as no one had missed the dress until the day after it was back from the cleaners.

The system worked well enough, and Cynthia and Betty understood one another. It was Betty who had the entrée to these parties, and who knew all the rich men who forgathered at them, and Cynthia knew better than to fall out with her friend. She had nothing but her weekly wage, and as most of this went on make-up, stockings, perfumes and so on, she was without other means. When they were on a party together, and money was required for something, it was Betty who paid. It suited her to pay, and it suited Cynthia. Neither wished to do without the other, but where Cynthia could not have managed without Betty's financial help, Betty on the other hand, could have managed without Cynthia. There were other girls who would, no doubt, have been pre-pared to 'loan' model dresses from shops where they worked; other girls who would get Betty out of a scrape by the odd little lie on the telephone over a confused date; yes, Betty would always manage while she was financially self-sufficient. And Cynthia knew it, and knew that the day was soon coming when Betty would be on the rocks. Then, perhaps, she would not take orders from her – give up the best man at Betty's whim – bear her rudeness and other pettinesses without a grumble.

So now she returned to the sitting-room and insisted that Martyn should have one more drink for the road while Betty hurried Sheldon out to the lift.

'John, I want to know more about Martyn Saunders,' she said, without preamble. 'Is he married?'

Sheldon looked at her with a grin.

'I don't think so. I don't know him very well. Just ran into him at the club. As a matter of fact, I only asked him along to-night because he was looking so gloomy. I think he's suffering from woman-trouble. Someone let him down, or something of that sort. Don't know any details. Cut me short when I asked questions, and said he wanted to forget the whole thing.'

Betty's face brightened. If Martyn was not married and on the rebound – why not rebound on her?

'Then I suppose you don't know much about him – what he's doing – his job and all that?' she asked.

'I think he's a vet,' said Sheldon. 'I heard one of the other fellows talking about him. Got a practice down in the country some-where, and doing very well, in spite of his disability.'

'He's on holiday then?' Betty pursued.

'Well, as a matter of fact, I think someone said he'd sold his practice. I don't know. Anyway, he must have some money to be staying at the club. It's devilishly expensive there nowadays. Look here, Betty, just what are you up to?'

'Nothing!' said Betty. 'Except that I *was* once engaged to him and naturally I'm still fond of him. In fact, I've regretted for a long time that the engagement was broken. It was all a stupid quarrel, and we were both too proud to make it up. It seems petty now when one is older and sees the thing in its proper light. I'd like to be friends again.'

'Come off it, Betty. You know me too well for that sort of blind. You want to know whether he's worth hooking, isn't that it?'

Betty frowned.

'Really, John, you can be extremely vulgar,' she said. 'You have such a nasty mind, you have to put the worst construction on things. People like you just don't know the meaning of the word love. Marriage is something you don't begin to understand. Martyn and I loved one another. We ought to have been married years ago.'

Sheldon shot her a quizzical look.

'Then why the probing into his past history?'

'Because obviously there's no use my breaking my heart over him if he's married in the meanwhile, is there?'

Sheldon shrugged his shoulders.

'Betty, if I thought you had a heart, I should never believe that any man could break it. Anyway, my dear, it's all your business and I shan't interfere. Now where are those other two?'

Martyn came down in the lift with Cynthia, wishing heartily that she would not lean against him. There was plenty of room and he could only draw one inference from her nearness – that she wanted it this way.

But he didn't want it. He disliked her and found her irritating, with her affected ways and speech, and her calculated femininity. It seemed to him almost a crime to think of this girl and Luisa at the same time, yet he could not help but compare Luisa's fresh beauty and naturalness with this sophisticated, insinuating glamorous woman beside him. He knew now, at such close quarters, that her red hair must be dyed. It had none of the golden lights of Luisa's glorious hair – none of the sweet fresh smell. He felt suffocated by the scent Cynthia was using, and was glad when the lift reached the ground floor, and they joined Sheldon and Betty.

Betty manœuvred to sit next to him in the Daimler at the back while Cynthia, with Sheldon driving, sat in front. A glass screen divided them and Betty spoke softly, having no fear of being overheard.

'Martyn, it is wonderful to see you again,' she said. 'I've wanted to so often, and never known where to get hold of you. You know, I've spent years reproaching myself for the appalling way I behaved last time we met. I've no right to expect you to forgive me.'

'My dear Betty,' Martyn said awkwardly, 'it's all very long ago and quite forgotten.'

'Perhaps you have forgotten, but I couldn't forget,' Betty said, quickly. 'You see, Martyn, I knew how crazy I was the moment you walked out of the door. I wanted to call you back, but my pride wouldn't let me. And many a time I started to write to you, and again my stupid girlish pride refused to allow me to do so. I'm older now. I know better than to let my pride stand in the way of real love – of happiness. So I am apologizing after all these years. Will you forgive me, Martyn? You see, I've never stopped loving you from that day to this.'

CHAPTER XVI

Martyn had been listening to Betty's words in dumb horror. For some strange reason, it appalled him to hear her say she loved him – had loved him all this time after all. He found it hard to believe – did not wish to believe it, either. He felt utterly wretched and very confused. Such a short while ago he would have given his life to hear those words from her. And now he felt he would give nearly as much to have avoided hearing them. They sounded so trite and shallow from Betty's pouting painted red lips.

He ran his hand across his forehead wearily. It all boiled down in the end to the fact that he loved Luisa – and therefore Betty meant nothing – less than nothing to him. Those years when he had thought himself in love with Betty were washed away as if they had never been. He did not want to remember them – far less to revive them.

'Betty, I'm very sorry you feel like this,' he said awkwardly. 'You see, I think it is only fair to be honest about such things. I'm in love with – with someone else.'

A frown crossed swiftly over the girl's face and her eyes narrowed. Martyn was not looking at her and did not see the hard determined expression in them. When he felt her hand on his and looked up, her face was soft and sad and sympathetic.

'Since we're being honest, Martyn, I must say it's a great blow to me. But my happiness doesn't really count any more. I deserve this, I know. I treated you so badly I couldn't expect you to go on caring about me. But at least promise me we can be friends, Martyn. That's all I ask.'

'Of course!' Martyn said, biting his lip. He was glad that her tone had become lighter and more impersonal. He had no wish to quarrel with Betty, and was quite content that they should part this evening as friends rather than enemies. He was not a person to bear grudges, and Betty was obviously sorry for all that had happened.

'Then I'm forgiven, Martyn?' Betty asked.

'Of course!' Martyn said again.

'I'm so glad,' Betty went on, and moved a little closer to him. 'Now you must tell me all about this other girl, Martyn. Don't think I shall be jealous, or anything like that. Now we are going to be friends, you must treat me like a sister. Tell me all about her. Does she love you very much? Are you going to be married soon?'

'I'm sorry, Betty, but honestly I'd rather not talk about it. You see, it's – it's all rather complicated.'

Betty's eyebrows raised sharply.

'You mean she's already married?'

Martin shook his head.

'No – but … there are other complications.'

Betty opened her mouth to press the questions further, but closed it again on second thought. This was no place to hear Martyn's story. In a few minutes they would be arriving at the party. It would be far better to wait until a little later when Martyn had had a few drinks, and was feeling confidential and mellow, and sorry for himself. Then they could slip away unobserved and there were endless possibilities.

She gave Martyn's hand a quick squeeze, and said softly:

'I'm so sorry, Martyn. Please believe that. We won't talk about it again. To-night we are going to enjoy ourselves and forget all our worries. Sheldon always gives such wonderful parties. We'll have a hilarious time, and pretend we're a couple of kids without a care in the world. Yes?'

Martyn turned and smiled at her and said:

'Thanks, Betty. I'm glad we can be friends. I'll try and see we both have a good evening.'

And he did make an effort to join in the fun – if it could be called fun. Sheldon's friends were a hard-drinking, rather vulgar crowd – chiefly men and women who hung on because there was something to be had out of him for nothing, and one or two others who enjoyed the noisy atmosphere and loose morality. Long before midnight, couples were dancing with their arms around one another's necks; others were sitting about kissing unashamedly in public, drinking in between whiles and laughing raucously at private jokes. It seemed almost a crime to compare this evening with the last he had spent in town – alone with Luisa.

The whole scene repelled Martyn. The girls with their heavy make-up, their daring frocks and complete lack of reserve, revolted him. The thick smoky atmosphere permeated with the smell of spilt drink and stale perfume, sickened him. And all the time at his side was Betty, with another glass of champagne for him, another little reminder to 'cheer up' and enjoy himself.

He drank several glasses of champagne, but they did not appear to have much effect on him. None of the expected exhilaration was forthcoming. Soon he realized that he and Betty were about the only two sober members of the party.

Betty had been watching his face for her opportunity. She saw that Martyn had had enough and that if she did not suggest a departure, he would soon leave himself. Martyn had, in fact, reached the end of his endurance. He was about to excuse himself to Betty when she said:

'Martyn, don't think me very rude and ungrateful, but I really can't bear this any more. All these awful people drunk and the smoke and everything ... could you please take me home?'

He looked very relieved and apologetic.

'My dear, I've only refrained from suggesting the same thing because I thought you were enjoying yourself. Of course, we'll go immediately.'

In the taxi going towards Betty's flat, she leant against him, saying in a small pathetic voice:

'I'm afraid I'm getting too old for those sorts of parties, Martyn. I always hope I'm going to enjoy them and I never do. I suppose it would all have seemed very exciting and thrilling when one was younger. Perhaps I'm blasée now.'

'No, I don't think so. I think we're just not blasée enough,' Martyn replied. 'We realize there are much better values in life.'

He thought of the Vicarage, and Luisa, and Bridget and the way the stocks would smell outside the surgery window at this time of night, and was swept with a longing for it all that was almost a physical pain. If only he could be back to that evening when he and Luisa had declared their love for each other! What years ago it seemed now. Where was Luisa at this moment? In bed, asleep, dreaming her young innocent youthful dreams, unaware that he existed, unknowing and uncaring of his loneliness?

"Oh, Luisa, Luisa!" he thought. "I would have given this left hand willingly for you, and now I would give the right hand, too, if it could bring back your memory and your love for me."

'Here we are, Martyn,' Betty said, suddenly, breaking in on his thoughts. 'You'll come up, won't you, for a drink?'

'I don't think I will, thank you very much,' Martyn said. 'I'm really rather tired. I think I'll go back to the club.'

'Where's that, sir?' asked the taxi driver. 'I'm not going back Piccadilly way. I'm on my way home, now. Hammersmith direction.'

'My club is nearly at Hyde Park,' Martyn said anxiously. 'Couldn't you turn back just that far? I'll pay double fare.'

The driver remained adamant.

'Sorry, sir. It's past midnight.'

'It's no good arguing with him, Martyn,' Betty broke in. 'Pay him off and come up to the flat. We can telephone for a taxi from there.'

Martyn felt annoyed, and at the same time, resigned. He had not wanted to go up to Betty's flat at this time of night. Apart from the conventional angle, he was extremely tired and he did not want any more to drink; nor did he wish to get involved in a long conversation with her. All he wanted was to go home to bed and sleep – to forget all his worries and unhappiness and this evening.

But the position was pretty hopeless. He was at least four miles from the club, and the buses had long since stopped running. Clearly there were no taxis about either. The sensible thing to do was to accept Betty's suggestion, and go to her flat and telephone for a taxi or hired car from there.

He paid off the taxi and followed Betty up in the lift. She was silent and, unobserved by him, was watching his face. How could she make this evening end up the way she wanted it – herself in Martyn's arm? If only she could achieve this, she had enough confidence in her own powers to be certain she could revive all the old passionate memories – to make him fall in love with her again. For Betty, love was an emotion of the senses. It went no deeper and it never occurred to her that there was more in love than just sex. Martyn had said he was in love with another girl – but Betty was not particularly perturbed by this statement. She was still pretty – she knew Martyn and how best to arouse his feelings. If she could just get him to kiss her once – then she was sure she could banish this other girl from his mind without difficulty. She little realized how utterly impossible such a thing was – even for a woman with all the virtues and charms which Betty lacked.

She unlocked the door of the flat and Martyn followed her in. He made no effort to take off his coat, and looked around the room for the telephone.

'I'll get you a drink and then you can telephone,' Betty said, leaving Martyn no option but to sit down while she poured him a generous whisky. She brought it over to him and sat down on the arm of his chair, holding her own glass between small white fingers with brilliant red tips.

'You know, Martyn, we should have left that party hours ago,' she said softly. 'This is much more fun, isn't it?'

'I'm afraid – I'm rather dull company for you,' Martyn said, wondering how he could get up to the telephone without appearing too rude.

'Nonsense, Martyn. You've got a complex. As a matter of fact, I don't find you a bit dull. But then I'm used to you, remember?'

As Martyn did not reply, she changed the topic of conversation.

'Tell me about your girl, Martyn,' she said. 'She must be pretty wonderful for you to care so much for her.'

Martyn toyed with his glass and thought of Luisa.

'Yes, she is wonderful,' he said, more to himself than to Betty.

'Tell me about her,' Betty said. 'I suppose

314

she loves you very much, too.'

'She did,' Martyn replied. 'Now, since the accident, she thinks she's in love with some other fellow. Unless a miracle happens, she'll marry him.'

'Accident?' Betty prompted, curious now to know the whole story.

'Yes, she fell from her horse and lost her memory. She looks on me as a complete stranger. She simply remembers nothing about me or the last seven years of her life.'

'But how awful!' said Betty. 'Isn't there a chance of her recovering?'

'There's always a chance,' said Martyn. 'But it's weeks now. And in the meantime, she has fallen in love with this other chap.'

'Then you meant when you said only a miracle could prevent her marriage, that unless she recovers very soon and remembers how she felt about you, she'll marry the other man?'

'That's about it,' said Martyn.

Betty felt a moment's complete satisfaction. With this other girl married, she would have no further competition with Martyn. The field would be hers. She decided to play her game slowly. She would not rush things now after all. There would be time enough once this girl was married. Then she, Betty, would catch him on the rebound. He would turn to her then for comfort and understanding and sympathy.

'I'm wretchedly sorry, Martyn. It's the darndest luck,' she said. 'If there were anything I could do to put things right, believe me I'd do it this minute.'

'There's nothing anyone can do,' Martyn said, hopelessly. 'I'm going to get out of this country altogether as soon as she's married. Until then, I'll wait – for the miracle to happen. I can't go until then.'

'Of course not,' said Betty. 'I'll hold thumbs up for you, Martyn. Are you sure nothing can be done for her – an operation?'

'The doctors advised against it. You see, Luisa doesn't realize she's lost her memory. They think the shock might be very harmful if she found out. Personally, I think an operation is the only answer. It isn't fair to let her go on in this day dream. Any time she might recover, and if she has married this fellow, it may be too late. Quite apart from my own point of view, it isn't fair to ruin her life. Oh, it's an appalling muddle. I've thought and thought about it, but there isn't a thing I can do. I have no right to interfere. I can do nothing but wait – and hope. And I'm beginning to give up hope. It's really all my fault. I should have broken my engagement to Bridget as soon as I realized I loved Luisa. Then this might never have happened. Luisa was upset – she rushed out to a friend, and on the way back, the accident happened. If she hadn't been worried... Oh, it's no good thinking about it.'

'No, that's the worst thing to do, Martyn. Try to forget it for a little while. You look terribly tired and ill, Martyn. You need a holiday. A change. Maybe a trip abroad would be a good thing for you.'

'It's kind of you to bother about my troubles,' said Martyn. 'I am tired, Betty. It's very good of you to put up with me. I think I'd better try and get this taxi now and go home. Maybe it will all seem better in the morning.'

'Yes, have a good night's sleep, and then I'm going to insist you take me out to lunch. It'll keep you from thinking too much on your own. Now, I won't take any refusal, Martyn. I'm your doctor now. I won't have you moping. I'll call for you at your club at half past twelve.'

Martyn stood up. Betty was really being very kind and sympathetic, and he ought to be grateful to her. He must have been very dull company for her all evening. The least he could do was agree to give her lunch to-morrow.

'Don't trouble to come to the club. I'll meet you at the Hungaria,' he said. 'I shall look forward to it.'

'So shall I, Martyn,' said Betty. 'Now, for a taxi!'

Ten minutes later, Martyn was on his way back to his club, and Betty was sitting on her bed, smiling to herself. She would get Martyn where she wanted him in the end. He was so gullible – so easily taken in. And at lunch to-morrow, she would make another date. The Hungaria – Martyn must have money to burn. In the old days it had been some small local restaurant, where the prices were low. Martyn couldn't be doing so badly. A trip abroad…

She undressed slowly, and curled up in her bed like a cat contemplating a bowl of cream. She would have slept even better had she known that Fate was preparing to play into her hand – giving her the trump cards, and a certain chance to win.

There had been no telephone call from Martyn for Bridget; no letter announcing his whereabouts, either the day of Luisa's arrival home, nor the two days following. Luisa felt that she could not bear to wait a moment longer.

'I must find him somehow,' she said to Bridget, her face white and drawn with anxiety. 'Surely there is some way – he can't have disappeared for ever.'

'Lis, don't worry so,' Bridget said, trying to calm Luisa. 'Martyn promised he'd get in touch with me. In any case, he must have intended doing so, because he asked me to write and tell him if ever I had good news of you. Besides, all his clothes, his books, his instruments are here. He'll come back.'

Luisa tried to accept this, because deep in her heart she too felt sure Martyn must return. Or even should he have decided to start life somewhere else, he would write eventually to Bridget, to send on his things. There was so much to clear up. He just could not disappear. Besides, there was the lease of the house. He had always paid his rent six months in advance, but the rent would be due again soon. He would have to communicate with his bank...

'Bridget!' Luisa shouted. 'Martyn's bank. I can trace him that way.'

She ran upstairs to find her accounts file, and searched feverishly for the bank's name and address. At last she gave a triumphant cry.

'I've found it,' she cried. 'I'm going to London first thing to-morrow morning.'

'Steady on, Luisa,' Bill said. 'Wouldn't it be best to telephone the bank first, and ascertain whether they do know his where-abouts? It would save you a long journey there unnecessarily.'

'I'll telephone now,' Luisa cried. 'Thanks for the idea, Bill.'

The exchange seemed to take an eternity to get her the number. Then the cashier kept her waiting while he put her through to the manager. At last she was able to ask for Martyn's whereabouts.

'It's very urgent,' she said, and her voice sounded so shaky and desperate, the bank manager did not hesitate to tell her that Martyn had called on the previous day to cash a cheque, and had given his address for the next three weeks at his club.

Luisa jotted down the name and address, and ran back to Bill and Bridget.

'He's staying at his club,' she cried, her face flushed with excitement. 'I'll catch the early train. I can be up in town by eleven, and I shall be with him for lunch. Oh, Bill, Bridget! I'm so happy, I could die!'

Luisa slept little that night. She had laid out for the morning a smart little suit, and her only pair of nylons, her best shoes and bag. She had washed and set her hair until it shone with a glorious red-gold light, and given herself a manicure. Then, these little details accomplished, there was nothing else for her to do but try and sleep.

But sleep would not come. She lay awake hour after hour, excitement making her feverish and restless. Never had the hours seemed to drag so slowly. To-morrow! To-morrow! she thought. Oh, Martyn, dearest love. To-morrow we shall be together again, and nothing shall ever part us any more.

At last to-morrow came, and although Bridget forced her to eat a little toast, Luisa felt she could not face a cooked breakfast, and Bill was forced to drive her down to the station in Martyn's car long before the train was due.

'Are you absolutely sure you ought to go alone?' he asked her again. 'You look very white, Luisa. I think you should have agreed to let Bridget go with you.'

'No, I'm all right, thanks to both of you for your offer,' Luisa said. 'I'm quite well again now, Bill. Besides, I shall be home to-night – with Martyn. He must come back with me. To-night we'll have a wonderful party – the four of us.'

And then the train came into the station, and Luisa was on her way to London.

Her first disappointment came when she reached the club, to learn that Martyn had already gone out.

'I'm afraid he didn't mention where he was going, Miss,' said the receptionist. And seeing the disappointment on her face, he said kindly: 'Perhaps Mr Sheldon could help you. He and Mr Saunders were talking last night. There's just a chance he might have mentioned his plans to him.'

'Thank you,' said Luisa. 'Would you ask Mr Sheldon to be so kind as to come here for a few minutes?'

Two minutes later, John Sheldon was introducing himself to Luisa.

'I'm looking for Mr Saunders,' she explained. 'It's rather urgent. I must find him to-day. The receptionist thought you might happen to know where he'd gone.'

John Sheldon looked at Luisa approvingly. Stunningly pretty girl, he thought. No doubt this was Saunders' little bit of woman-trouble. Didn't blame the fellow. Deuced pretty girl.

'I'm frightfully sorry, but I really don't know where he is. Haven't seen him this morning. Was up late, you know. Bit of a hangover and all that. Saunders came on the party, too. Left early I think. Now come to think of it...' he broke off, remembering that Martyn had left with Betty and feeling that this was perhaps not quite the right thing to tell this girl. All the same, chances were Martyn was round at Betty's flat. Could be. He'd taken quite an interest in her, judging from the fact they remained together at the party. And they were old friends, too.

'Look here,' he said. 'It may be a wild goose-chase, but Saunders met an old friend of his at the party last night. He may have fixed some appointment, and have gone round there now. You could try, if you like. I'm not doing anything. I could run you round in my car.'

Luisa tried to control her impatience. She did not much like the look of this man, but at least he was doing his best to help her find Martyn.

'It's very good of you to offer, but I can take a taxi,' she said firmly. 'If you'd just be so good as to give me the address...'

'Of course,' said Sheldon, feeling that after all he'd be better having a sniff of the hair of the dog that had bit him than go gallivanting around to Betty's and get mixed up in a female squabble. He gave Luisa the address of Betty's flat, and saw her into a taxi.

As the car pulled up outside the block of flats, Luisa tried not to allow herself to get too excited. Martyn might not be here after all. If he were not, she would have to go back to the club, and wait there until he came in. But if he were here ... in a few minutes she would see him.

She over-tipped the taxi-driver and hurried up in the lift. Outside the flat she hesitated for a moment, longing to ring the bell, and perhaps hear Martyn's voice, and yet longing to prolong this moment of supreme happiness. Then she pressed the bell and waited.

Betty opened the door. She was still in her dressing-gown, having woken late, but she was well made-up, and had on her best négligé, for this might be Martyn. She stared at Luisa in surprise.

'This is number fifty-four,' she said, feeling annoyed that this was not Martyn after all but someone at the wrong number.

Luisa looked hastily at the slip of paper Sheldon had given her and ascertained that the number was fifty-four.

'I'm sorry to trouble you,' she said, nervously. 'A Mr Sheldon gave me your address. He said he thought I might find Martyn – Mr Saunders here.'

Betty's eyes narrowed.

'Martyn?' she said. 'He's not here right now. What do you want him for?'

'I – I rather wanted to see him – urgently,' Luisa said, feeling acutely embarrassed. 'I'm so sorry to trouble you. If he's not here, it really doesn't matter…'

'Wait a minute,' Betty said. 'I think you'd better come in and we'll see if we can get this straightened out. You can tell me who you are, and perhaps I can help you.'

She stood aside, and Luisa had no option but to go in. She looked around the sitting-room in distaste. There were unemptied ash trays everywhere. Half-empty glasses, and a bottle of whisky still sat on a table. The air in the room was stuffy with the smell of perfume and smoke.

'Afraid it's rather untidy,' Betty said. 'Had a party last night. Only just come to. I'll open a window.'

Luisa sat down, feeling suddenly tired and a little faint.

'Do you think I could have a glass of water?' she asked. 'I've not been very well – the train journey upset me. I'm sorry to trouble you.'

Betty stared at Luisa, suspicion suddenly

gathering to certainty. This girl – she hadn't been well. She'd come to London suddenly – to find Martyn who wasn't expecting her. Suppose this was the girl who had lost her memory – what had Martyn called her – Luisa. Suppose this were Luisa with her memory back.

"Steady now, Betty," she told herself. "Play your cards carefully. This might be the making of you."

'Would you like a little brandy,' she asked, her voice sympathetic and kind. 'You do look faint.'

'I'd rather have water,' Luisa said.

Betty fetched a glass of water from the kitchen, and gave it to Luisa.

'There, you look better now,' she said. 'Now tell me what it's all about.'

'I'm afraid you must think it very odd,' said Luisa. 'You see, it's like this. I – I had an accident and lost my memory. I only recovered last Thursday. When I went back to my home where Martyn was practising as a veterinary surgeon, he had gone. We – we were in love with one another. I've been trying to find him. He doesn't know I'm better. I really ought not to have come to town alone to-day. I'm supposed to be resting, but I couldn't wait to see him. That's why I came along here instead of waiting at Martyn's club.'

'I see,' said Betty, slowly. 'Then you must

be Luisa. Martyn told me about you. Perhaps he told you about me. I'm Betty.'

Luisa jumped up, faced the other girl, her face flushing.

'Betty!' she repeated. 'So you're the girl who treated him so badly. You're the girl who might have ruined his life – except he was so much better off without you, that you really succeeded in saving his life. Well, I'm sorry I ever came here. I hope I'll never have the doubtful pleasure of meeting you again. Now if you'll excuse me...'

'Just one moment before you go,' said Betty, her voice cold and utterly cruel. 'I quite understand the way you feel, and I return the compliment. But I suggest that although you don't deserve such solicitude, you might as well avoid waiting at Martyn's club the whole day. You can catch the next train back instead. You see, Martyn and I became engaged last night. As a matter of fact, I'm meeting him at the Hungaria for a celebration lunch. And if you don't believe me, there's the telephone. Ring the Hungaria – and see.'

CHAPTER XVII

Luisa swayed a little on her feet, but with a great effort she managed to remain standing. Her hands were clenched at her sides, and her face was chalk white.

'I don't believe you. I don't believe Martyn was here at all. It isn't possible!' she whispered.

Betty surveyed her with a little smile twisting the corners of her mouth.

'Would you know Martyn's gold pencil if you saw it?'

Luisa nodded. Her eyes followed Betty's slim figure as she went across to the little table where Martyn had telephoned last night for a taxi.

'There!' said Betty, triumphantly. 'You know, I wouldn't be such a fool as to lie to you. After all, you need only go to the Hungaria at lunch time, and ask Martyn for yourself. Or wait for him at his club. But I haven't lied, Unfortunately for you, Martyn has ceased to care about you – if he ever did. As a matter of fact, he's really been in love with me all this time.'

'I don't understand!' Luisa said, weakly. 'I thought you broke your engagement to him.'

'I did!' Betty said, calmly. 'But I was young and pretty, and having a good time in those days. I didn't want to settle down. Now I do. And that's all there is to it. I love Martyn, and we shall be married as soon as possible.'

'Love him!' Luisa cried, fiercely. 'I don't believe you know the meaning of the word.'

Betty gave a hard little laugh.

'And you do, I suppose – you, with your sweet innocent little airs and graces. Well, I'm the one Martyn has chosen, so I don't see it makes much odds who loves him more – you or I. The fact remains that I shall be his wife. You know, I'm almost sorry for you. It must be quite disturbing to lose your memory, and then recover in time to find you've lost your man!'

She gave another little laugh, but something in Luisa's expression caused the smile to fade slowly from her face.

'I'm going now,' Luisa said. 'You may think it odd, but I wish you every happiness – for Martyn's sake. But if you let him down – or ever hurt him in the slightest way, I'm warning you that you shall pay for it. I'll find out some way or another.'

And she turned and walked out of the room, out of the flat, closing the door quietly behind her.

For a moment, Betty remained where she was, staring at the closed door. She felt the slightest twinge of fear at what she had done. Not fear of Luisa, but fear in case Luisa might after all take up the challenge and go to the Hungaria to see Martyn. Or wait for him at his club.

Then slowly the smile returned to her face. She would keep the appointment at the Hungaria early, and persuade Martyn to take her somewhere else. Then with a little ingenuity she could keep him away from the club. It was unlikely Luisa would wait for him until late at night. Besides, the girl was obviously proud.

But she need not have worried. Luisa had accepted Betty's story and was on her way back to the station to catch the next train home. It never occurred to her, having seen Martyn's pencil in the flat, that he might have been there on some perfectly innocent mission. That Betty should be lunching with him and was prepared for her to go along and check the fact was, in her mind, conclusive. Martyn had reverted to his first love. And he had loved Betty or he couldn't have been so hurt by her.

She tried desperately to understand Martyn, to make excuses for him, but somehow the very thought of him marrying Betty was utterly repulsive. How *could* he love her? Surely he must see how cruel and self-centred and shallow she was? How cheap with her négligés and perfumes and smoky little sitting-room. That Martyn wished to make Betty his wife and the mother of his children was simply unbelievable, and yet it did not occur to her to doubt the evidence that he did so intend.

As the train hurried her back towards her home, Luisa felt more and more wretched, more tired and ill and beaten. In her depression, she began to think about that never-to-be-forgotten evening with Martyn, and to question her memory of it. He could not have meant what he said. Perhaps he had not really said them at all. Had his love for her been but a few moments of wild passion after all?

Her mind turned wearily round the subject. One thing only she could not bear to think about – her own frightful loss. She had loved Martyn – desperately and wholly, as she would never love another man. Since she had been well again, she had lived for the moment when she could see his face, tell him how deeply she cared for him, and beg him never to allow them to be separated again. It had never occurred to her even for a second that Martyn might not want her. Bridget had repeatedly told her how Martyn had suffered because she would in her illness shy away from him. Bridget had said it was because of her he had gone away; because of her he had broken his engagement. He had told Bridget time and time again how much he loved her, Luisa. And now, quite suddenly, he had become re-engaged to Betty – to the girl he said he had forgotten.

"Am I going out of my mind again?" she asked herself. "I'm tired – terribly tired. If only I could lie down and sleep and forget this nightmare."

Another woman in the carriage looked at Luisa anxiously. This girl was terribly white and seemed ill. There were deep shadows under her eyes, and she was shivering violently.

'Can I do anything for you? You look ill!' she said to Luisa kindly.

Luisa opened her eyes and tried to smile.

'I'm all right. I haven't been very well. I'm going home now. Perhaps – if I should fall asleep, you would wake me at Chippenham. I'm getting out there. I'm rather tired…'

'I'm getting out there myself,' said the older woman, looking at Luisa anxiously. The girl must be very tired indeed, she thought, to find such difficulty staying awake even while she talked. 'Are you being met?'

Luisa shook her head.

'No! I'll take a taxi from the station – Hunstanton Vicarage…' and this time her eyes closed and her head fell back against the cushioned seat.

The older woman watched wondering if the girl had fainted but not liking to interfere, in case she were just tired. At Chippenham, she shook Luisa gently by the shoulder, but the girl did not wake.

'So she is ill!' she thought. And putting her head out of the window, she quickly called a porter.

'My friend is ill. I must have help immediately. Will you get another porter and carry her to a taxi,' she said.

Many curious glances were cast at Luisa's inert form, and her flustered companion, but neither took any notice. Within a very short while, the taxi was riding quickly in the direction of Hunstanton Vicarage.

It so happened that Jim Mathers had taken the opportunity of Luisa's absence to drive over to the Vicarage himself, to see Bridget, with whom he wished to have a long talk. He had not seen Luisa since the day of their return from the seaside, and he was anxious about her, but had not enquired before for fear of embarrassing her. He was, therefore, on the spot when Bridget called to him.

'Jim, come quickly. Luisa's ill. Someone has kindly brought her out here in a taxi from the station. She collapsed in the train.'

With an anxious look at Luisa's inert form, Jim hurried forward to assist the driver. Bridget looked after the kindly stranger, and insisted she should come in for a cup of tea, if she was not in a hurry, but Luisa's train companion said she would take the taxi back into Chippenham, and left with many good wishes for Luisa's recovery.

It was not until two hours later that Luisa recovered consciousness. Jim had telephoned immediately for the doctor, who had given her an injection.

'Nothing to worry too much about. Intense fatigue. Might call it a minor relapse, but I don't think her memory will be affected. Main thing is no worry and complete rest. What did she want to career off to London for? I told her to rest.'

Fortunately he did not wait for an answer, and leaving instructions for Bridget to telephone him if Luisa did not wake up within the next three hours, or if she seemed unwell on waking, he left the two of them by Luisa's bed.

'Something must have happened,' Bridget said. 'I can't understand it. Where's Martyn? Didn't she see him after all? I'm worried, Jim. I feel everything can't be well after all.'

'Don't worry, Bridget,' Jim said, with a conviction he did not have. 'I'm certain she'll be all right. You run along and tell Bill what's happened. I'll stay by Luisa.'

Bill was in the kitchen with Bridget, watching her prepare the supper when Jim came running in with the news that Luisa was awake and asking for her.

'She seems all right,' he said, quietly. 'Just asked me to fetch you.'

Bridget hurried into Luisa's room, and bent over the bed.

'How are you, Lis?' she asked, gently.

'I suppose I must have fainted in the train. How did I get here?' Luisa asked.

'You just fell asleep. The doctor has been to see you and said you were over-tired. Some strange woman who was in the same carriage brought you here in a taxi. Fortunately you had told her where you lived.'

Luisa nodded.

'Yes, I remember. I was feeling ghastly – so terribly tired...'

Bridget looked at her anxiously. There was a dead tone to Luisa's voice, that sounded unnatural.

'Just lie still and rest, Lis,' she said. 'I'll bring you a little supper if you think you can eat it.'

'No, I couldn't eat anything,' Luisa said. 'Bridget?'

'Yes, Lis?'

'I didn't see Martyn after all.'

'Didn't you, Luisa?'

'No! You see, I found out before I could see him that he had become engaged again to Betty – you remember – the girl he loved before he came here?'

'Yes, I remember,' Bridget said, trying to keep her voice calm. What an appalling calamity. No wonder Luisa was suffering from shock. It was unbelievable. 'Are you certain there hasn't been a mistake, Lis? Who told you? I'm sure it can't be true! Martyn had long since got over her. He told me he'd never really loved her. He loved you, Luisa. I know he did. It wasn't a week ago he told me so, in this very house, and I'd swear my life away he wasn't pretending. He was desperate about you. You *must* be mistaken, Lis.'

'I'm not mistaken,' Luisa said, in that same dead little voice. 'You see, I saw Betty myself.'

'Then she's lying,' Bridget said, fiercely. 'I don't believe it, Luisa. You may, but I don't. I shall see Martyn myself. I won't believe it until he tells me so.'

'Bridget, please! I tell you it is true. You see, he'd been to her flat the night before. He left his pencil there, and I saw it. He was lunching with her at the Hungaria to celebrate the engagement. Betty told me I could go with her if I didn't believe her. She would hardly bluff that far.'

Bridget stared at Luisa in utter dismay. Things certainly looked black, but even now she could not believe Martyn capable of such a sudden change of heart. There could be no doubt at all – not even the slightest little doubt, that he had been in love with Luisa, and desperately unhappy because of her illness. He'd gone away because he couldn't stand the house without Lis. No, it didn't make sense.

Bridget sat down on the edge of the bed and took Luisa's ice-cold hand in her own.

'Lis, that girl could have been bluffing. It is possible. And even if Martyn had been to her flat, it may all have been perfectly innocent.'

For the first time, Luisa's voice showed some expression.

'Nothing that happened in her flat could be perfectly innocent,' she said, her tone scathing and bitter.

'Then Martryn could have been duped. She may have got him there on some pretence or other. If you love him, Luisa, surely you have more faith in him?'

Luisa was silent. Her voice was almost inaudible when she replied.

'Perhaps I should, Bridget. But Martyn seems to have fallen in and out of love quite a number of times lately. With you when Betty let him down, then with me. And now her again.'

'He was never in love with me, and you know it, Lis,' Bridget said, 'and I don't think he ever cared about her, either. It was just a case of a strong physical attraction, and Martyn being too gullible to see through it. She's trapped him again while he was miserable and unhappy about you.'

'Why should she want to? She chucked him over once.'

'Because it suits her for some reason. From what I gathered, Betty sounds a pretty ghastly type of person. You met her, Lis.

What is she like?'

'Pretty, shallow, hard as nails, and calculating,' Luisa said. The ghost of a smile flickered over her white little face. 'But then I'm biased, aren't I? I'd be jealous of her if I didn't despise her to much.'

Bridget gave a triumphant little cry.

'There, Luisa, you've answered your own doubts. If she's all you say, it's just the sort of thing she'd tell you to get rid of you. She's after Martyn for some reason of her own. I'm certain of it. Where is Martyn staying? I'm going to telephone him to find out if this is true.'

'He's at his club,' Luisa said, giving the name and address. 'But if you do this, Bridget, you must promise me one thing. You are not to tell him I was up there to-day. I don't think Betty will have told him. If she has, it doesn't matter. But I'd rather he didn't know – if he is engaged to her.'

'All right, I'll be tactful,' Bridget promised, and hurried out to the telephone.

But although she rang three times – the last at nearly midnight, the answer was always the same...

'I'm sorry, Miss, but Mr Saunders hasn't come in yet. Shall I take a message?'

'No,' said Bridget, quietly with a sinking heart. 'I'll ring again.'

Betty was in the best of spirits during her

lunch with Martyn, and pretended not to notice that he was quiet and unresponsive. She kept the conversation impersonal, and tried to talk of light inconsequent things which might amuse him.

Over coffee, she asked him what plans he had for the afternoon.

'Well, none really,' Martyn admitted, having failed to think up some engagement quickly enough.

'Then I'm not going to allow you to mope by yourself,' Betty said, with a gay little laugh. 'I've been given two complimentary tickets for a pre-view of a French film. I believe it's very good. Now be a dear, Martyn, and say you'll go with me. I'm dying to see it, but I simply won't go unescorted.'

'Isn't it – rather a lovely afternoon for a film show?' Martyn asked, lamely.

'Nonsense!' Betty replied, smiling at him in playful disapproval. 'You know what this weather is like. It'll be raining before tea. Now do be a dear, Martyn. I'd so love to go.'

Seeing no way out, Martyn allowed himself to be hurried off to the film show.

"It'll pass a few hours," he told himself. "And then I'll plead a headache or something and go back to the club. I must telephone Bridget and ask her if there is any news. I don't suppose there is, but in any case, she ought to know where I'm staying – just in case."

The film was quite enjoyable but he was not, after all, able to slip away to the club. Betty had met some friends in the foyer who insisted they should go along to some flat or other for a drink. Betty linked her arm in his, and without being publicly rude to her, he could barely refuse to go. As they got into a taxi he did manage to whisper to her that he didn't feel too well, but her reply was that a drink would do him good in that case.

It was even more difficult to get away from the party. A vast amount of drink was circulating and more and more people arrived. Martyn waited an opportunity to slip away unnoticed, but Betty was never absent from his side. She was introducing him to crowds of people, and every time he attempted to slip away she found someone else who was 'dying to meet him'.

The party must have gone on until six or later when someone suggested a show and someone else rang up for two boxes and Martyn was swept off in the crowd, Betty and another woman either side of him, refusing to allow him to leave them.

'You've got to come, Martyn,' Betty said, laughing, but her voice firm. 'He wants to go away by himself and mope, and I'm determined he shan't.'

'Of course he shan't!' said a chorus of people, all very merry and happy as a result of several drinks.

To keep Martyn with them then became the main purpose of at least eight people, and there was no arguing with them. Thoroughly annoyed, but preferring not to become involved in a drunken quarrel, Martyn acquiesced and found himself in a box watching a variety show. After the show, he gave up the idea of trying to get back to the club and not caring any more what this mad crowd of people did with him, he allowed himself to be rushed off to dinner and on to a night club to drink and dance.

It was nearly one o'clock in the morning when at last, thoroughly annoyed with Betty and the whole stupid drunken party in which she had involved him, he at last managed to get away without being noticed. Betty had gone off to powder her nose with one or two of the other women, and the man at his table was too drunk to know where *he* was, let alone mind about Martyn.

He slipped a couple of notes on the table for his share of the party, and with a great sense of relief, walked out into the fresh air.

He refused a waiting taxi and walked back along the deserted streets to the club. He was utterly tired and wretched and fed up with everything and everybody. Betty had no doubt meant well, but the day had been dull and meaningless for him. It seemed that whichever way he turned, life had nothing to offer him. He thought of the Vicarage and his work, and then of Betty and the crowd of people he had met, and knew that he could not bear another day in town. He could not forget Luisa here, even although there was nothing that could possibly remind him of her.

"I must get back to my work," he thought. "Perhaps that is the way to find peace again. I'll get in touch with Bridget and ask her to send my equipment to the club. Then I'll go abroad. I'll start again. Surely somewhere in the world there is peace and happiness for me!"

But Fate was playing against him. Had he arrived home a little earlier – one half hour earlier – he would still have been too late for Bridget's telephone call, but the receptionist would have told him about it. Now, when he arrived back, the receptionist had gone to bed and there was only the night porter awake.

Martyn said a quick good night, and went slowly up the stairs to bed.

CHAPTER XVIII

Bill, Bridget and Jim were sitting in the dining-room over after-lunch coffee. Mrs Jennings had cleared the table and they knew they would not be disturbed.

'I'm so worried about Luisa,' Bridget said, voicing all their thoughts. 'She just lies there, hardly saying a word, her eyes open but at the same time – dead.'

'If only you hadn't made that promise last night,' Bill said. 'I can't help feeling that you're wrong about Martyn. I admit I don't know the chap very well – in fact my one meeting with him could hardly be called pleasant. But from what you say, darling, he doesn't sound the sort of chap to do wild things on impulse.'

'Perhaps it was wrong of me to promise not to try to contact him again,' Bridget said with a frown. 'In fact, I'm regretting it already. But Jim will bear me out when I say I just had to promise last night. Luisa was in a dreadful state.'

'I think if Bridget had refused to give her word, it might have been dangerous. Luisa was near to hysteria. After all she has been through, it simply wasn't worth risking.'

Bridget sighed. If only she had not mentioned to Luisa that she intended telephoning Martyn. Then she would not have raised her hopes. But she herself had felt so convinced that one call – one word with Martyn would straighten the whole thing out. Then, each time she had had to return to Luisa with the same story – Martyn was not at his club and they did not know when he would return. And at midnight, Luisa had burst into tears – hard, choking sobs that racked her body, and had begged Bridget to let the whole thing be.

'He's with Betty somewhere. I know it, Bridget. I knew this morning that she wasn't lying. She wouldn't have dared. Promise me you won't telephone him. I don't want him to know how I feel. Please, Bridget, promise.'

Bridget had argued that she could contact Martyn on quite a different subject – his instruments, perhaps, and leave it to him to announce his engagement, but Luisa would have none of it.

'No! He may ask after me out of courtesy and then you would not know what to say. You're such a bad liar. No, Bridget, I won't allow it.'

And eventually Jim had taken Bridget aside and whispered that it was best to promise for the time being. They could argue about it in a day or two when Luisa was better.

But this morning she did not seem any

stronger, even if she seemed no worse. The doctor came and ordered rest and no worry, but Bridget and Jim felt that what Luisa needed was something to think about – something to take her mind off Martyn – and Betty.

'If only she would say something – or cry again,' she said. 'But she just lies there, white and still and only answers in that quiet dead voice.'

The three sat in silence, wondering what was to be done.

'Perhaps Martyn would come down of his own accord,' Bill suggested after a moment or two.

'That might be pretty ghastly for Luisa – if he is really engaged to Betty,' Jim said. 'We could hardly keep his appearance a secret, could we?'

Bridget nodded.

'Jim, did you tell your mother about all this when you went home last night?'

'Yes! She refused to believe Martyn was in love with Betty. She thinks as you do, that he loved Luisa all along.'

'She hadn't any suggestions?'

'None, except that one of us try to contact him, but now that's impossible.'

'Unless we break our promise. After all, only Bridget actually gave her word. Neither Jim nor I did,' said Bill.

'Is that fair?' Bridget asked.

'I don't know,' Bill went on. 'If Luisa didn't know about it, it couldn't hurt her and it might save her so much unhappiness – and perhaps making her ill again.'

'Let's not think of such a dreadful thing,' said Jim.

'If you did contact Martyn, Bill, what could you say to him?'

'Well, he doesn't know about our engagement for one thing, darling,' Bill said, with a tender look at his fiancée. 'And then I can mention Luisa's recovery, say we are going to give a celebration party and would he like to come. If he is engaged to this Betty woman, he'll excuse himself on those grounds. He's hardly likely to come back without telling us, is he?'

'It won't do!' said Jim, thoughtfully. 'What about the telephone extension in Luisa's room? She'd be bound to hear.'

'Then I'll go to town,' Bill said. 'He needn't know why I went up. Come to that, I've been meaning to go to get Bridget an engagement ring, haven't I, darling? We might both go. Then Luisa wouldn't suspect anything either. We can have been passing his club, and looked him up to tell him the good news.'

'How do you know where he is staying?' Bridget asked. 'We can hardly tell him Luisa telephoned his bank and passed it on to us, can we?'

Bill sighed.

'Oh, heavens!' he said, with a grin. 'Deception isn't so easy after all. There's a snag at every turn. Well, all I can say is that we'll have to be more pointed. Bridget called his bank to give her his address because she wanted to tell him about us.'

'That's good enough,' said Jim. 'Personally, I'd like to be going up to see him myself. I'd tell him a thing or two about the way he's treated Luisa.'

'You don't trust him, do you, Jim?' Bridget asked.

Jim shrugged his shoulders.

'Don't take any notice of me. I'm jealous, I expect.'

'Poor old Jim,' Bridget said, putting an affectionate hand on his. 'You've really had the worst of this all along, haven't you?'

'I'm quite happy so long as Luisa is,' said Jim, flatly. 'But I can't bear to see her so unhappy. It's worse than when she was ill.'

'We'll soon clear it all up to-morrow,' said Bill. 'You'd better go and break the news to Luisa that we're going to town to-morrow to buy the ring. Let's hope she doesn't get suspicious about it.'

But all Luisa said was:

'How nice for you, Bridget. Don't worry about me. I'll be all right.'

'Jim is going to spend the day with you,' Bridget said. 'You'd like that, wouldn't you?'

347

But Luisa only nodded her head, and closed her eyes again as if she wished to sleep.

Bridget closed the door behind her and left her alone with her thoughts.

The next day, Bill and Bridget went to London and called at Martyn's club.

But there was a big disappointment awaiting them.

'Mr Saunders went out early yesterday morning with a young lady, who called for him,' said the receptionist, in answer to their enquiries. 'He said he'd be back to lunch, but he never came. About tea time, the young lady called with a note from him asking us to pack his luggage and give it to the young lady to take away and we've not heard another word since, sir.'

'The young lady,' Bridget pursued. 'Do you remember her name?'

'Miss Betty Simms, I think it was, Miss, or Simmonds. I can't quite remember. A short blonde girl.'

Bridget looked at Bill in dismay, and he at her.

'Shall we leave a message in case he comes back?' Bridget asked.

Bill gave a worried sigh.

'Things don't look too promising,' he said. 'I suppose now we've gone so far, we might as well. Ask him to drop a line to the Vicarage, as you want to get in touch with him about some business.'

Bridget hastily scribbled a note to this effect, and left it in case Martyn should return. Then she and Bill went out of the club and into Green Park, where they sat down on one of the benches to talk things over.

'Seems as if Jim's suspicions – and Luisa's, are right, after all,' Bill said.

'I still can't believe it, although I admit everything points to the worst conclusion. But one thing puzzles me, Bill. Why did she – Betty – call for his luggage? Why didn't he call for it himself?'

'Don't ask me!' Bill said. 'The whole thing is a hopeless mystery. Perhaps he was doing something else – arranging plans – I don't know. Looks as if they decided to elope or something. He had gone off to book plane tickets and she went for the luggage.'

Bridget smiled.

'What an imagination, Bill. All the same, that would explain it. But there must be some other explanation. I'm sure Martyn isn't the kind of person to elope. He's much too serious and quiet. I can't imagine him rushing off all in a minute to marry the girl he used to be engaged to. Unless he was afraid she'd let him down again.'

'Now you're beginning to admit there might be something in the engagement after all. This morning you refused to even contemplate it.'

Bridget gave a deep sigh.

'Well, Martyn is clearly involved with her in some way, even if it's not an engagement or elopement,' she said. 'The pencil Luisa saw proved that Martyn had been to her flat. And now we know she's been to his club to collect his luggage. She must have known where he was going. Bill! If we could find out where she lives! We could say we were relatives or something, and make her tell us where he is.'

'Now, steady on, Bridget. We can't just go poking about into other people's lives. We must keep this in perspective. Firstly, suppose Martyn is with Betty? We'd look a couple of fools then, wouldn't we – relatives! And if they are going away together, eloping – or what you will, then presumably they don't wish anyone to interfere.'

'But if they aren't!' Bridget persisted. 'If she has Martyn locked up in her flat!'

They both laughed. Betty hardly sounded the criminal type or Martyn the kind of person to allow himself to be abducted against his will.

'It isn't funny!' Bridget said, after a moment. 'I think really and truly that we've come to a dead end. I just don't see what we can do. After all, Martyn is a free man. We've no hold on him, or any right to track him down like this. It's just that I feel in my bones that something is wrong somewhere. Perhaps it's my woman's instinct. But I'm *sure* he still loves Luisa.'

'You've been reading too many mystery novels,' Bill teased her. 'Betty – the villainess, abducts Martyn, hero, and locks him up in her flat, then proceeds to collect his luggage and remove all traces of his whereabouts. No, darling, I think we've just got to face the fact that Martyn has gone off with her somewhere, for some reason of his own. There's absolutely nothing more we can do about it. Besides, my angel, you promised Luisa *you* wouldn't try to contact Martyn. I'm the one who should be doing it, and I just can't think of a thing to do.'

Bridget was silent for a moment. Then she stood up and said softly:

'Poor Luisa! I'm so terribly sorry for her, Bill. I think I feel her unhappiness more because I'm so happy myself. I do love you, Bill.'

'And I love you, my darling,' he said. 'And now before we leave it too late, we're going to find that ring.'

Arm in arm, they walked through the avenue of trees and out of the park.

Martyn, meantime, was lying in the emergency ward of one of the London hospitals, feeling more than sorry for himself. The morning following the party with Betty, he had gone down to breakfast feeling tired and a little sick. He put it down to some 'hooch' he may have drunk the day previously, and in his mind this suspicion was confirmed when he had a sudden attack of violent cramp. Sitting in the lounge feeling utterly rotten, Martyn was more than annoyed to receive a message from the porter that Betty was waiting to see him in the hall.

'Tell her I'm ill, or something,' he said, clenching his teeth, as another attack of cramp caught him in the stomach.

Betty, however, was not to be put off. Pushing past the porter, she went through into the lounge and found Martyn, bent almost double in his chair.

'Martyn, my poor dear! Whatever is wrong with you?' she asked, her tone warm and sympathetic. 'You look perfectly ghastly.'

'I feel it,' he said, too annoyed with her and feeling too rotten to rise to his feet. 'Really, Betty, you ought not to push your way in here like this. They don't really allow women in the lounge before midday.'

'I know, my sweet, but when that man said you were ill, I just had to come. What is it – hangover?'

'I don't know,' Martyn said, brusquely. 'I should think it's caused by something I ate or drank last night. I wouldn't have been surprised if that drink we had with your film friends was all hooch.'

She sat down and surveyed him anxiously. Martyn was clearly not at all pleased to see her. But then, he did look ill.

'I can't understand it,' she said. 'I feel all right. If it is poisoning, Martyn, you ought to see a doctor.'

Marty bent double again in another spasm of pain. He really did feel ghastly.

'Don't know any doctors in town,' he said, between clenched teeth.

'Well, I know a perfect wizard,' Betty said. 'You wait here, Martyn, while I get a taxi. We'll go straight round to his surgery. I can always get him to fix a moment for me.'

Too ill to argue, Martyn remained in his chair until Betty returned to say the taxi was waiting.

'Do you think you can walk?' she asked, seeing Martyn's white face clearly screwed up with pain.

'I suppose so!' was Martyn's reply.

But when he stood up, the pain was frightful, and he doubled up again. Betty called the porter, and together they helped him to the taxi.

On the way, Martyn lay back, drawing deep breaths between bouts of pain, and wondering if he were going to die. He felt horribly sick again and hoped that he wouldn't disgrace himself in front of Betty. Not that he really cared. It was her fault he was being jolted about like this.

Betty chattered away in a sweet sympathetic voice, but her charm was lost on Martyn. He was immensely thankful when the taxi pulled up somewhere in Harley Street, and Betty said they had arrived.

'You'll find some money in my left pocket,' he told her, gasping as another pain racked through him.

Betty paid off the taxi and Martyn hobbled to the door, feeling that an eternity of agony passed, while he waited for it to open. They were shown into the waiting room, and he lay back in a chair while Betty spoke in an undertone to the nurse.

Presently a bell rang and Betty and the nurse came and forced him to his feet and up an interminable flight of stairs. The door opened from the inside and he collapsed forward into the doctor's arms.

When he next remembered who and where he was, the doctor was saying:

'He'll have to go into the emergency ward immediately. I'll operate in an hour's time. Can't take any chances. Don't want him down with peritonitis.'

He turned and saw Martyn's eyes were open.

'Pain very bad?' he asked.

Martyn nodded.

'Nothing to worry about. Perfectly ordinary appendix. I'm going to operate on you later. I'm afraid you'll have to go into a public ward. No other beds available.'

'I – don't – mind!' Martyn gasped.

'He'll need one or two things in hospital,' the doctor went on.

'I'll fetch them from his club,' Betty said. 'Could you sign a note saying it's all right, Martyn? They may not trust me. Make a list of what you want.'

'No, just take everything,' said the doctor. 'Save time. Here, drink this, Mr Saunders, it may relieve the pain a little, until the ambulance comes.'

When Martyn could next think clearly, he was coming round from the anaesthetic, and a nurse was sitting beside his bed, which was surrounded by screens. He lay still, watching her face and recalling what had happened. The nurse saw his eyes open and smiled at him.

'Feeling better?' she asked. 'Would you like a drink?'

Martyn nodded, and the nurse poured a glass of water. His throat felt dry and he was becoming conscious of a pain in his stomach.

'It – hurts!' he said.

The nurse smiled again.

'Of course it does, but you'll soon be better. Mr Meakin made a wonderful job of you. The appendix burst on the table just after he'd taken it out. Another minute or two and you'd have had peritonitis. Now lie down and see if you can sleep a little. Your young lady is coming to see you after tea. You spoke of her several times when you were coming round. "Luisa," you kept saying, "Luisa". Such a pretty name!'

'Luisa – coming here?' Martyn asked. 'Are you sure?'

The nurse looked at him anxiously.

'Isn't that the young lady's name – the one who brought you in here?'

Martyn lay back on his pillow, and closed his eyes, disappointment welling over him. He must have been mad to imagine that Luisa was here. Still dreaming. Luisa had lost her memory, and was away at the seaside with Jim Mathers. It was Betty who was coming to see him after tea.

'Please, I'd rather not see anyone,' he said. 'I don't feel up to it. Please.'

'Of course not, if you don't wish to see her,' the nurse said, soothingly. 'Now you go to sleep.'

She wondered privately, as she sat by Martyn's sleeping form, who was this girl 'Luisa' who meant so much to him? And the other blonde girl, who had brought him in – who was she? Mr Saunders obviously didn't care a row of pins for her. It was all rather romantic. Martyn himself was romantic, with his dark curly hair and dark eyes, and that one missing arm. Obviously a war hero.

She wondered whether the girl, Luisa, would come to see him, or if they had quarrelled. She mused away the hours until she went off duty and another nurse came on.

The next morning Martyn felt distinctly better. There was a large bunch of roses by his bed, with a note from Betty saying:

'Get well soon, darling, from your Betty.'

He looked at them with a worried frown. Betty had really been extremely good to him, but he wished in a way that he wasn't under any obligation to her. It made things so awkward. He could not close his eyes to the fact that ever since the night he had met her, she had been only too anxious to see more of him. She had told him in the taxi that she still loved him, and now this note – it was damnably awkward. The more so because he couldn't raise even a spark of feeling for her. If he had his own way, he'd never see her again. But he couldn't do that. Betty had called the hospital three times yesterday enquiring after him. It was through her he had got to a good doctor in time. And now, in a few hours, it would be visiting hours, and clearly he could not refuse to see her.

The screens had been taken away from his bed, and he had made the acquaintance of his neighbours. It reminded him of the months he had spent in hospital, after they had amputated his arm. Then he had lain hour upon hour, longing for the sight of Betty, who never came, longing for the letters she never wrote. And now here he was, wondering how he could avoid seeing her.

"What a mess I've made of my life!" he thought wretchedly, "I nearly ruined Bridget's life, too. I wonder how she is and what has happened to her. I wonder if she has met her Bill again. I wonder if Luisa has married Jim yet."

The last thought was so unbearable that he tried to think of something else. But lying there, hour upon hour, not feeling well enough to read or listen to the wireless, or talk to his ward companions, the thought kept recurring, until Martyn decided he must know what had happened, whatever the result.

He beckoned to the nurse on duty and asked for some writing paper and a pencil. Then, awkwardly, he started to compose a letter to Bridget. It was not easy. He tore up several attempts and then started again:

Dear Bridget,

I meant to write sooner to tell you I was staying at my club, but somehow it never got done. Now I have landed up in the Lady Elizabeth hospital with an appendix – or I should say, without one now. I've been wondering how things are going at the Vicarage, and feeling a little guilty about my practice, and also leaving you to cope with accounts and so on. I think when I'm better I shall come down for a short while and clear things up. I still have not decided what to do in the future, but I am contemplating emigrating and starting life again in one of the colonies.

Please drop me a line here, if you have time, to tell me your news and, if any, news of Luisa. I still cannot bring myself to leave the country while there is hope of her recovery and while she is still unmarried. Perhaps this is not the case, and she is already Jim's wife. Anyway, let me know what goes on.

Yours,
Martyn.

He put it in an envelope and addressed it to Bridget at Hunstanton Vicarage. If Betty were coming to see him, she could post it on her way out of the hospital, he thought.

Betty arrived in due course, dressed in a very 'new look' outfit, with an elaborately veiled hat, and carrying another bunch of flowers. Many of the men in the ward turned to admire her, but Martyn had to force a smile of welcome to his face.

'Martyn, darling,' she said. 'I'm so glad you're better. What a frightful thing to have happened to you, poor sweet. How are you feeling?'

'Not too bad, thanks, and thanks, too, for the flowers. You really shouldn't have bothered,' he said.

Betty sat down on the edge of the bed, and

took his hand in hers.

'How could I help bothering, Martyn dear?' she said, softly. 'You know how I feel about you. I didn't mean to talk about it again, but I've been so worried about you. It showed me all too clearly how much you mean to me. Suppose you'd died.'

'Now, look here, Betty, I'm more than grateful for all you've done for me, but there wasn't a chance of my dying. Besides, you know – well, it seems so ungrateful after your kindness – and I am very fond of you,' he lied. 'But, well, you know how it is, Betty. I'm still in love with Luisa – and I always shall love her.'

Betty concealed her annoyance.

'Of course, I understand,' she said. 'But that doesn't prevent me feeling as I do about you. I'm quite happy to remain your friend, Martyn. Besides, who knows what may happen in the future?'

She did not specify her meaning, but it was clear to Martyn that she was referring to Luisa's possible marriage. Betty obviously hoped that if Luisa married, he would turn to her. But he did not feel well enough, nor was this the place, to discuss the matter further. When he was better, and out of the ward, he would tell Betty exactly how he felt, and make it clear to her that it was useless her expecting anything more from him in the future.

He changed the conversation.

'I wonder if you'd post this letter?' he asked her.

Betty looked at the name and address, and nodded her head.

'Of course!' she said. But her mind was working quickly, and she recalled that Luisa had come up from the country – that Martyn had been living at Hunstanton Vicarage. This letter must not on any account go to its addressee, she thought. It would be one of those lost in the post. No one would suspect. So many letters went astray nowadays. She could not risk Luisa learning through any source that Martyn was not, after all, engaged.

But at last, after all this time, Fate decided to take a favourable hand in Martyn's life.

'I'm just going off duty, Mr Saunders,' said the nurse who had brought him the pencil and writing pad. 'Shall I post your letter for you?'

'Thank you very much,' Martyn said. 'I had given it to Miss Simmonds, but it might catch an earlier post if you're going now.'

And Betty had no alternative but to hand it over.

CHAPTER XIX

Bridget came down the stairs, and saw the envelope lying on the hall mat. As she stooped to pick it up, she recognized Martyn's handwriting, and her heart jumped with hope. Then she took hold of herself and told herself not to hope for too much. This might merely be the confirmation of all their fears.

When she and Bill had returned home yesterday evening, neither had been happy in spite of the fact that they had chosen a charming little garnet engagement ring and celebrated their engagement with dinner and a show. At the back of both their minds had lain the thought of Luisa, pale, listless, silent in her bed at the Vicarage, all too clearly not wishing to get well; the thought of their morning and Martyn's disappearance – with Betty. Bridget who was deeply fond of Luisa, and already involved in her affairs, found now that she could not realize her own happiness to the full until Luisa was happy, too. And Bill, loving Bridget, and pitying Luisa, found his own spirits damped, and had to make an effort to play his part in their celebration.

Now, by the afternoon post, a letter had come from Martyn, and Bridget felt instinctively that the news it contained was vital. It would decide Luisa's future – one way or another.

Afraid to open it and read the worst, Bridget went into the garden to find Bill, who was in a deck-chair, reading a book.

'A letter from Martyn,' she told him, sitting down beside him. 'You open it, Bill. Read it to me.'

'But it's addressed to you, darling,' Bill said. 'It may be personal.'

'I'd still want you to see it,' Bridget said.

He took it from her and opened it, and read aloud Martyn's pencilled note. When he had finished, he looked at Bridget and saw tears in her eyes.

'Seems as if you were right, after all,' he said.

Bridget smiled at him.

'I still don't quite understand where Betty comes into the picture, but I'm convinced now that I was right – or that my instincts were right. I always felt so certain he loved Luisa.'

Bill grinned.

'You weren't so certain when we came home last night. Poor chap, having his appendix out. That accounts for the girl collecting his luggage from the club.'

'Bill, shall I take the letter and show it to

364

Luisa?' Bridget asked. 'It's going to be such a wonderful surprise for her. And I must give the good news of her recovery to Martyn. What a wonderful surprise that will be for him.'

'I don't see why she shouldn't see the letter. After all, I hardly think there's any doubt about the fact that he loves her. If only Luisa were stronger and up and about, she could have gone to him. Now they will have to wait until he is convalescing and can come down here.'

'I believe you're allowed up after an appendix in about ten days,' Bridget said. 'He can't be seriously ill if he's writing letters. Bill, I think I'll go up to town again and see him. Luisa may have a number of messages for him, and he's bound to want to know all the details. It would take ages to tell him the whole story in a letter.'

'Go by all means, if you want to, darling. But in a way, I think it might be better to let Luisa tell him. After all, it's their life, their future. Suppose we show Luisa his letter now and ask her what she'd like us to do?'

Bridget smiled at Bill tenderly.

'You're always right,' she said. 'I was carried away by enthusiasm. It will mean so much to me to see them both happy again.'

'I know, dearest. That's one of the things I love about you – your unselfishness and kindness to other people.'

Arm in arm, they went into the house and into Luisa's room.

She did not look up as they entered, but lay quite still, her eyes closed.

Bridget bent over her.

'Are you sleeping, Luisa?' she asked, softly.

Luisa opened her eyes and shook her head.

'Then, Lis, dear, I've got something to show you – something that is going to make you terribly, terribly happy. It's good news, Lis, from Martyn.'

For the first time since her return from London, Luisa appeared to have some life in her. Her eyes widened and a look flashed across her face – an expression of hope.

'News – of Martyn?' she repeated.

Bridget handed her the letter and then quietly left the room with Bill, realizing that Luisa would probably wish to be alone.

Luisa read the letter twice, and then buried her face in her pillow, and wept – not tears of sorrow, but tears of happiness and some, too, of self-condemnation. She should have had more faith in Martyn and his love for her. He had never wavered in his feelings for her, in spite of her engagement to Jim and the way she had unwittingly treated him during her illness. But she had doubted him and lain here these three days trying to hate him.

'Oh, Martyn, Martyn!' she whispered his name aloud 'My darling Martyn. Forgive me. Forgive me.'

She lay quietly for a while, realizing her own intense happiness and feeling new life surging through her. She no longer felt ill and listless, and she longed to be up and away to London, to the hospital to see him. Poor Martyn, lying in bed with his appendix out. She smiled tenderly, thinking of him helpless and alone and miserable, and knowing that it lay in her power to bring happiness to him again.

She called Bridget, who came running in to her.

'Bridget, I must go to him,' she said, urgently.

Bridget shook her head.

'You can't, Lis, dear. You're not well enough. Besides, Martyn wouldn't want it if he knew the doctor had ordered complete rest.'

'But Bridget, I have to see him – to tell him. Do you realize he doesn't even know I'm better – that I'm home – that I love him?'

Bridget nodded.

'You can write to him, Lis, or if you like I'll go and tell him. He can come here to convalesce. If you spend this next week getting well again, when you do see him you will be up and about and have some colour in your cheeks, and look beautiful again. He would be horribly shocked to see you as you are now. Just look at yourself, Lis.' And she handed her a mirror.

Luisa stared at her own pale reflection, at the enormous eyes, shadowed with sleeplessness and fatigue. Her hair looked dull and lifeless, and she saw she was almost plain. She gave a horrified exclamation.

'He mustn't see me like this,' she cried.

'Then do as I say and get well now,' Bridget suggested.

Luisa nodded her head.

'I'll write to him, Bridget. I'll write him a long letter and tell him everything that has happened. Now. Oh, Bridget, I'm so terribly happy.'

Bridget disappeared to find writing paper and envelope, and as soon as she returned, Luisa sat up in bed and started her letter. Bridget went back to Bill to tell him that already there was a change in Luisa – there was colour in her cheeks, a sparkle in her eyes.

When Bridget went back an hour later, the letter lay finished, sealed and ready for posting, by Luisa's bed, and Luisa herself was fast asleep. Bridget took the letter and went straight off with Bill to the post.

Meantime Martyn was beginning to recover. While he had been suffering from the after effects of his anaesthetic, he had been content to lie quietly and do little. But now he was making a rapid recovery and the long hours of idleness irked him and made him miserable. He had too much that was unhappy to think about. For a while he would read his books, listen to the wireless or talk to his companions. But always during the day there were long hours when he would lie on his back – thinking, remembering, wondering what to do about the future.

Betty had come to see him every visiting time and this, too, was beginning to irk him. She was always so full of tenderness and sympathy and ill-concealed affection. He didn't want any of those things from her, and at the same time he felt under an obligation to her which forced him to be polite. But he felt his temper fraying and he knew that if she came once more first in and last to go, he would be rude to her. If only she would leave him alone!

And then his special little nurse, who had been with him immediately after his operation, had brought him Luisa's letter. Luisa had never written to him before – except once from Monte Carlo, and he had long since thrown that letter away. He did not recognize her handwriting and wondered at first if it was Bridget's. When he tore the envelope, and looked at the end to see Luisa's signature, his heart leapt wildly, and the colour rushed to his face.

'Nurse,' he cried, wildly. 'It's from *her* – from Luisa.'

She smiled kindly at him, enjoying her part in his romance.

'Well, go on, read it!' she teased him, and left him alone to do so.

My darling Martyn, Luisa had written,

I am writing this from the Vicarage, where I returned two weeks ago. You will understand in a minute why I have not contacted you sooner. To start at the beginning, I was, as you know, on holiday with Jim and Mrs Mathers. While we were there, we met Bill, Bridget's ex-boy-friend, whom you will no doubt remember. He, of course, knew nothing of my loss of memory and started to talk about Bridget and you and that time we all met. Then my memory began to come back and by the evening I had remembered everything. Imagine how painful was the recovery when I was so far away from you, whom I still loved, and to find myself engaged to Jim, with all the realization of what this must have caused you in pain and worry. Jim was wonderful, and released me instantly from my engagement, and I had but one thought then – to come back to the Vicarage to you.

Bill travelled with us, and at home a fresh shock awaited me – or should I say dis-appointment. You had broken your engagement to Bridget and left the day before our arrival. I should add here that this was good news for Bill, who has subsequently become engaged to Bridget after all, and they are very much in love, and perfectly happy. I know you will be pleased to hear this.

To go on with our *story, the first thing I did was to try to find you. I discovered through your bank that you were staying at the club, so I decided to go to town and meet you there. When I arrived, you had left the club. In my anxiety to see you, I made enquires as to your whereabouts, and a man called Sheldon told me you might be at some address which he wrote down for me. Not knowing where I was going, I took a taxi to this address, and found myself in Betty Simmonds' flat. At first it never occurred to me to suspect you, but after some conversation, she told me that you and she had become engaged the previous night, and that she was lunching with you that day to celebrate. Even then I didn't believe her, but she offered the telephone to me and said I could check up on the table you had booked at the Hungaria, or if I preferred, go there to hear the truth from you. I see now that this was nothing but a tremendous bluff, but naturally at the time I was so hurt and shocked, I could not bring myself to see you. I could think only of my hurt pride.*

I went home by the next train, and fainted on the way. A stranger took me to the Vicarage, where I was put to bed. When I recovered, I told Bridget about the day, but she refused to believe you were engaged, and insisted on telephoning you at the club. She rang three times but you were out, and of course, I put two and two together and assumed you were with Betty. Bridget told me to-day, that she had then decided to go to town with Bill, without letting me know. She still believed Betty's story untrue, and meant to see you to confirm it. But once again you were not at the club, and all they could tell her was that a Miss Simmons had left the club with you, and later came back for your luggage. So then, she, too, began to think there was some truth in Betty's story.

I knew nothing of her visit to town, of course. I was lying here in bed, feeling too miserable to care, and I wanted to die. It seemed so ghastly, Martyn, my dearest, to have recovered my memory, only to find I had lost the man I loved. Without you I have no future, no happiness.

Then at last came your letter to Bridget, which I read half an hour ago. I can still hardly believe all this is true, and that you are in hospital thinking of me, and that soon perhaps you will be coming back here. I want to come to you, but the doctor has forbidden it.

I know now that Betty was bluffing – that for some reason of her own she lied that day. I ought to have known you would never return to her after the things you told me about her. I suppose she hoped she would get rid of me, and perhaps trap you into an engagement before you saw or heard of me again. And to a point she succeeded. I shall find it hard to forgive her for keeping us *apart, even although, thank God, it has not been for so very long.*

Write to me, dearest Martyn. Come to me as soon as you can. I love you, and shall love you always. Fate has cruelly kept us apart by devious means, but now our road is clear, and I am yours, if you want me, beloved.

Yours,
Luisa

At first, Martyn knew nothing but happiness, blinding, overwhelming happiness, that Luisa's letter had brought to him. She had recovered. She was free of Jim – free to marry him, and she still loved him.

And then he thought of Betty, and in that moment of blinding anger, he could have killed her. She had come near to ruining his life for a second time, and with her lies and deceit she seemed better out of the world. He thought with a repercussion of fear, how nearly he might have lost Luisa, by giving Betty that letter to Bridget to post. Only God had intervened in the shape of his little nurse, who had taken the letter from her.

Silently Martyn said a prayer of thanks, and then he knew that Betty did not matter. She was coming to see him this afternoon, and it would be the last time he would ever set eyes on her. Whatever lay behind her scheming, it would never bear fruit now, he thought grimly. Then his mind went back to

Luisa, and his face softened, and he pulled over his writing pad, and started to reply to her.

Betty arrived before he had finished his letter. He did not answer her greeting, and the smile faded from her face. She had, in fact, been living in daily fear since the nurse had posted that letter, that Martyn might learn the truth from Luisa. She screwed up her courage and continued her visits, hoping against hope that he might show some sign of turning to her before her deception could be discovered. She had acted on impulse that day in the flat with Luisa, and had not had time to consider the repercussions. Now she was badly scared.

She looked at Martyn's grim, silent face, and said slowly:

'What's wrong, Martyn dear? Don't you feel well?'

His lips tightened.

'No!' he said. 'Having to breathe the same air as you makes me rather sick.'

'Martyn!' she cried. 'Whatever do you mean?'

'I think you know very well what I mean, Betty,' he said, his face white with anger. 'I don't understand why you have been trying to ruin my life a second time. Knowing you, I suppose it can only be just viciousness. But to go to such lengths to ruin two people's happiness – it's beyond me. I thought I had learnt all that was beastly about you when our engagement ended last time. Now I know I was wrong. I had only seen half of your nastiness.'

Betty sat down weakly in a chair, wanting to burst into tears, and perhaps claim Martyn's sympathy, and soften him this way, but unable to make a scene in a public ward.

'You don't understand,' she said, in a small voice. 'I lied to Luisa because I was in love with you. A woman will do anything – however awful – to keep the man she loves. It was all because I loved you, Martyn. Surely you see that?'

'Loved me!' Martyn said, his voice hard and scornful. 'You defile the word, Betty. I doubt if you know what it means – unless with regard to yourself. No doubt you do love yourself. All you think about is your happiness – your comfort – your stupid, selfish, lying little schemes. Well, it's the last time I shall have any part in your life. You can get out – now, this minute, and I'm warning you before you go, that if you ever attempt, now or later, to have anything to do with Luisa's life or mine, I won't answer for my actions. I'll kill you with my own hand, rather than have you speak one word to Luisa. You see, even one word from your lips would pollute the air she had to breathe. Now get out – quick!'

'But Martyn...' Betty began, when he

broke in with a quiet savageness that really frightened her.

'Get out! Now! Or I'll have you thrown out!'

And she knew then that she had lost, and afraid to turn on him and return his insults, she could do nothing but walk with as much dignity as she could muster, out of the ward, and out of Martyn's life.

The little nurse came over to his bed and smiled down at him.

'Miss Simmonds didn't stay very long to-day, did she?' she said.

Martyn lit a cigarette.

'No, and she won't be coming again. Nurse, how long will it be before I can get out of this damned bed? Did the doctor say when I can go home? I must get home soon.'

'I'm afraid it'll be another week, Mr Saunders,' the nurse said, sympathetically. 'But perhaps less if you keep quiet and obey orders. Besides – she'll wait, won't she?'

He grinned suddenly.

'Yes, she'll wait. But I haven't seen her for so long. Nurse, can you post this letter when you go off duty? I've nearly finished it.'

'I'll post your epistle,' she said, with a smile at the heap of closely written pages on his bed table. 'But I go in ten minutes, so you'd better hurry up.'

Half an hour later, Martyn's letter was on its way to Luisa, who was anxiously watching every post.

Luisa was up and around the house, busy spring-cleaning and making herself a new dress.

Bridget was worried that she was over-doing it, but the doctor shook his head and said:

'Leave her alone. It'll do her good. She's making a splendid recovery. It's just what she needs. The more work, the less worry.'

'She's not worried!' Bridget replied, with a smile. 'Just excited. Mr Saunders comes back to-morrow.'

'Mr Saunders!' said the doctor. 'So that's it. Well, well, you young people do surprise me. I thought you were engaged to him, my dear?'

'That was a mistake!' Bridget explained. 'I've really been in love with Bill all along.'

'The nice young man with the freckled face?' asked the doctor, and was amused to see the colour come to Bridget's cheeks. 'Well, I haven't time to stay here teasing you about your young man. There's no need to worry about Luisa. She's as right as rain. In fact, I don't think there's any need for me to call again. Wish her the best of luck for me, and I shall expect to be asked to the wedding.'

'You will be!' said Bridget, and showed the doctor to his car.

As the doctor's car drove away, Bridget turned to go indoors, when she heard the sound of a second engine. Suspecting it might be Jim, she waited to see a taxi turn into the drive. Two minutes later, Martyn climbed out of the car and was saying:

'Got out a day early, Bridget, where is she?'

Bridget recovered from her surprise and pleasure, and told Martyn Luisa was in the sitting-room drying her hair in front of the fire.

'She'll be furious with you, Martyn, for turning up like this. This hair washing was for to-morrow. And she has a special dress she says she must wear, too.'

'I can't help it,' Martyn said, feeling as excited as a small boy coming home for the holidays. 'I can't wait until to-morrow now. Bridget, I'm damned glad to see you, and congratulations. I couldn't be more pleased it's worked out this way for you.'

'Thank you, Martyn!' she said, simply. And stood back to let him go through the door.

Outside the sitting-room, Martyn paused, his breath catching in his throat, and his heart beating painfully. Then very quietly he opened the door and looked inside.

Luisa was kneeling on the floor, her head turned away from him, as her beautiful red-gold hair hung in a cloud in front of the fire.

She did not look up, thinking it must be Bridget or Bill. When no one spoke, she turned her head and looked over her shoulder – and saw Martyn.

At first the colour rushed from her face, and then a glorious red spread into her cheeks. A smile of welcome came into her eyes, and she held out her arms to him.

Martyn went forward and knelt down beside her putting his arm gently round her shoulders beneath the fine silk of her hair.

'Luisa! Luisa!' he whispered, and then his lips were on hers, and her eyes closed as she surrendered herself to the wonder of his kiss.

When he released her, she leant back against his arm, and her hands went to his head, tracing the lines of his face as if to refresh her memory of him.

'Martyn, my dearest love,' she said, softly. 'I'm so wonderfully, unbelievably happy. I can hardly believe you are really here. Is it true, or am I dreaming?'

He smiled down at her, his eyes full of love.

'I couldn't wait another day. I made my doctor's life such hell badgering him to let me go, that he turned me out this morning for the sake of peace. Luisa, you look so beautiful with your hair like that. You are the most beautiful girl on earth.'

She looked away from him then, suddenly

shy and self-conscious. She was wearing one of last year's summer frocks, and there was no make-up on her face. She did not know that with her brilliant eyes and pink cheeks, she was utterly desirable.

'Oh, Martyn – my grey dress!' she said. 'I wanted to wear it to welcome you to-morrow.'

'Then I'll go away and come back to-morrow,' he said, teasing her.

She clung to him then, and cried:

'No, never again. Never leave me again, Martyn. I couldn't bear it.'

He bent his head and kissed her, gently this time, and with great tenderness.

'Luisa, my little love, will you marry me?' he asked.

'Yes, Martyn, yes! Whenever you want,' she told him.

'To-morrow?' he persisted.

'To-morrow, if you want,' Luisa repeated.

Martyn gave a sudden joyous laugh.

'Oh, Luisa, I'm so happy. I'm so much in love with you. I'll get a special licence. We'll be married the day after to-morrow. Here, in the local church. Peter Morrell will come down and be my best man. Do you remember our day in London – his studio?'

'Yes, darling,' she agreed, her gaze never leaving his face.

'And you shall have to-morrow in which to choose a wedding gown,' he continued. 'For

I know you would like to be married in white, and then I should have the most glorious bride in the world. Can you find a wedding dress in a day?'

'I can do anything for you,' was Luisa's reply.

'Then kiss me again, my very dearest,' said Martyn, huskily, 'For we two have been long parted, and I want convincing that you are here in the circle of my arm again.'

So she raised her lips and kissed him, shyly at first but with growing passion, and then gently, with love and tenderness. And dear faithful Boot, who was lying on the rug in front of the fire, wagged his old tail with a continuous thump upon the floor to show how much he, at any rate, approved. Then with that queer canine tact, he struggled to his feet, and ambled slowly from the room.

The publishers hope that this book has given you enjoyable reading. Large Print Books are especially designed to be as easy to see and hold as possible. If you wish a complete list of our books please ask at your local library or write directly to:

Magna Large Print Books
Magna House, Long Preston,
Skipton, North Yorkshire.
BD23 4ND

This Large Print Book, for people
who cannot read normal print,
is published under the auspices of

THE ULVERSCROFT FOUNDATION